PART I

CHAPTER I

A STRANGER

THE young man who, at the end of September, 1924, dismounted from a taxicab in South Square, Westminster, was so unobtrusively American that his driver had some hesitation in asking for double his fare. The young man had no hesitation in refusing it.

"Are you unable to read!" he said, softly. "Here is four shillings."

With that he turned his back and looked at the house before which he had descended. This first private English house he had ever proposed to enter inspired him with a certain uneasiness, as of a man who expects to part with a family ghost. Comparing a letter with the number chased in pale brass on the door, he murmured: "It surely is," and rang the bell.

While waiting for the door to be opened, he was conscious of extreme quietude, broken by a clock chiming four as if with the voice of Time itself. When the last boom died, the door yawned inwards, and a man, almost hairless, said:

"Yes, sir?"

The young man removed a soft hat from a dark head.

"This is Mrs. Michael Mont's house?"

"Correct, sir."

"Will you give her my card, and this letter?"

"'Mr. Francis Wilmot, Naseby, S. C.' Will you wait in here, sir?"

Ushered through the doorway of a room on the right, Francis Wilmot was conscious of a commotion close to the ground, and some teeth grazing the calf of his leg.

3

"Dandie!" said the voice of the hairless man, "you little devil! That dog is a proper little brute with strangers, sir. Stand still! I've known him bite clean through a lady's stockings."

Francis Wilmot saw with interest a silver-grey dog nine inches high and nearly as broad, looking up at him with lustrous eyes above teeth of extreme beauty.

"It's the baby, sir," said the hairless man, pointing to a sort of nest on the floor before the fireless hearth; "he *will* go for people when he's with the baby. But once he gets to smelling your trousers, he's all right. Better not touch the baby, though. Mrs. Mont was here a minute ago; I'll take your card up to her."

Francis Wilmot sat down on a settee in the middle of the room; and the dog lay between him and the baby.

And while the young man sat he gazed around him.

The room was painted in panels of a sub-golden hue, with a silver-coloured ceiling. A clavichord, little golden ghost of a piano, stood at one end. Glass lustres, pictures of flowers and of a silvery-necked lady swinging a skirt and her golden slippers, adorned the walls. The curtains were of gold and silver. The silver-coloured carpet felt wonderfully soft beneath his feet, the furniture was of a golden wood.

The young man felt suddenly quite homesick. He was back in the living-room of an old 'Colonial' house, in the bend of a lonely South Carolina river, reddish in hue. He was staring at the effigy of his high-collared, red-coated great-grandfather, Francis Wilmot, Royalist major in the War of Independence. They always said it was like the effigy he saw when shaving every morning; the smooth dark hair drooping across his right temple, the narrow nose and lips, the narrow dark hand on the sword-hilt or the razor, the slits of dark eyes gazing steadily out. Young Francis was seeing the darkies working in the

cotton-fields under a sun that he did not seem to have
seen since he came over here; he was walking with his
setter along the swamp edge, where Florida moss festooned the tall dolorous trees; he was thinking of the
Wilmot inheritance, ruined in the Civil War, still decayed
yet precious, and whether to struggle on with it, or to sell
it to the Yank who wanted a week-end run-to from his
Charleston dock job, and would improve it out of recognition. It would be lonely there, now that Anne had
married that young Britisher, Jon Forsyte, and gone away
north, to Southern Pines. And he thought of his sister,
thus lost to him, dark, pale, vivid, 'full of sand.' Yes!
this room made him homesick, with its perfection, such
as he had never beheld, where the only object out of
keeping was that dog lying on its side now, and so thick
through that all its little legs were in the air. Softly he
said:

"It's the prettiest room I ever was in."

"What a perfectly charming thing to overhear!"

A young woman, with crinkly chestnut hair above a
creamy face, with smiling lips, a short straight nose, and
very white dark-lashed eyelids active over dark hazel
eyes, stood near the door. She came towards him, and
held out her hand.

Francis Wilmot bowed over it, and said, gravely:

"Mrs. Michael Mont?"

"So Jon's married your sister. Is she pretty?"

"She is so."

"Very?"

"Yes, indeed."

"I hope baby has been entertaining you."

"He's just great."

"He is, rather. I hear Dandie bit you?"

"I reckon he didn't break the cuticle."

"Haven't you looked? But he's quite healthy. Sit

down, and tell me all about your sister and Jon. Is it a marriage of true minds?"

Francis Wilmot sat down.

"It certainly is. Young Jon is a pretty white man, and Anne——"

He heard a sigh.

"I'm very glad. He says in his letter that he's awfully happy. You must come and stay here. You can be as free as you like. Look on us as an hotel."

The young man's dark eyes smiled.

"That's too good of you! I've never been on this side before. They got through the war too soon."

Fleur took the baby out of its nest.

"*This* creature doesn't bite. Look—two teeth, but they don't antagonise—isn't that how you put it?"

"What is its name?"

"Kit—for Christopher. We agreed about its name luckily. Michael—my husband—will be in directly. He's in Parliament, you know. They're not sitting till Monday —Ireland, of course. We only came back for it from Italy yesterday. Italy's so wonderful—you must see it."

"Pardon me, but is that the Parliament clock that chimes so loud?"

"Big Ben—yes. He marks time for them. Michael says Parliament is the best drag on Progress ever invented. With our first Labour Government, it's been specially interesting this year. Don't you think it's rather touching the way this dog watches my baby? He's got the most terrific jaw!"

"What kind of dog is he?"

"A Dandie Dinmont. We did have a Peke. It was a terrible tragedy. He *would* go after cats; and one day he struck a fighting Tom, and got clawed over both eyes— quite blinded—and so——"

The young man saw her eyes suddenly too bright. He

made a soft noise, and said gently: "That was too bad."

"I had to change this room completely. It used to be Chinese. It reminded me too much."

"This little fellow would chaw any cat."

"Luckily he was brought up with kittens. We got him for his legs—they're so bowed in front that he can hardly run, so he just suits the pram. Dan, show your legs!"

The Dandie looked up with a negative sound.

"He's a terrible little 'character.' Do tell me, what's Jon like now? Is he still English?"

The young man was conscious that she had uttered at last something really in her mind.

"He is; but he's a dandy fellow."

"And his mother? She used to be beautiful."

"And is to this day."

"She would be. Grey, I suppose, by now?"

"Yes. You don't like her?"

"Well, I hope she won't be jealous of your sister!"

"I think, perhaps, you're unjust."

"I think, perhaps, I am."

She sat very still, her face hard above the baby's. And the young man, aware of thoughts beyond his reach, got up.

"When you write to Jon," she said, suddenly, "tell him that I'm awfully glad, and that I wish him luck. I shan't write to him myself. May I call you Francis?"

Francis Wilmot bowed. "I shall be proud, ma'am."

"Yes; but you must call me Fleur. We're sort of related, you know."

The young man smiled, and touched the name with his lips.

"Fleur! It's a beautiful name!"

"Your room will be ready when you come back. You'll have a bathroom to yourself, of course."

He put his lips to the hand held out.

"It's wonderful," he said. "I was feeling kind of home-sick; I miss the sun over here."

In going out, he looked back. Fleur had put her baby back in its nest, and was staring straight before her.

CHAPTER II

CHANGF

BUT more than the death of a dog had caused the re-garnishing of Fleur's Chinese room. On the evening of her twenty-second birthday Michael had come home saying:

"Well, my child, I've chucked publishing. With old Danby always in the right—it isn't a career."

"Oh! Michael, you'll be bored to death."

"I'll go into Parliament. It's quite usual, and about the same screw."

He had spoken in jest. Six days later it became apparent that she had listened in earnest.

"You were absolutely right, Michael. It's the very thing for you. You've got ideas."

"Other people's."

"And the gift of the gab. We're frightfully handy for the House, here."

"It costs money, Fleur."

"Yes; I've spoken to father. It was rather funny—there's never been a Forsyte, you know, anywhere near Parliament. But he thinks it'll be good for me; and that it's all baronets are fit for."

"One has to have a Seat, unfortunately."

"Well, I've sounded your father, too. He'll speak to people. They want young men."

"Ah! And what are my politics?"

"My dear boy, you must know—at thirty."

"I'm not a Liberal. But am I Labour or Tory?"

"You can think it out before the next election!"

Next day, while he was shaving, and she was in her bath, he cut himself slightly and said:

"The land and this unemployment is what I really care about. I'm a Foggartist."

"What?"

"Old Sir James Foggart's book. You read it."

"No."

"Well, you said so."

"So did others."

"Never mind—his eyes are fixed on 1944, and his policy's according. Safety in the Air, the Land, and Child Emigration; adjustment of Supply and Demand within the Empire; cut our losses in Europe; and endure a worse Present for the sake of a better Future. Everything, in fact, that's unpopular, and said to be impossible."

"Well, you could keep all that to yourself till you get in. You'll have to stand as a Tory."

"How lovely you look!"

"If you get in, you can disagree with everybody. That'll give you a position from the start."

"Some scheme!" murmured Michael.

"You can initiate this—this Foggartism. He isn't mad, is he?"

"No, only too sane, which is much the same thing of course. You see we've got a higher wage-scale than any other country except America and the Dominions; and it isn't coming down again; we really group in with the new countries. He's for growing as much of our food as we can, and pumping British town children, before they're spoiled, into the Colonies, till Colonial demand for goods equals our supply. It's no earthly, of course, without whole-hearted co-operation between the Governments within the Empire."

"It sounds very sensible."

"We published him, you know, but at his own expense.

It's a 'faith and the mountain' stunt. He's got the faith all right, but the mountain shows no signs of moving."

Fleur stood up. "Well," she said, "that's settled. Your father says he can get you a nomination as a Tory, and you can keep your own views to yourself. You'll get in on the human touch, Michael."

"Thank you, ducky. Can I help dry you?" . . .

Before redecorating her Chinese room, however, Fleur had waited till after Michael was comfortably seated for a division which professed to be interested in agriculture. She chose a blend between Adam and Louis Quinze. Michael called it the 'bimetallic parlour'; and carried off 'The White Monkey' to his study. The creature's pessimism was not, he felt, suited to political life.

Fleur had initiated her 'salon' with a gathering in February. The soul of society had passed away since the Liberal *débâcle* and Lady Alison's politico-legal coterie no longer counted. Plainer people were in the ascendant. Her Wednesday evenings were youthful, with age represented by her father-in-law, two minor ambassadors, and Pevensey Blythe, editor of 'The Outpost.' So unlike his literary style that he was usually mistaken for a Colonial Prime Minister, Blythe was a tall man with a beard, and grey bloodshot eyes, who expressed knowledge in paragraphs that few could really understand. "What Blythe thinks to-day, the Conservative Party will not think to-morrow," was said of him. He spoke in a small voice, and constantly used the impersonal pronoun.

"One is walking in one's sleep," he would say of the political situation, "and will wake up without any clothes on."

A warm supporter of Sir James Foggart's book, characterising it as "the masterpiece of a blind archangel," he had a passion for listening to the clavichord, and was invaluable in Fleur's 'salon.'

Freed from poetry and modern music, from Sibley Swan, Walter Nazing and Hugo Solstis, Fleur was finding time for her son—the eleventh baronet. He represented for her the reality of things. Michael might have posthumous theories, and Labour predatory hopes, but for her the year 1944 would see the eleventh baronet come of age. That Kit should inherit an England worth living in was of more intrinsic importance than anything they proposed in the Commons and were unable to perform. All those houses they were going to build, for instance—very proper, but a little unnecessary if Kit still had Lippinghall Manor and South Square, Westminster, to dwell in. Not that Fleur voiced such cynical convictions, or admitted them even to herself. She did orthodox lip-service to the god Progress.

The Peace of the World, Hygiene, Trade, and the End of Unemployment, preoccupied all, irrespective of Party, and Fleur was in the fashion; but instinct, rather than Michael and Sir James Foggart, told her that the time-honoured motto: 'Eat your cake and have it,' which underlay the platforms of all Parties, was not 'too frightfully' sound. So long as Kit had cake, it was no good bothering too deeply about the rest; though, of course, one must seem to. Fluttering about her 'salon'—this to that person, and that to the other, and to all so pretty, she charmed by her grace, her common-sense, her pliancy. Not infrequently she attended at the House, and sat, not listening too much to the speeches, yet picking up, as it were, by a sort of seventh sense (if women in Society all had six, surely Fleur had seven) what was necessary to the conduct of that 'salon'—the rise and fall of the Governmental barometer, the catchwords and clichés of policy; and, more valuable, impressions of personality, of the residuary man within the Member. She watched Michael's career, with the fostering eye of a godmother

who has given her godchild a blue morocco prayer-book,
in the hope that some day he may remember its existence.
Although a sedulous attendant at the House all through
the spring and summer, Michael had not yet opened his
mouth, and so far she had approved of his silence, while
nurturing his desire to know his own mind by listening
to his wanderings in Foggartism. If it were indeed the
only permanent cure for Unemployment, as he said, she
too was a Foggartist; common-sense assuring her that
the only real danger to Kit's future lay in that national
malady. Eliminate Unemployment, and nobody would
have time to make a fuss. But her criticisms were often
pertinent:

"My dear boy, does a country ever sacrifice the present
for the sake of the future?" or: "Do you really think
country life is better than town life?" or: "Can you imagine sending Kit out of England at fourteen to some
Godforsaken end of the world?" or: "Do you suppose
the towns will have it?" And they roused Michael to
such persistence and fluency that she felt he would really
catch on in time—like old Sir Giles Snoreham, whom they
would soon be making a peer, because he had always
worn low-crowned hats and advocated a return to han-
som cabs. Hats, buttonholes, an eyeglass—she turned
over in her mind all such little realities as help a political
career.

"Plain glass doesn't harm the sight; and it really has
a focussing value, Michael."

"My child, it's never done my dad a bit of good; I
doubt if it's sold three copies of any of his books. No!
If I get on, it'll be by talking."

But still she encouraged him to keep his mouth shut.

"It's no good starting wrong, Michael. These Labour
people aren't going to last out the year."

"Why not?"

"Their heads are swelling, and their tempers going. They're only on sufferance; people on sufferance have got to be pleasant or they won't be suffered. When they go out, the Tories will get in again and probably last. You'll have several years to be eccentric in, and by the time they're out again, you'll have your licence. Just go on working the human touch in your constituency; I'm sure it's a mistake to forget you've got constituents."

Michael spent most week-ends that summer working the human touch in mid-Bucks; and Fleur spent most week-ends with the eleventh baronet at her father's house near Mapledurham.

Since wiping the dust of the City off his feet, after that affair of Elderson and the P. P. R. S., Soames had become almost too countrified for a Forsyte. He had bought the meadows on the far side of the river and several Jersey cows. Not that he was going in for farming or nonsense of that sort, but it gave him an interest to punt himself over and see them milked. He had put up a good deal of glass, too, and was laying down melons. The English melon was superior to any other, and every year's connection with a French wife made him more and more inclined to eat what he grew himself. After Michael was returned for Parliament, Fleur had sent him Sir James Foggart's book, 'The Parlous State of England.' When it came, he said to Annette:

"I don't know what she thinks I want with this great thing!"

"To read it, Soames, I suppose."

Soames sniffed, turning the pages.

"I can't tell what it's all about."

"I will sell it at my bazaar, Soames. It will do for some good man who can read English."

From that moment Soames began almost unconsciously to read the book. He found it a peculiar affair, which gave most people some good hard knocks. He began to enjoy them, especially the chapter deprecating the workman's dislike of parting with his children at a reasonable age. Having never been outside Europe, he had a somewhat sketchy idea of places like South Africa, Australia, Canada, and New Zealand; but this old fellow Foggart, it appeared, had been there, and knew what he was talking about. What he said about their development seemed quite sensible. Children who went out there put on weight at once, and became owners of property at an age when in England they were still delivering parcels, popping in and out of jobs, hanging about street corners, and qualifying for unemployment and Communism. Get them out of England! There was a startling attraction in the idea for one who was English to a degree. He was in favour, too, of what was said about growing food and making England safe in the air. And then, slowly, he turned against it. The fellow was too much of a Jeremiah altogether. He complained to Fleur that the book dealt with nothing but birds in the bush; it was unpractical. What did Old Mont say?

"He won't read it; he says he knows old Foggart."

"H'm!" said Soames: "I shouldn't be surprised if there were something in it, then." That little-headed baronet was old-fashioned! "Anyway it shows that Michael's given up those Labour fellows."

"Michael says Foggartism will be Labour's policy when they understand all it means."

"How's that?"

"He thinks it's going to do them much more good than anybody else. He says one or two of their leaders are beginning to smell it out, and that the rest of the leaders are bound to follow in time."

"In that case," said Soames, "it'll never go down with their rank and file." And for two minutes he sat in a sort of trance. Had he said something profound, or had he not?

Fleur's presence at week-ends with the eleventh baronet was extremely agreeable to him. Though at first he had felt a sort of disappointment that his grandchild was not a girl—an eleventh baronet belonged too definitely to the Monts—he began, as the months wore on, to find him 'an engaging little chap,' and in any case, to have him down at Mapledurham kept him away from Lippinghall. It tried him at times, of course, to see how the women hung about the baby—there was something very excessive about motherhood. He had noticed it with Annette; he noticed it now with Fleur. French—perhaps! He had not remembered his own mother making such a fuss; indeed, he could not remember anything that happened when he was one. A week-end, when Madame Lamotte, Annette and Fleur were all hanging over his grandson— three generations of maternity concentrated on that pudgy morsel, reduced him to a punt, fishing for what he felt sure nobody would eat.

By the time he had finished Sir James Foggart's book, the disagreeable summer of 1924 was over, and a more disagreeable September had set in. The mellow golden days that glow up out of a haze which stars with dew-drops every cobweb on a gate, simply did not come. It rained, and the river was so unnaturally full, that the newspapers were at first unnaturally empty—there was literally no news of drought; they filled up again slowly with reports of the wettest summer 'for thirty years.' Calm, greenish with weed and tree shadow, the river flowed unendingly between Soames' damp lawn and his damp meadows. There were no mushrooms. Blackberries tasted of rain. Soames made a point of eating one every year; and, by the flavour, could tell what sort of year it had been. There was a good deal of 'old-man's-beard.'

In spite of all this, however, he was more cheerful than he had been for ages. Labour had been 'in,' if not in real power, for months, and the heavens had only lowered. Forced by Labour-in-office to take some notice of politics, he would utter prophecies at the breakfast-table. They varied somewhat, according to the news; and, since he always forgot those which did not come true, he was constantly able to tell Annette that he had told her so. She took no interest, however, occupied, 'like a woman, with her bazaars and jam-making, running about in the car, shopping in London, attending garden-parties'; and, in spite of her tendency to put on flesh, still remarkably handsome. Jack Cardigan, his niece Imogen's husband, had made him a sixty-ninth-birthday present of a set of golf-clubs. This was more puzzling to Soames than anything that had ever happened to him. What on earth was he to do with them? Annette, with that French quickness which so often annoyed him, suggested that he should use them. She was uncomfortable! At his age—! And then, one week-end in May the fellow himself had come down with Imogen, and, teeing a ball up on half a molehill, had driven it across the river.

"I'll bet you a box of cigars, Uncle Soames, that you don't do that before we leave on Monday."

"I never bet," said Soames, "and I don't smoke."

"Time you began both. Look here, we'll spend to-morrow learning to knock the ball!"

"Absurd!" said Soames.

But in his room that night he had stood in his pyjamas swinging his arms in imitation of Jack Cardigan. The next day he sent the women out in the car with their lunch; he was not going to have them grinning at him. He had seldom spent more annoying hours than those which followed. They culminated in a moment when at last he hit the ball, and it fell into the river three yards from the near bank. He was so stiff next morning in arms and ribs, that Annette had to rub him till he said:

"Look out! you're taking the skin off!"

He had, however, become infected. After destroying some further portions of his lawn, he joined the nearest Golf Club, and began to go round by himself during the luncheon-hour, accompanied by a little boy. He kept at it with characteristic tenacity, till by July he had attained a certain proficiency; and he began to say to Annette that it would do her all the good in the world to take it up, and keep her weight down.

"*Merci*, Soames," she would reply; "I have no wish to be the figure of your English Misses, flat as a board before and behind." She was reactionary, 'like her nation'; and Soames, who at heart had a certain sympathy with curves, did not seriously press the point. He found that the exercise jogged both his liver and his temper. He began to have colour in his cheeks. The day after his first nine-hole round with Jack Cardigan, who had given him three points per hole and beaten him by nine holes, he received a package which, to his dismay, contained a box of cigars. What the fellow was about, he could not imagine! He only discovered when, one evening a few days later, sitting at the window of his picture-gallery, he found that he had one in his mouth. Curiously enough, it did not make him sick. It produced rather something of the feeling he used to enjoy after 'doing Coué'—now comparatively out of fashion, since an American, so his sister Winifred said, had found a shorter cut. A suspicion, however, that the family had set Jack Cardigan on, prevented him from indulging his new sensation anywhere but in his picture-gallery; so that cigars gathered the halo of a secret vice. He renewed his store stealthily. Only when he found that Annette, Fleur, and others had known for weeks, did he relax his rule, and say openly that the vice of the present day was cigarettes.

"My dear boy," said Winifred, when she next saw him, "everybody's saying you're a different man!"

Soames raised his eyebrows. He was not conscious of any change.

"That chap Cardigan," he said, "is a funny fellow! . . . I'm going to dine and sleep at Fleur's; they're just back from Italy. The House sits on Monday."

"Yes," said Winifred; "very fussy of them—sitting in the Long Vacation."

"Ireland!" said Soames, deeply. "A pretty pair of shoes again!" Always had been; always would be!

CHAPTER III

MICHAEL TAKES 'A LUNAR'

MICHAEL had returned from Italy with the longing to 'get on with it,' which results from Southern holidays. Countryman by upbringing, still deeply absorbed by the unemployment problem and committed to Foggartism, as its remedy, he had taken up no other hobby in the House, and was eating the country's bread, if somewhat unbuttered, and doing nothing for it. He desired, therefore, to know where he stood, and how long he was going to stand there.

Bent on 'taking this lunar'—as 'Old Forsyte' would call it—at his own position, he walked away from the House that same day, after dealing with an accumulated correspondence. He walked towards Pevensey Blythe, in the office of that self-sufficing weekly: 'The Outpost.' Sunburned from his Italian holiday and thinned by Italian cookery, he moved briskly, and thought of many things. Passing down on to the Embankment, where a number of unemployed birds on a number of trees were also wondering, it seemed, where they stood and how long they were going to stand there, he took a letter from his pocket to read a second time.

"12 Sapper's Row,
Camden Town.

"Honourable Sir,

"Being young in 'Who's Who,' you will not be hard, I think, to those in suffering. I am an Austrian woman who married a German eleven years ago. He was an actor on the English stage, for his father and mother, who are no more living, brought him to England quite young. Interned he was, and his health broken up. He has the neurasthenie very bad so he cannot be trusted for any work. Before the war he was always in a part, and we had some good money; but this went partly when I was left with my child alone, and the rest was taken by the P. T., and we got very little back, neither of us being English. What we did get has all been to the doctor, and for our debts, and for burying our little child, which died happily, for though I loved it much this life which we have is not fit for a child to live. We live on my needle, and that is not earning much, a pound a week and some-times nothing. The Managers will not look at my hus-band all these years, because he shakes suddenly, so they think he drinks, but, Sir, he has not the money to buy it. We do not know where to turn, or what we do. So I thought, dear Sir, whether you could do anything for us with the P. T.; they have been quite sympatical; but they say they administrate an order and cannot do more. Or if you could get my husband some work where he will be in open air—the doctor say that is what he want. We have nowhere to go in Germany or in Austria, our well-loved families being no more alive. I think we are like many, but I cannot help asking you, Sir, because we want to keep living if we can, and now we are hardly having any food. Please to forgive me my writing, and to be-lieve your very anxious and humble

ANNA BERGFELD."

'God help them!' thought Michael, under a plane-tree close to Cleopatra's Needle, but without conviction. For in his view God was not so much interested in the fate of individual aliens as the Governor of the Bank of Eng-land in the fate of a pound of sugar bought with the fraction of a Bradbury; He would not arbitrarily inter-fere with a ripple of the tides set loose by His arrangement of the Spheres. God, to Michael, was a monarch strictly

limited by his own Constitution. He restored the letter
to his pocket. Poor creatures! But really, with 1,200,000
and more English unemployed, mostly due to that confounded Kaiser and his Navy stunt—! If that fellow and
his gang had not started their Naval rivalry in 1899,
England would have been out of the whole mess, or,
perhaps, there never would have been a mess!

He turned up from the Temple station towards the
offices of 'The Outpost.' He had 'taken' that weekly for
some years now. It knew everything, and managed to
convey a slight impression that nobody else knew anything; so that it seemed more weighty than any other
weekly. Having no particular Party to patronise, it
could patronise the lot. Without Imperial bias, it professed a special knowledge of the Empire. Not literary,
it made a point of reducing the heads of literary men—
Michael, in his publishing days, had enjoyed every opportunity of noticing that. Professing respect for Church
and the Law, it was an adept at giving them 'what-for.'
It fancied itself on Drama, striking a somewhat Irish
attitude towards it. But, perhaps, above all, it excelled
in neat detraction from political reputations, keeping
them in their place, and that place a little lower than
'The Outpost's.' Moreover, from its editorials emanated
that 'holy ghost' of inspired knowledge in periods just a
little beyond average comprehension, without which no
such periodical had real importance.

Michael went up the stairs two at a time, and entered
a large square room, where Mr. Blythe, back to the door,
was pointing with a ruler to a circle drawn on a map.

"This is a bee map," said Mr. Blythe to himself.
"Quite the bee-est map I ever saw."

Michael could not contain a gurgle, and the eyes of
Mr. Blythe came round, prominent, epileptic, richly en-
circled by pouches.

CHAPTER IV

MERE CONVERSATION

WHEN they came in, Fleur was returning down-
stairs from showing the young man to his room.
Already fully dressed for the evening, she had but little
on, and her hair was shingled. . . .

"My dear girl," Michael had said, when shingling came
in, "to please me, don't! Your *nuque* will be too bristly
for kisses."

"My dear boy," she had answered, "as if one could
help it! You're always the same with any new fashion!"

She had been one of the first twelve to shingle, and was
just feeling that without care she would miss being one
of the first twelve to grow some hair again. Marjorie
Ferrar, 'the Pet of the Panjoys,' as Michael called her,
already had more than an inch. Somehow, one hated
being distanced by Marjorie Ferrar. . . .

Advancing to her father, she said:

"I've asked a young American to stay, Dad; Jon Forsyte has married his sister, out there. You're quite brown,
darling. How's mother?"

Soames only gazed at her.

And Fleur passed through one of those shamed moments, when the dumb quality of his love for her seemed
accusing the glib quality of her love for him. It was not
fair—she felt—that he should look at her like that; as
if she had not suffered in that old business with Jon more
than he; if she could take it lightly now, surely he could!
As for Michael—not a word!—not even a joke! She bit
her lips, shook her shingled head, and passed into the
'bimetallic parlour.'

27

Dinner began with soup and Soames deprecating his own cows for not being Herefords. He supposed that in America they had no Herefords?

Francis Wilmot believed that they were going in for Holsteins.

"Holsteins!" repeated Soames: "They're new since my young days. What's their colour?"

"Parti-coloured," said Francis Wilmot. "The English grass is just wonderful."

"Too damp, with us," said Soames: "We're on the river."

"The river Thames? What size will that be, where it hasn't a tide?"

"Just there—not more than a hundred yards."

"Will it have fish?"

"Plenty."

"And it'll run clear, won't it—not red; our Southern rivers have a red colour. And your trees will be willows and poplars and elms."

Soames stared. He was a good deal puzzled. He had never been in America. The inhabitants were human, of course, but peculiar and all alike, with more face than feature, heads fastened upright on their backs, and shoulders too square to be real. Their voices clanged in their mouths; they pronounced the words 'very' and 'America' in a way that he had tried to imitate without success; their dollar was too high, and they all had motor-cars; they despised Europe, came over in great quantities, and took back all they could; they talked all the time, and were not allowed to drink. This young man cut across all these preconceptions. He drank sherry and only spoke when he was spoken to. His shoulders looked natural; he had more feature than face; and his voice was soft. Perhaps, at least, he despised Europe.

"I suppose," he said, "you find England very small."

"No, sir. I find London very large; and you certainly have the loveliest kind of a countryside."

Soames looked down one side of his nose. "Pretty enough!" he said.

Then came turbot and a silence, broken, low down, behind his chair.

"That dog!" said Soames, impaling a morsel of fish he had set aside as uneatable.

"No, Dad! He just wants to know you've seen him!"

Soames stretched down a finger, and the Dandie fell on his side.

"He never eats," said Fleur; "but he has to be noticed."

A small covey of partridges came in, cooked.

"Is there any particular thing you want to see over here, Mr. Wilmot?" said Michael. "There's nothing very un-American left. You're just too late for Regent Street."

"I want to see the Beefeaters; and Cruft's Dog Show; and your blood horses; and the Derby."

"Darby!" Soames corrected: "You can't stay for that —it's not till next June."

"My cousin Val will show you race-horses," said Fleur. "He married Jon's sister, you know."

A 'bombe' appeared. "You have more of this in America, I believe," said Soames.

"We don't have much ice-cream in the South, sir; but we have special cooking—very tasty."

"I've heard of terrapin."

"Well, *I* don't get frills like that. I live away back, and have to work pretty hard. My place is kind of homey; but I've got some mighty nice darkies that can cook fine—old folk that knew my grannies. The old-time darky is getting scarce, but he's the real thing."

A Southerner!

Soames had been told that the Southerner was a gentleman. He remembered the 'Alabama,' too; and his father, James, saying: "I told you so" when the Government ate humble pie over that business.

In the savoury silence that accompanied soft roes on toast, the patter of the Dandie's feet on the parquet floor could be plainly heard.

"This is the only thing he likes," said Fleur. "Dan! go to your master. Give him a little bit, Michael." And she stole a look at Michael, but he did not answer it.

On their Italian holiday, with Fleur in the throes of novelty, sun and wine warmed, disposed to junketing, amenable to his caresses, he had been having his real honeymoon, enjoying, for the first time since his marriage, a sense of being the chosen companion of his adored. And now had come this stranger, bringing reminder that one played but second fiddle to that young second cousin and first lover; and he couldn't help feeling the cup withdrawn again from his lips. She had invited this young man because he came from that past of hers whose tune one could not play. And, without looking up, he fed the Dandie with tid-bits of his favourite edible.

Soames broke the silence.

"Take some nutmeg, Mr. Wilmot. Melon without nutmeg—" . . .

When Fleur rose, Soames followed her to the drawing-room; while Michael led the young American to his study.

"You knew Jon?" said Francis Wilmot.

"No; I never met him."

"He's a great little fellow; and some poet. He's growing dandy peaches."

"Is he going on with that, now he's married?"

"Surely."

"Not coming to England?"

"Not this year. They have a nice home—horses and dogs. They have some hunting there, too. Perhaps he'll bring my sister over for a trip, next fall."

"Oh!" said Michael. "And are you staying long, yourself?"

"Why! I'll go back for Christmas. I'd like to see Rome, and Seville; and I want to visit the old home of my people, down in Worcestershire."

"When did they go over?"

"William and Mary. Catholics—they were. Is it a nice part, Worcestershire?"

"Very; especially in the Spring. It grows a lot of fruit."

"Oh! You still grow things in this country?"

"Not many."

"I thought that was so, coming on the cars, from Liverpool. I saw a lot of grass and one or two sheep, but I didn't see anybody working. The people all live in the towns, then?"

"Except a few unconsidered trifles. You must come down to my father's; they still grow a turnip or two thereabouts."

"It's sad," said Francis Wilmot.

"It is. We began to grow wheat again in the war; but they've let it all slip back—and worse."

"Why was that?"

Michael shrugged his shoulders: "No accounting for statesmanship. It lets the Land go to blazes when in office; and beats the drum of it when in opposition. At the end of the war we had the best air force in the world, and agriculture was well on its way to recovery. And what did they do? Dropped them both like hot potatoes. It was tragic. What do you grow in Carolina?"

"Just cotton, on my place. But it's mighty hard to make cotton pay nowadays. Labour's high."

"High with you, too?"

"Yes, sir. Do they let strangers in to your Parliament?"

"Rather. Would you like to hear the Irish debate? I can get you a seat in the Distinguished Strangers' gallery."

"I thought the English were stiff; but it's wonderful the way you make me feel at home. Is that your father-in-law—the old gentleman?"

"Yes."

"He seems kind of rarefied. Is he a banker?"

"No. But now you mention it—he ought to be."

Francis Wilmot's eyes roved round the room and came to rest on 'The White Monkey.'

"Well, now," he said, softly, "that, surely, is a wonderful picture. Could I get a picture painted by that man, for Jon and my sister?"

"I'm afraid not," said Michael. "You see, he was a Chink—not quite of the best period; but he must have gone West five hundred years ago at least."

"Ah! Well, he had a great sense of animals."

"We think he had a great sense of human beings."

Francis Wilmot stared.

There was something, Michael decided, in this young man unresponsive to satire.

"So you want to see Cruft's Dog Show?" he said. "You're keen on dogs, then?"

"I'll be taking a blood-hound back for Jon, and two for myself. I want to raise blood-hounds."

Michael leaned back, and blew out smoke. To Francis Wilmot, he felt, the world was young, and life running on good tires to some desirable destination. In England——!

"What is it you Americans want out of life?" he said abruptly.

"Well, I suppose you might say we wanted success—in the North, at all events."

"*We* wanted that in 1824," said Michael.

"Oh! And nowadays?"

"We've had success, and now we're wondering whether it was worth it."

"Well," said Francis Wilmot, "we're sort of thinly populated, compared with you."

"That's it," said Michael. "Every seat here is booked in advance; and a good many sit on their own knees. Will you have another cigar, or shall we join the lady?"

CHAPTER V

SIDE-SLIPS

IF Providence was completely satisfied with Sapper's Row, Camden Town, Michael was not. What could justify those twin dismal rows of three-storied houses, so begrimed that they might have been collars washed in Italy? What possible attention to business could make these little ground-floor shops do anything but lose money? From the thronged and tram-lined thoroughfare so pregnantly scented with fried fish, petrol, and old clothes, who would turn into this small backwater for sweetness or for profit? Even the children, made with heroic constancy on its second and third floors, sought the sweets of life outside its precincts; for in Sapper's Row they could neither be run over nor stare at the outside of Cinemas. Hand-carts, bicycles, light vans which had lost their nerve and taxicabs which had lost their way, provided all the traffic; potted geraniums and spotted cats supplied all the beauty. Sapper's Row drooped and withered.

Michael entered from its west end, and against his principles. Here was overcrowded England, at its most dismal, and here was he, who advocated a reduction of its population, about to visit some broken-down aliens with the view of keeping them alive. He looked into three of the little shops. Not a soul! Which was worst? Such little shops frequented, or—deserted? He came to No. 12, and looking up, saw a face looking down. It was wax white, movingly listless, above a pair of hands sewing at a garment. 'That,' he thought, 'is my "obedient humble" and her needle.' He entered the shop below, a hair-dresser's, containing a dirty basin below a dusty mirror, suspicious towels, bottles, and two dingy chairs.

In his shirt-sleeves, astride one of them, reading 'The Daily Mail,' sat a shadowy fellow with pale hollow cheeks, twisted moustache, lank hair, and the eyes, at once knowing and tragic, of a philosopher.

"Hair cut, sir?"

Michael shook his head.

"Do Mr. and Mrs. Bergfeld live here?"

"Up-stairs, top floor."

"How do I get up?"

"Through there."

Passing through a curtained aperture, Michael found a stairway and, at its top, stood, hesitating. His conscience was echoing Fleur's comment on Anna Bergfeld's letter: "Yes, I dare say; but what's the good?" when the door was opened, and it seemed to him almost as if a corpse were standing there, with a face as though some one had come knocking on its grave, so eager and so white.

'Mrs. Bergfeld? My name's Mont. You wrote to me."

The woman trembled so, that Michael thought she was going to faint.

"Will you excuse me, sir, that I sit down?" And she dropped on to the end of the bed. The room was spotless, but, besides the bed, held only a small deal washstand, a pot of geranium, a tin trunk with a pair of trousers folded on it, a woman's hat on a peg, and a chair in the window covered with her sewing.

The woman stood up again. She seemed not more than thirty, thin but prettily formed; and her oval face, without colour except in her dark eyes, suggested Rafael rather than Sapper's Row.

"It is like seeing an angel," she said. "Excuse me, sir."

"Queer angel, Mrs. Bergfeld. Your husband not in?"

"No, sir. Fritz has gone to walk."

"Tell me, Mrs. Bergfeld. If I pay your passages to Germany, will you go?"

"We cannot get a passport now; Fritz has been here twenty years, and never back; he has lost his German nationality, sir; they do not want people like us, you know."

Michael stivered up his hair.

"Where are you from yourself?"

"From Salzburg."

"What about going back there?"

"I would like to, but what would we do? In Austria every one is poor now, and I have no relative left. Here at least we have my sewing."

"How much is that a week?"

"Sometimes a pound; sometimes fifteen shillings. It is bread and the rent."

"Don't you get the dole?"

"No, sir. We are not registered."

Michael took out a five-pound note and laid it with his card on the wash-stand. "I've got to think this over, Mrs. Bergfeld. Perhaps your husband will come and see me." He went out quickly, for the ghostly woman had flushed pink.

Repassing through the curtained aperture, he caught the hair-dresser wiping out the basin.

"Find 'em in, sir?"

"The lady."

"Ah! Seen better days, I should say. The 'usband's a queer customer; 'alf off his nut. Wanted to come in here with me, but I've got to give this job up."

"Oh! How's that?"

"I've got to have fresh air—only got one lung, and that's not very gaudy. I'll have to find something else."

"That's bad, in these days."

The hair-dresser shrugged his bony shoulders. "Ah!" he said. "I've been a hair-dresser from a boy, except for the war. Funny place this, to fetch up in after where I've been. The war knocked me out." He twisted his little thin moustache.

"No pension?" said Michael.

"Not a bob. What I want to keep me alive is something in the open."

Michael took him in from head to foot. Shadowy, narrow-headed, with one lung.

"But do you know anything about country life?"

"Not a blessed thing. Still, I've got to find something, or peg out."

His tragic and knowing eyes searched Michael's face.

"I'm awfully sorry," said Michael. "Good-bye!"

The hair-dresser made a queer jerky little movement.

Emerging from Sapper's Row into the crowded, roaring thoroughfare, Michael thought of a speech in a play he had seen a year or two before. "The condition of the people leaves much to be desired. I shall make a point of taking up the cudgels in the House. I shall move—!" The condition of the people! What a remote thing! The sportive nightmare of a few dreaming nights, the skeleton in a well-locked cupboard, the discomforting rare howl of a hungry dog! And probably no folk in England less disturbed by it than the gallant six hundred odd who sat with him in 'that House.' For to improve the condition of the people was their job, and that relieved them of a sense of nightmare. Since Oliver Cromwell some sixteen thousand, perhaps, had sat there before them, to the same end. And was the trick done—not bee likely! Still *they* were really working for it, and other people were only looking on and telling them how to do it!

Thus was he thinking, when a voice said:

"Not got a job about you, sir?"

Michael quickened his steps, then stood still. He saw that the man who had spoken, having cast his eyes down again, had missed this sign of weakness; and he went back to him. They were black eyes in a face round and pasty like a mince pie. Decent and shabby, quiet and forlorn, he wore an ex-Service-man's badge.

"You spoke to me?" said Michael.

"I'm sure I don't know why, sir; it just hopped out of me."

"No work?"

"No; and pretty low."

"Married?"

"Widower, sir; two children."

"Dole?"

"Yes; and fair sick of it."

"In the war, I see?"

"Yes, Messpot."

"What sort of job do you want?"

"Any mortal thing."

"Give me your name and address."

"Henry Boddick, 94 Waltham Buildings, Gunnersbury."

Michael took it down.

"Can't promise anything," he said.

"No, sir."

"Good luck, anyway. Have a cigar?"

"Thank you, and good luck to *you*, sir."

Michael saluted, and resumed his progress; once out of sight of Henry Boddick, he took a taxi. A little more of this, and he would lose the sweet reasonableness without which one could not sit in 'that House'!

'For Sale or to Let' recorded recurrently in Portland Place, somewhat restored his sense of balance.

That same afternoon he took Francis Wilmot with him to the House, and leaving him at the foot of the Distinguished Strangers' stairway, made his way on to the floor.

He had never been in Ireland, so that the debate had for him little relation to reality. It seemed to illustrate, however, the obstacles in the way of agreement on any mortal subject. Almost every speech emphasized the paramount need for a settlement, but declared the impossibility of 'going back' on this, that or the other factor which precluded such settlement. Still, for a debate on Ireland it seemed good-tempered; and presently they would all go out and record the votes they had determined on before it all began. He remembered the thrill with which he had listened to the first debates after his election; the impression each speech had given him that somebody must certainly be converted to something; and the reluctance with which he had discovered that nobody ever was. Some force was at work far stronger than any eloquence, however striking or sincere. The clothes were washed elsewhere; in here they were but aired before being put on. Still, until people put thoughts into words, they didn't know what they thought, and sometimes they didn't know afterwards. And for the hundredth time Michael was seized by a weak feeling in his legs. In a few weeks he himself must rise on them. Would the House accord him its "customary indulgence"; or would it say: 'Young fellow—teaching your grandmother to suck eggs—shut up!'

He looked around him.

His fellow members were sitting in all shapes. Chosen of the people, they confirmed the doctrine that human nature did not change, or so slowly that one could not see the process—he had seen their prototypes in Roman statues, in mediæval pictures. . . . 'Plain but pleasant,' he thought, unconsciously reproducing George Forsyte's description of himself in his palmy days. But did they take themselves seriously, as under Burke, as under Gladstone even?

The words "customary indulgence" roused him from reverie; for they meant a maiden speech. Ha! yes! The member for Cornmarket. He composed himself to listen. Delivering himself with restraint and clarity, the speaker seemed suggesting that the doctrine 'Do unto others as ye would they should do unto you' need not be entirely neglected, even in Ireland; but it was long—too long— Michael watched the House grow restive. 'Alas! poor brother!' he thought, as the speaker somewhat hastily sat down. A very handsome man rose in his place. He congratulated his honourable friend on his able and well-delivered effort, he only regretted that it had nothing to do with the business in hand. Exactly! Michael slipped out. Recovering his 'distinguished stranger,' he walked away with him to South Square.

Francis Wilmot was in a state of some enthusiasm.

"That was fine," he said. "Who was the gentleman under the curtains?"

"The Speaker?"

"No; I mean the one who didn't speak."

"Exactly; he's the dignity of the House."

"They ought to feed him oxygen; it must be sleepy under there. I liked the delegate who spoke last. He would 'go' in America; he had big ideas."

"The idealism which keeps you out of the League of Nations, eh?" said Michael with a grin.

Francis Wilmot turned his head rather sharply.

"Well," he said, "we're like any other people when it comes down to bed-rock."

"Quite so," said Michael, "idealism is just a by-product of geography—it's the haze that lies in the middle distance. The farther you are from bed-rock, the less quick you need be to see it. We're twenty sea-miles more idealistic about the European situation than the French. And you're three thousand sea-miles more idealistic than we are. But when it's a matter of niggers, we're three thousand sea-miles more idealistic than you; isn't that so?"

Francis Wilmot narrowed his dark eyes.

"It is," he said. "The farther north we go in the States, the more idealistic we get about the nigger. Anne and I've lived all our life with darkies, and never had trouble; we love them and they love us; but I wouldn't trust myself not to join in lynching one that laid his hands on her. I've talked that over many times with Jon. He doesn't see it that way; he says a darky should be tried like a white man; but he doesn't know the real South. His mind is still three thousand sea-miles away."

Michael was silent. Something within him always closed up at mention of a name which he still spelt mentally with an h.

Francis Wilmot added ruminatively: "There are a few saints in every country proof against your theory; but the rest of us aren't above human nature."

"Talking of human nature," said Michael, "here's my father-in-law!"

CHAPTER VI

SOAMES KEEPS HIS EYES OPEN

SOAMES, having prolonged his week-end visit, had been spending the afternoon at the Zoological Gardens, removing his great-nephews, the little Cardigans, from the too close proximity of monkeys and cats. After standing them once more in Imogen's hall, he had roosted at his Club till, idly turning his evening paper, he had come on this paragraph, in the 'Chiff-chaff' column:

"A surprise for the coming Session is being confectioned at the Wednesday gatherings of a young hostess not a hundred miles from Westminster. Her husband, a prospective baronet lately connected with literature, is to be intrusted with the launching in Parliament of a policy which enjoys the peculiar label of Foggartism, derived from Sir James Foggart's book called 'The Parlous State of England.' This amusing alarum is attributed to the somewhat fantastic brain which guides a well-known weekly. We shall see what comes of it. In the meantime the enterprising little lady in question is losing no chance of building up her 'salon' on the curiosity which ever surrounds any buccaneering in politics."

Soames rubbed his eyes; then read it again with rising anger. 'Enterprising little lady is losing no chance of building up her "salon."' Who had written that? He put the paper in his pocket—almost the first theft he had ever committed—and all the way across St. James's Park in the gathering twilight he brooded on that anonymous paragraph. The allusion seemed to him unmistakable, and malicious into the bargain. 'Lion-hunter' would not have been plainer. Unfortunately, in a primary sense 'lion-hunter' was a compliment, and Soames doubted whether its secondary sense had ever been 'laid down' as libellous. He was still brooding deeply, when the young men ranged alongside.

"Well, sir?"

"Ah!" said Soames. "I want to speak to you. You've got a traitor in the camp." And, without meaning to at all, he looked angrily at Francis Wilmot.

"Now, sir?" said Michael, when they were in his study. Soames held out the folded paper.

Michael read the paragraph and made a face.

"Whoever wrote that comes to your evenings," said Soames; "that's clear. Who is he?"

"Very likely a she."

"D'you mean to say they print such things by women?"

Michael did not answer. Old Forsyte was behind the times.

"Will they tell me who it is, if I go down to them?" asked Soames.

"No, fortunately."

"How d'you mean 'fortunately'?"

"Well, sir, the Press is a sensitive plant. I'm afraid you might make it curl up. Besides, it's always saying nice things that aren't deserved."

"But this—" began Soames; he stopped in time, and substituted: "Do you mean that we've got to sit down under it?"

"To lie down, I'm afraid."

"Fleur has an evening to-morrow."

"Yes."

"I shall stay up for it, and keep my eyes open."

Michael had a vision of his father-in-law, like a plain-clothes man in the neighbourhood of wedding-presents.

But in spite of assumed levity, Michael had been hit. The knowledge that his adored one had the collector's habit, and flitted, alluring, among the profitable, had, so

far, caused him only indulgent wonder. But now it seemed
more than an amusing foible. The swiftness with which
she turned her smile off and on as though controlled by a
switch under her shingled hair; the quick turns of her
neck, so charming and exposed; the clever roving, disguised so well but not quite well enough, of the pretty
eyes; the droop and flutter of their white lids; the expres-
sive hands grasping, if one could so call such slim and
dainty apprehensions, her career—all this suddenly caused
Michael pain. Still she was doing it for him and Kit!
French women, they said, co-operated with their husbands in the family career. It was the French blood in
her. Or perhaps just idealism, the desire to have and be
the best of whatever bunch there was about! Thus
Michael, loyally. But his uneasy eyes roved from face to
face of the Wednesday gathering, trying to detect signs
of quizzicality.

Soames followed another method. His mind, indeed,
was uncomplicated by the currents awash in that of one
who goes to bed with the object of his criticism. For him
there was no reason why Fleur should not know as many
aristocrats, labour members, painters, ambassadors, young
fools, and even writing fellows, as might flutter her fancy.
The higher up they were, the less likely, he thought with
a certain naïveté, they would be to borrow money or get
her into a mess. His daughter was as good or better than
any of them, and his deep pride was stung to the quick
by the notion that people should think she had to claw
and scrape to get them round her. It was not she who
was after them, but they who were after her! Standing
under the Fragonard which he had given her, grizzled,
neatly moustached, close-faced, chinny, with a gaze concentrated on nothing in particular, as of one who has
looked over much and found little in it, he might have
been one of her ambassadors.

A young woman, with red-gold hair, about an inch long on her de-shingled neck, came and stood with her back to him, beside a soft man, who kept washing his hands. Soames could hear every word of their talk.

"Isn't the little Mont amusing? Look at her now, with 'Don Fernando'—you'd think he was her only joy. Ah! There's young Bashly! Off she goes. She's a born little snob. But that doesn't make this a 'salon,' as she thinks. To found a 'salon' you want personality, and wit, and the 'don't care a damn' spirit. She hasn't got a scrap. Besides, who is she?"

"Money?" said the soft man.

"Not so very much. Michael's such dead nuts on her that he's getting dull; though it's partly Parliament, of course. Have you heard them talk this Foggartism? All food, children, and the future—the very dregs of dulness."

"Novelty," purred the soft man, "is the vice of our age."

"One resents a nobody like her climbing in on piffle like this Foggartism. Did you read the book?"

"Hardly. Did you?"

"No jolly fear! I'm sorry for Michael. He's being exploited by that little snob."

Penned without an outlet, Soames had begun breathing hard. Feeling a draught, perhaps, the young woman turned to encounter a pair of eyes so grey, so cold, in a face so concentrated, that she moved away. "Who was that old buffer?" she asked of the soft man, "he gave me 'the jim-jams.'"

The soft man thought it might be a poor relation—he didn't seem to know anybody.

But Soames had already gone across to Michael.

"Who's that young woman with the red hair?"

"Marjorie Ferrar."

"She's the traitress—turn her out!"

Michael stared.

"But we know her quite well—she's a daughter of Lord Charles Ferrar, and——"

"Turn her out!" said Soames again.

"How do you know, sir?"

"I've just heard her use the very words of that paragraph, and worse."

"But she's our guest."

"Pretty guest!" growled Soames through his teeth.

"One can't turn a guest out. Besides, she's the granddaughter of a marquess and the pet of the Panjoys—it would make the deuce of a scandal."

"Make it, then!"

"We won't ask her again; but, really, that's all one can do."

"Is it?" said Soames; and walking past his son-in-law, he went towards the object of his denunciation. Michael followed, much perturbed. He had never yet seen his father-in-law with his teeth bared. He arrived in time to hear him say in a low but quite audible voice:

"You were good enough, madam, to call my daughter a snob in her own house."

Michael saw the de-shingled neck turn and rear, the hard blue eyes stare with a sort of outraged impudence; he heard her laugh, then Soames saying:

"You are a traitress; be so kind as to withdraw."

Of the half-dozen people round, not a soul was missing it! Oh, hell! And he the master of the house! Stepping forward, he put his arm through that of Soames:

"That'll do, sir," he said, quietly; "this is not a Peace Conference."

There was a horrid hush; and in all the group only the soft man's white hands, washing each other, moved.

Marjorie Ferrar took a step towards the door.

"I don't know who this person is," she said; "but he's a liar."

"I reckon not."

At the edge of the little group was a dark young man. His eyes were fixed on Marjorie Ferrar's, whose eyes in turn were fixed on his.

And, suddenly, Michael saw Fleur, very pale, standing just behind him. She must have heard it all! She smiled, waved her hand, and said:

"Madame Carelli's going to play."

Marjorie Ferrar walked on towards the door, and the soft man followed her, still washing those hands, as if trying to rid them of the incident. Soames, like a slow dog making sure, walked after them; Michael walked after him. The words "How amusing!" floated back, and a soft echoing snigger. Slam! Both outer door and incident were closed.

Michael wiped his forehead. One half of the brain behind admired his father-in-law; the other thought: 'Well, the old man *has* gone and done it!' He went back into the drawing-room. Fleur was standing near the clavichord, as if nothing had happened. But Michael could see her fingers crisping at her dress; and his heart felt sore. He waited, quivering, for the last chord.

Soames had gone up-stairs. Before 'The White Monkey' in Michael's study, he reviewed his own conduct. He regretted nothing. Red-headed cat! 'Born snob!' 'Money? Not very much.' Ha! 'A nobody like her!' Granddaughter of a marquess, was she? Well, he had shown the insolent baggage the door. All that was sturdy and all that was acrid in his blood, all that resented patronage and privilege, the inherited spirit of his forefathers, moved within him. Who were the aristocracy, to give themselves airs? Jackanapes! Half of 'em descendants of those who had got what they had by robbery or jobbery! That one should call his daughter, *his* daughter, a snob! He wouldn't lift a finger, wouldn't cross a road, to meet the Duke of Seven Dials himself! If Fleur liked to amuse herself by having people round her, why shouldn't she? His blood ran suddenly a little cold. Would she say that he had spoiled her 'salon'? Well! He couldn't help it if she did; better to have had the thing out, and got rid of that cat, and know where they all were. 'I shan't wait up for her,' he thought. 'Storm in a teacup'!

The thin strumming of the clavichord came up to him out on the landing, waiting to climb to his room. He wondered if these evenings woke the baby. A gruff sound at his feet made him jump. That dog lying outside the baby's door! He wished the little beggar had been downstairs just now—he would have known how to put his teeth through that red-haired cat's nude stockings. He passed on up, looking at Francis Wilmot's door, which was opposite his own.

That young American chap must have overheard something too; but he shouldn't allude to the matter with him; not dignified. And, shutting his door on the strumming of the clavichord, Soames closed his eyes again as best he could.

CHAPTER VII

SOUNDS IN THE NIGHT

MICHAEL had never heard Fleur cry, and to see her, flung down across the bed, smothering her sobs in the quilt, gave him a feeling akin to panic. She stopped at his touch on her hair, and lay still.

"Buck up, darling!" he said, gently. "If you aren't one, what does it matter?"

She struggled up, and sat cross-legged, her flushed face smudged with tears, her hair disordered.

"Who cares what one is? It's what one's labelled."

"Well, we've labelled her 'Traitress.'"

"As if that made it better! We all talk behind people's backs. Who minds that? But how can I go on when everybody is sniggering and thinking me a lion-hunting snob? She'll cry it all over London in revenge. How can I have any more evenings?"

Was it for her career, or his, that she was sorrowing? Michael went round to the other side of the bed and put his arms about her from behind.

"Never mind what people think, my child. Sooner or later one's got to face that anyway."

"It's you who aren't facing it. If I'm not thought nice, I can't *be* nice."

"Only the people who really know one matter."

"Nobody knows one," said Fleur, sullenly. "The fonder they are, the less they know, and the less it matters what they think."

Michael withdrew his arms.

She sat silent for so long that he went back to the other side of the bed to see if he could tell anything from her face resting moodily on her hands. The grace of her

49

body thus camped was such that his senses ached. And since caresses would only worry her, they ached the more.

"I hate her," she said, at last; "and if I can hurt her, I will."

He would have liked to hurt the 'pet of the Panjoys' himself, but it did not console him to hear Fleur utter that sentiment; it meant more from her than from himself, who, when it came to the point, was a poor hand at hurting people.

"Well, darling," he said, "shall we sleep on it?"

"I said I wouldn't have any more evenings; but I shall."

"Good!" said Michael; "that's the spirit."

She laughed. It was a funny hard little sound in the night. And with it Michael had to remain discontented.

All through the house it was a wakeful night. Soames had the three o'clock tremors, which cigars and the fresh air wherein he was obliged to play his golf had subdued for some time past. He was disturbed, too, by that confounded great clock from hour to hour, and by a stealthy noise between three and four, as of some one at large in the house.

This was, in fact, Francis Wilmot. Ever since his impulsive denial that Soames was a liar, the young man had been in a peculiar state of mind. As Soames surmised, he too had overheard Marjorie Ferrar slandering her hostess; but in the very moment of his refutation, like Saul setting forth to attack the Christians, he had been smitten by blindness. Those blue eyes, pouring into his the light of defiance, had finished with a gleam which seemed to say: 'Young man, you please me!' And it haunted him. That lissome nymph—with her white skin and red-gold hair, her blue eyes full of insolence, her red lips full of joy, her white neck fragrant as a pinewood in sunshine— the vision was abiding. He had been watching her all through the evening; but it was uncanny the way she had left her image on his senses in that one long moment, so that now he got no sleep. Though he had not been introduced, he knew her name to be Marjorie Ferrar, and he thought it 'fine.' Countryman that he was—she was unlike any woman he had known. And he had given her the lie direct! This made him so restless that he drank the contents of his water-bottle, put on his clothes, and stole down-stairs. Passing the Dandie, who stirred as though muttering: 'Unusual! But I know those legs!' he reached the hall, where a milky glimmer came in through the fanlight. Lighting a cigarette, he sat down on the marble coat-sarcophagus. It cooled his anatomy so that he got off it, turned up the light, saw a telephone directory resting beside him, and mechanically sought the letter 'F.' There she was! "Ferrar, Marjorie, 3, River Studios, Wren Street." Switching off the light, he slipped back the door-chain, and stole out. He knew his way to the river, and went towards it.

It was the hour when sound, exhausted, has laid its head on the pillow, and one can hear a moth pass. London, in clear air, with no smoke going up, slept beneath the moon. Bridges, towers, water, all silvered, had a look as if withdrawn from man. Even the houses and the trees enjoyed their moony hour apart, and seemed to breathe out with Francis Wilmot a stanza from 'The Ancient Mariner':

> 'O Sleep, it is a blessèd thing,
>   Beloved from pole to pole!
> To Mary Queen the praise be given,
> She sent the gentle sleep from heaven
>   That slid into my soul!'

He turned at random to the right along the river. Never in his life had he walked through a great city at the dead hour. Not a passion alive, nor a thought of gain; haste asleep, and terrors dreaming; here and there, no

A tallish man was standing in the middle of the little room, thin and upright, with a moustache brushed arrogantly off his lips, and a single eyeglass which seemed to have grown over the right eye, so unaided was it. There were corrugations in his thin weathered cheeks, and in his thick hair flecked at the sides with grey. Soames had no difficulty in disliking him at sight.

"Mr. Forsyte, I believe?"

Soames inclined his head.

"You made use of an insulting word to my daughter last night in the presence of several people."

"Yes; it was richly deserved."

"You were not drunk, then?"

"Not at all," said Soames.

His dry precision seemed to disconcert the visitor, who twisted his moustache, frowned his eyeglass closer to his eye, and said:

"I have the names of those who overheard it. You will be good enough to write to each of them separately withdrawing your expression unreservedly."

"I shall do nothing of the kind."

A moment's silence ensued.

"You are an attorney, I believe?"

"A solicitor."

"Then you know the consequences of refusal."

"If your daughter likes to go into Court, I shall be happy to meet her there."

"You refuse to withdraw?"

"Absolutely."

"Good evening, then!"

"Good evening."

For two pins he would have walked round the fellow, the bristles rising on his back, but, instead, he stood a little to one side to let him out. Insolent brute! He could so easily hear again the voice of old Uncle Jolyon, characterising some person of the eighties as 'a pettifogging little attorney.' And he felt that, somehow or other, he must relieve his mind. 'Old Mont' would know about this fellow—he would go across and ask him.

At 'The Aeroplane' he found not only Sir Lawrence Mont, looking almost grave, but Michael, who had evidently been detailing to his father last evening's incident. This was a relief to Soames, who felt the insults to his daughter too bitterly to talk of them. Describing the visit he had just received, he ended with the words:

"This fellow—Ferrar—what's his standing?"

"Charlie Ferrar? He owes money everywhere, has some useful horses, and is a very good shot."

"He didn't strike me as a gentleman," said Soames.

Sir Lawrence cocked his eyebrow, as if debating whether he ought to answer this remark about one who had ancestors, from one who had none.

"And his daughter," said Soames, "isn't a lady."

Sir Lawrence wagged his head.

"Single-minded, Forsyte, single-minded; but you're right; there's a queer streak in that blood. Old Shropshire's a dear old man; it skipped his generation, but it's there—it's there. His aunt——"

"He called me an attorney," said Soames with a grim smile, "and she called me a liar. I don't know which is worse."

Sir Lawrence got up and looked into St. James's Street. Soames had the feeling that the narrow head perched up on that straight thin back counted for more than his own, in this affair. One was dealing here with people who said and did what they liked and damned the consequences; this baronet chap had been brought up in that way himself, no doubt, he ought to know how their minds worked.

Sir Lawrence turned.

"She may bring an action, Forsyte; it was very public. What evidence have you?"

"My own ears."

Sir Lawrence looked at the ears, as if to gauge their length.

"M'm! Anything else?"

"That paragraph."

"She'll get at the paper. Yes?"

"The man she was talking to."

Michael ejaculated: "Philip Quinsey—put not your trust in Gath!"

"What more?"

"Well," said Soames, "there's what that young American overheard, whatever it was."

"Ah!" said Sir Lawrence: "Take care she doesn't get at *him*. Is that all?"

Soames nodded. It didn't seem much, now he came to think of it!

"You say she called you a liar. How would it be to take the offensive?"

There was a silence; then Soames said: "Women? No!"

"Quite right, Forsyte! They have their privileges still. There's nothing for it but to wait and see how the cat jumps. Traitress! I suppose you know how much the word costs?"

"The cost," said Soames, "is nothing; it's the publicity!"

His imagination was playing streets ahead of him. He saw himself already in 'the box,' retailing the spiteful purrings of that cat, casting forth to the public and the papers the word 'snob,' of his own daughter; for if he didn't, he would have no defence. Too painful!

"What does Fleur say?" he asked, suddenly, of Michael.

"War to the knife."

Round and About

Soames jumped in his chair.

"Ah!" he said: "That's a woman all over—no imagination!"

"That's what I thought at first, sir, but I'm not so sure. She says if Marjorie Ferrar is not taken by the short hairs, she'll put it across everybody—and that the more public the thing is, the less harm she can do."

"I think," said Sir Lawrence, coming back to his chair, "I'll go and see old Shropshire. My father and his shot woodcock together in Albania in 'fifty-four."

Soames could not see the connection, but did not snub the proposal. A marquess was a sort of gone-off duke; even in this democratic age, he would have some influence, one supposed.

"He's eighty," went on Sir Lawrence, "and gets gout in the stomach, but he's as brisk as a bee."

Soames could not be sure whether it was a comfort.

"The grass shall not grow, Forsyte. I'll go there now."

They parted in the street, Sir Lawrence moving north —towards Mayfair.

The Marquess of Shropshire was dictating to his secretary a letter to his County Council, urging on them an item of his lifelong programme for the electrification of everything. One of the very first to take up electricity, he had remained faithful to it all his brisk and optimistic days. A short, bird-like old man, in shaggy Lovat tweeds, with a blue tie of knitted silk passed through a ring, bright cheeks and well-trimmed white beard and moustache, he was standing in his favourite attitude, with one foot on a chair, his elbow on his knee, and his chin on his hand.

"Ah! young Mont!" he said: "Sit down."

Sir Lawrence took a chair, crossed his knees, and threaded his finger-tips. He found it pleasing to be called 'young Mont,' at sixty-six or so.

"Have you brought me another of your excellent books?"

"No, Marquess; I've come for your advice."

"Ah! Go on, Mr. Mersey: 'In this way, gentlemen, you will save at least three thousand a year to your rate-payers; confer a blessing on the countryside by abolishing the smoke of four filthy chimneys; and make me your obliged servant   SHROPSHIRE.'

"Thank you, Mr. Mersey. Now, my dear young Mont?"

Having watched the back of the secretary till it vanished, and the old peer pivot his bright eyes, with their expression of one who means to see more every day, on the face of his visitor, Sir Lawrence took his eyeglass between thumb and finger, and said:

"Your granddaughter, sir, and my daughter-in-law want to fight like billy-o."

"Marjorie?" said the old man, and his head fell to one side like a bird's. "I draw the line—a charming young woman to look at, but I draw the line. What has she done now?"

"Called my daughter-in-law a snob and a lion-hunter; and my daughter-in-law's father has called your granddaughter a traitress to her face."

"Bold man," said the marquess; "bold man! Who is he?"

"His name is Forsyte."

"Forsyte?" repeated the old peer; "Forsyte? The name's familiar—now where would that be? Ah! Forsyte and Treffry—the big tea men. My father had his tea from them direct—real caravan; no such tea now. Is that the——?"

"Some relation, perhaps. This man is a solicitor—retired; chiefly renowned for his pictures. A man of some substance, and probity."

"Indeed! And *is* his daughter a—a lion-hunter?"

Sir Lawrence smiled.

"She's a charmer. Likes to have people about her. Very pretty. Excellent little mother; some French blood."

"Ah!" said the marquess: "the French! Better built round the middle than our people. What do you want me to do?"

"Speak to your son Charles."

The old man took his foot off the chair, and stood nearly upright. His head moved sideways with a slight continuous motion.

"I never speak to Charlie," he said, gravely. "We haven't spoken for six years."

"I beg your pardon, sir. Didn't know. Sorry to have bothered you."

"No, no; pleasure to see you. If I run across Marjorie, I'll see—I'll see. But, my dear Mont, what shall we do with these young women—no sense of service; no continuity; no hair; no figures? By the way, do you know this Power Scheme on the Severn?" He held up a pamphlet: "I've been at them to do it for years. My Colliery among others could be made to pay with electricity; but they won't move. We want some Americans over here."

Sir Lawrence had risen; the old man's sense of service had so clearly taken the bit between its teeth again. He held out his hand.

"Good-bye, Marquess; delighted to see you looking so well."

"Good-bye, my dear young Mont; command me at any time, and let me have another of your nice books."

They shook hands; and from the Lovat clothes was disengaged a strong whiff of peat. Sir Lawrence, looking back, saw the old man back in his favourite attitude, foot

on chair and chin on hand, already reading the pamphlet.
'Some boy!' he thought; 'as Michael would say. But
what has Charlie Ferrar done not to be spoken to for six
years? Old Forsyte ought to know. . . .'

In the meantime Old Forsyte and Michael were walking homewards across St. James's Park.

"That young American," said Soames; "what do you
suppose made him put his oar in?"

"I don't know, sir; and I don't like to ask."

"Exactly," said Soames, glumly. There was, indeed,
something repulsive to him in treating with an American
over a matter of personal dignity.

"Do they use the word 'snob' over there?"

"I'm not sure; but, in the States to hunt lions is a form
of idealism. They want to associate with what they think
better than themselves. It's rather fine."

Soames did not agree; but found difficulty in explain-
ing why. Not to recognise any one as better than himself,
or his daughter, had been a sort of guiding principle, and
guiding principles were not talked about. In fact, it was
so deep in him that he hadn't known of it.

"I shan't mention it," he said, "unless he does. What
more can this young woman do? She's in a set, I suppose?"

"The Panjoys——"

"Panjoys!"

"Yes, sir; out for a good time at any cost—they don't
really count, of course. But Marjorie Ferrar is frightfully
in the limelight. She paints a bit; she's got some standing with the Press; she dances; she hunts; she's something
of an actress; she goes everywhere week-ending. It's the
week-ends that matter, where people have nothing to do
but talk. Were you ever at a week-end party, sir?"

Round and About 61

"I ?" said Soames: "Good Lord—no !"

Michael smiled—incongruity, indeed, could go no farther.

"We must get one up for you at Lippinghall."

"No, thank you."

"You're right, sir; nothing more boring. But they're the *coulisses* of politics. Fleur thinks they're good for me. And Marjorie Ferrar knows all the people we know, and lots more. It *is* awkward."

"I should go on as if nothing had happened," said Soames: "But about that paper? They ought to be warned that this woman is venomous."

Michael regarded his father-in-law quizzically.

On entering, they found the man-servant in the hall.

"There's a man to see you, sir, by the name of Bugfill."

"Oh! Ah! Where have you put him, Coaker?"

"Well, I didn't know what to make of him, sir, he shakes all over. I've stood him in the dining-room."

"Excuse me, sir," said Michael.

Soames passed into the 'parlour,' where he found his daughter and Francis Wilmot.

"Mr. Wilmot is leaving us, Father. You're just in time to say good-bye."

If there were moments when Soames felt cordial, they were such as these. He had nothing against the young man; indeed, he rather liked the look of him; but to see the last of almost anybody was in a sense a relief; besides, there was this question of what he had overheard, and to have him about the place without knowing would be a continual temptation to compromise with one's dignity and ask him what it was.

"Good-bye, Mr. Wilmot," he said; "if you're interested in pictures—" he paused, and, holding out his hand, added, "you should look in at the British Museum."

Francis Wilmot shook the hand deferentially.

"I will. It's been a privilege to know you, sir."

Soames was wondering why, when the young man turned to Fleur.

"I'll be writing to Jon from Paris, and I'll surely send your love. You've been perfectly wonderful to me. I'll be glad to have you and Michael visit me any time you come across to the States; and if you bring the little dog, why—I'll just be honoured to let him bite me again."

He bowed over Fleur's hand, kissed it, and was gone, leaving Soames staring at the back of his daughter's neck.

"That's rather sudden," he said, when the door was closed; "anything upset him?"

She turned on him, and said coldly:

"Why did you make that fuss last night, Father?"

The injustice of her attack was so palpable that Soames bit his moustache in silence. As if he could help himself, when she was insulted in his hearing!

"What good do you think you've done?"

Soames, who had no notion, made no attempt to enlighten her. He only felt sore inside.

"You've made me feel as if I couldn't look anybody in the face. But I'm going to, all the same. If I'm a lion-hunter and a snob, I'll do it thoroughly. Only I do wish you wouldn't go on thinking I'm a child and can't defend myself."

And still Soames was silent, sore to the soles of his boots.

Fleur flashed a look at him, and said:

"I'm sorry, but I can't help it; everything's queered"; and she too went out of the room.

Soames moved blindly to the window and stood looking out. He saw a cab with luggage drive away; saw some pigeons alight, peck at the pavement, and fly off again; he saw a man kissing a woman in the dusk; a policeman light his pipe and go off duty. He saw many human and interesting things; he heard Big Ben chime. Nothing in it all! He was staring at a silver spoon. He himself had put it in her mouth at birth.

CHAPTER IX

POULTRY AND CATS

HE who had been stood in the dining-room, under the name of Bugfill, was still upright. Rather older than Michael, with an inclination to side-whisker, darkish hair, and a pale face stamped with that look of schooled quickness common to so many actors but unfamiliar to Michael, he was grasping the edge of the dining-table with one hand, and a wide-brimmed black hat with the other. The expression of his large, dark-circled eyes was such that Michael smiled and said:

"It's all right, Mr. Bergfeld, I'm not a Manager. Do sit down, and smoke?"

The visitor silently took the proffered chair and cigarette with an attempt at a fixed smile. Michael sat on the table.

"I gather from Mrs. Bergfeld that you're on the rocks."

"Fast," said the shaking lips.

"Your health, and your name, I suppose?"

"Yes."

"You want an open-air job, I believe? I haven't been able to think of anything very gaudy, but an idea did strike me last night in the stilly watches. How about raising poultry—everybody's doing it."

"If I had my savings."

"Yes, Mrs. Bergfeld told me about them. I can inquire, but I'm afraid——"

"It's robbery." The chattered sound let Michael at once into the confidence of the many Managers who had refused to employ him who uttered it.

"I know," he said, soothingly, "robbing Peter to pay

Paul. That clause in the Treaty was a bit of rank barbarism, of course, camouflage it as they like. Still, it's no good to let it prey on your mind, is it?"

But his visitor had risen. "To take from civilian to pay civilian! Then why not take civilian life for civilian life? What is the difference? And England does it—the leading nation to respect the individual. It is abominable."

Michael began to feel that he was overdoing it.

"You forget," he said, "that the war made us all into barbarians, for the time being; we haven't quite got over it yet. And your country dropped the spark into the magazine, you know. But what about this poultry stunt?"

Bergfeld seemed to make a violent effort to control himself.

"For my wife's sake," he said, "I will do anything; but unless I get my savings back, how can I start?"

"I can't promise; but perhaps I could start you. That hair-dresser below you wants an open-air job, too. What's his name, by the way?"

"Swain."

"How do you get on with him?"

"He is an opinionated man, but we are good friends enough."

Michael got off the table. "Well, leave it to me to think it out. We shall be able to do something, I hope"; and he held out his hand.

Bergfeld took it silently, and his eyes resumed the expression with which they had first looked at Michael.

'That man,' thought Michael, 'will be committing suicide some day, if he doesn't look out.' And he showed him to the door. He stood there some minutes gazing after the German actor's vanishing form, with a feeling as if the dusk were formed out of the dark stories of such as he and the hair-dresser and the man who had whispered to him to stand and deliver a job. Well, Bart must lend him that bit of land beyond the coppice at Lip-pinghall. He would buy a War hut if there were any left, and some poultry stock, and start a colony—the Bergfelds, the hair-dresser, and Henry Boddick. They could cut the timber in the coppice, and put up the fowl-houses for themselves. It would be growing food—a prac-tical experiment in Foggartism! Fleur would laugh at him. But was there anything one could do nowadays that somebody couldn't laugh at? He turned back into the house. Fleur was in the hall.

"Francis Wilmot has gone," she said.

"Why?"

"He's off to Paris."

"What was it he overheard last night?"

"Do you suppose I asked?"

"Well, no," said Michael, humbly. "Let's go up and look at Kit, it's about his bath time."

The eleventh baronet, indeed, was already in his bath.

"All right, nurse," said Fleur, "I'll finish him."

"He's been in three minutes, ma'am."

"Lightly boiled," said Michael.

For one aged only fourteen months this naked infant had incredible vigour—from lips to feet he was all sound and motion. He seemed to lend a meaning to life. His vitality was absolute, not relative. His kicks and crows and splashings had the joy of a gnat's dance, or a jack-daw's gambols in the air. They gave thanks not for what he was about to receive, but for what he was receiving. White as a turtle-dove, with pink toes, darker in eyes and hair than he would be presently, he grabbed at the soap, at his mother, at the bath-towelling—he seemed only to need a tail. Michael watched him, musing. This mannikin, born with all that he could possibly wish for within his reach—how were they to bring him up? Were they fit to bring him up—they who had been born, like all their generation in the richer classes—emancipated, to parents properly broken-in to worship the fetich— Liberty? Born to everything they wanted, so that they were at wits' end to invent something they could not get; driven to restive searching by having their own way? The war had deprived one of one's own way, but the war had overdone it, and left one grasping at licence. And for those, like Fleur, born a little late for the war, the tale of it had only lowered what respect they could have for anything. With veneration killed, and self-denial 'off,' with atavism buried, sentiment derided, and the future in the air, hardly a wonder that modernity should be a dance of gnats, taking itself damned seriously! Such were the reflections of Michael, sitting there above the steam, and frowning at his progeny. Without faith was one fit to be a parent? Well, people were looking for faith again. Only they were bound to hatch the egg of it so hard that it would be addled long before it was a chicken. 'Too self-conscious!' he thought. 'That's our trouble!'

Fleur had finished drying the eleventh baronet, and was dabbing powder over him; her eyes seemed penetrating his skin, as if to gauge the state of health behind it. He watched her take the feet and hands one by one and examine each nail, lost in her scrutiny, unselfconscious in her momentary devotion! And oppressed by the difficulty, as a Member of Parliament, of being devoted, Michael snapped his fingers at the baby and left the nursery. He went to his study and took down a volume of the Encyclopædia Britannica containing the word Poultry. He read about Leghorns, Orpingtons, White Sussex, Bramaputras, and was little the wiser. He remembered that if you drew a chalk-line to the beak of a hen, the hen thought it was tied up. He wished somebody would draw a chalk-line to his beak. Was Foggartism a chalk-line? A voice said:

"Tell Fleur I'm going to her aunt's."

"Leaving us, sir?"

"Yes, I'm not wanted."

What had happened?

"You'll see her before you go, sir?"

"No," said Soames.

Had somebody rubbed out the chalk-line to Old Forsyte's nose?

"Is there any money in poultry-farming, sir?"

"There's no money in anything nowadays."

"And yet the Income Tax returns continue to rise."

"Yes," said Soames; "there's something wrong there."

"You don't think people make their incomes out more than they are?"

Soames blinked. Pessimistic though he felt at the moment, he could not take quite that low view of human nature.

"You'd better see that Fleur doesn't go about abusing that red-haired baggage," he said. "She was born with a silver spoon in her mouth; she thinks she can do what she likes." And he shut Michael in again.

Silver spoon in her mouth! How *àpropos!* . . .

After putting her baby into its cot Fleur had gone to the marqueterie bureau in the little sanctuary that would have been called a boudoir in old days. She sat there brooding. How could her father have made it all glaringly public? Couldn't he have seen that it was nothing so long as it was not public, but everything the moment it was? She longed to pour out her heart, and tell people her opinion of Marjorie Ferrar.

She wrote three letters—one to Lady Alison, and two to women in the group who had overheard it all last night. She concluded her third letter with the words: "A woman like that, who pretends to be a friend and sneaks into one's house to sting one behind one's back, is a snake of the first water. How Society can stick her, I can't think; she hasn't a moral about her nor a decent impulse. As for her charm—Good Lord!" Yes! And there was Francis Wilmot! She had not said all she wanted to say to him.

"MY DEAR FRANCIS," she wrote:

"I am so sorry you have to run away like this. I wanted to thank you for standing up for me last night. Marjorie Ferrar is just about the limit. But in London society one doesn't pay attention to backbiting. It has been so jolly to know you. Don't forget us; and do come and see me again when you come back from Paris.

Your very good friend,

FLEUR MONT."

In future she would have nothing but men at her evenings! But would they come if there were no women? And men like Philip Quinsey were just as snakelike. Besides, it would look as if she were really hurt. No! She would have to go on as before, just dropping people who were 'catty.' But who wasn't? Except Alison, and heavyweights like Mr. Blythe, the minor Ambassadors, and three or four earnest politicians, she couldn't be sure about any of them. It was the thing to be 'catty.' They all scratched other people's backs, and their faces too when they weren't looking. Who in Society was exempt from scratches, and who didn't scratch? Not to scratch a little was so dreadfully dull. She could not imagine a scratchless life except perhaps in Italy. Those Fra Angelico frescoes in the San Marco monastery! There was a man who did not scratch. St. Francis talking to his birds, among his little flowers, with the sun and the moon and the stars for near relations. Ste. Claire! Ste. Fleur— little sister of St. Francis! To be unworldly and quite good! To be one who lived to make other people happy! How new! How exciting, even—for about a week; and how dull afterwards! She drew aside the curtains and looked out into the Square. Two cats were standing in the light of a lamp—narrow, marvellously graceful, with their heads turned towards each other. Suddenly they began uttering horrible noises, and became all claws. Fleur dropped the curtain.

CHAPTER X

FRANCIS WILMOT REVERSES

ABOUT that moment Francis Wilmot sat down in the lounge of the Cosmopolis Hotel, and as suddenly sat up. In the middle of the parquet floor, sliding and lunging, backing and filling, twisting and turning in the arms of a man with a face like a mask, was she, to avoid whom, out of loyalty to Fleur and Michael, he had decided to go to Paris. Fate! For he could hardly know that she came there most afternoons during the dancing hours. She and her partner were easily the show couple; and, fond of dancing, Francis Wilmot knew he was looking at something special. When they stopped, quite close to him, he said in his soft drawl:

"That was beautiful."

"How do you do, Mr. Wilmot?"

Why! She knew his name! This was the moment to exhibit loyalty! But she had sunk into a chair next his.

"And so you thought me a traitress last night?"

"I did."

"Why?"

"Because I heard you call your hostess a snob."

Marjorie Ferrar uttered an amused sound.

"My dear young man, if one never called one's friends anything worse than that—! I didn't mean you to hear, or that poptious old person in the chin!"

"He was her father," said Francis Wilmot, gravely. "It hurt him."

"Well! I'm sorry!"

A hand without a glove, warm but dry, was put into his. When it was withdrawn the whole of his hand and arm were tingling.

71

"Do you dance?"

"Yes, indeed, but I wouldn't presume to dance with you."

"Oh! but you must."

Francis Wilmot's head went round, and his body began going round too.

"You dance better than an Englishman, unless he's professional," said her lips six inches from his own.

"I'm proud to hear you say so, ma'am."

"Don't you know my name? or do you always call women ma'am? It's ever so pretty."

"Certainly I know your name and where you live. I wasn't six yards from you this morning at four o'clock."

"What were you doing there?"

"I just thought I'd like to be near you."

Marjorie Ferrar said, as if to herself:

"The prettiest speech I ever heard. Come and have tea with me there to-morrow."

Reversing, side-stepping, doing all he knew, Francis Wilmot said, slowly:

"I have to be in Paris."

"Don't be afraid, I won't hurt you."

"I'm not afraid, but——"

"Well, I shall expect you." And, transferring herself again to her mask-faced partner, she looked back at him over her shoulder.

Francis Wilmot wiped his brow. An astonishing experience, another blow to his preconception of a stiff and formal race! If he had not known she was the daughter of a lord, he would have thought her an American. Would she ask him to dance with her again? But she left the lounge without another glance.

An up-to-date young man, a typical young man, would have felt the more jaunty. But he was neither. Six months' training for the Air Service in 1918, one visit to New York, and a few trips to Charleston and Savannah, had left him still a countryman, with a tradition of good manners, work, and simple living. Women, of whom he had known few, were to him worthy of considerable respect. He judged them by his sister, or by the friends of his dead mother, in Savannah, who were all of a certain age. A Northern lady on the boat had told him that Southern girls measured life by the number of men they could attract; she had given him an amusing take-off of a Southern girl. It had been a surprise to this young Southerner. Anne was not like that; she had never had the chance to be, anyway, having married at nineteen the first young man who had asked her!

By the morning's post he received Fleur's little letter. 'Limit!' Limit of what? He felt indignant. He did not go to Paris, and at four o'clock he was at Wren Street.

In her studio Marjorie Ferrar, clad in a flax-blue overall, was scraping at a picture with a little knife. An hour later he was her slave. Cruft's Dog Show, the Beef-eaters, the Derby—he could not even remember his desire to see them; he only desired to see one English thing—Marjorie Ferrar. He hardly remembered which way the river flowed, and by mere accident walked East instead of West. Her hair, her eyes, her voice—he 'had fallen for her!' He knew himself for a fool, and did not mind; farther man cannot go. She passed him in a little open car, driving it herself, on her way to a rehearsal. She waved her hand. Blood rushed to his heart and rushed away; he trembled and went pale. And, as the car vanished, he felt lost, as if in a world of shadows, grey and dreary! Ah! There was Parliament! And, near by, the one spot in London where he could go and talk of Marjorie Ferrar, and that was where she had misbehaved herself! He itched to defend her from the charge of being 'the limit.' He could perceive the inappropriateness of

The Silver Spoon

going back there to talk to Fleur of her enemy, but anything was better than not talking of her. So, turning into South Square, he rang the bell.

Fleur was in her 'parlour,' if not precisely eating bread and honey, at least having tea.

"Not in Paris? How nice! Tea?"

"I've had it," said Francis Wilmot, colouring. "I had it with *her*."

Fleur stared.

"Oh!" she said, with a laugh. "How interesting! Where did she pick you up?"

Without taking in the implication of the words, Francis Wilmot was conscious of something deadly in them.

"She was at the *thé dansant* at my hotel yesterday. She's a wonderful dancer. I think she's a wonderful person altogether; I'd like to have you tell me what you mean by calling her 'the limit'?"

"I'd like to have you tell me why this *volte face* since Wednesday night?"

Francis Wilmot smiled: "You people have been ever so kind to me, and I want you to be friends with her again. I'm sure she didn't mean what she said that night."

"Indeed! Did she tell you that?"

"Why—not exactly! She said she didn't mean us to hear them."

"No?"

He looked at her smiling face, conscious, perhaps, of deep waters, but youthfully, Americanly, unconscious of serious obstacle to his desire to smooth things out.

"I just hate to think you two are out after each other. Won't you come and meet her at my hotel, and shake hands?"

Fleur's eyes moved slowly over him from head to toe.

"You look as if you might have some French blood in you. Have you?"

"Yes. My grandmother was of French stock."

"Well, I have more. The French, you know, don't forgive easily. And they don't persuade themselves into believing what they want to."

Francis Wilmot rose, and spoke with a kind of masterfulness.

"You're going to tell me what you meant in your letter."

"Am I? My dear young man, the limit of perfection, of course. Aren't you a living proof?"

Aware that he was being mocked, and mixed in his feelings, Francis Wilmot made for the door.

"Good-bye," he said. "I suppose you'll have no use for me in future."

"Good-bye!" said Fleur.

He went out rueful, puzzled, lonelier even than when he went in. He was guideless, with no one to 'put him wise'! No directness and simplicity in this town. People did not say what they meant; and his goddess—as enigmatic and twisting as the rest! More so—more so—for what did the rest matter?

CHAPTER XI

SOAMES VISITS THE PRESS

SOAMES had gone off to his sister's in Green Street thoroughly upset. That Fleur should have a declared enemy, powerful in Society, filled him with uneasiness; that she should hold him accountable for it, seemed the more unjust, because in fact he was.

An evening spent under the calming influence of Winifred Dartie's common-sense, and Turkish coffee, which, though 'liverish stuff,' he always drank with relish, restored in him something of the feeling that it was a storm in a teacup.

"But that paper paragraph," he said, "sticks in my gizzard."

"Very tiresome, Soames, the whole thing; but I shouldn't bother. People skim those 'chiff-chaff' little notes and forget them the next moment. They're just put in for fun."

"Pretty sort of fun! That paper says it has a million readers."

"There's no name mentioned."

"These political people and whipper-snappers in Society all know each other," said Soames.

"Yes, my dear boy," said Winifred in her comfortable voice, so cosey, and above disturbance, "but nobody takes anything seriously nowadays."

She was sensible. He went up to bed in more cheerful mood.

But retirement from affairs had effected in Soames a deeper change than he was at all aware of. Lacking professional issues to anchor the faculty for worrying he had inherited from James Forsyte, he was inclined to pet any trouble that came along. The more he thought of that paragraph, the more he felt inclined for a friendly talk with the editor. If he could go to Fleur and say: "I've made it all right with those fellows, anyway. There'll be no more of that sort of thing," he would wipe out her vexation. If you couldn't make people in private think well of your daughter, you could surely check public expression of the opposite opinion.

Except that he did not like to get into them, Soames took on the whole a favourable view of 'the papers.' He read 'The Times'; his father had read it before him, and he had been brought up on its crackle. It had news—more news for his money than he could get through. He respected its leading articles; and if its great supplements had at times appeared to him too much of a good thing, still it was a gentleman's paper. Annette and Winifred took 'The Morning Post.' That also was a gentleman's paper, but it had bees in its bonnet. Bees in bonnets were respectable things, but personally Soames did not care for them. He knew little of the other papers except that those he saw about had bigger head-lines and seemed cut up into little bits. Of the Press as a whole he took the English view: It was an institution. It had its virtues, and its vices—anyway you had to put up with it.

About eleven o'clock he was walking towards Fleet Street.

At the office of 'The Evening Sun' he handed in his card and asked to see the Editor. After a moment's inspection of his top-hat, he was taken down a corridor and deposited in a small room. It seemed a 'wandering great place.' Some one would see him!

"Some one?" said Soames: "I want the Editor."

The Editor was very busy; could he come again when the rush was over?

"No," said Soames.

Would he state his business? Soames wouldn't.

The attendant again looked at his top-hat and went away.

Soames waited a quarter of an hour, and was then taken to a still smaller room, where a cheery-looking man in eyeglasses was turning over a book of filed cuttings. He glanced up as Soames entered, took his card from the table, and read from it:

"Mr. Soames Forsyte? Yes?"

"Are you the Editor?" asked Soames.

"One of them. Take a seat. What can I do for you?"

Impressed by a certain speed in the air, and desirous of making a good impression, Soames did not sit down, but took from his pocket-book the paragraph.

"I've come about this in your issue of last Thursday."

The cheery man put it up to his eyes, seemed to chew the sense of it a little with his mouth, and said: "Yes?"

"Would you kindly tell me who wrote it?"

"We never disclose the names of correspondents, sir."

"Well, as a matter of fact I know."

The cheery man's mouth opened, as if to emit the words: "Then why did you ask?" but closed in a smile instead.

"You'll forgive me," said Soames, "it quite clearly refers to my daughter, Mrs. Michael Mont, and her husband."

"Indeed! You have the advantage of me; but what's the matter with it? Seems rather a harmless piece of gossip."

Soames looked at him. He was too cheery!

"You think so?" he said, drily. "May I ask if you would like to have your daughter alluded to as an enterprising little lady?"

"Why not? It's quite a pleasant word. Besides, there's no name mentioned."

"Do you put things in," asked Soames, shrewdly, "in order that they may be Greek to all your readers?"

The cheery man laughed: "Well," he said, "hardly. But really, sir, aren't you rather thin-skinned?"

This was an aspect of the affair that Soames had not foreseen. Before he could ask this Editor chap not to repeat his offence, he had apparently to convince him that it *was* an offence; but to do that he must expose the real meaning of the paragraph.

"Well," he said, "if you can't see that the tone of the thing's unpleasant, I can't make you. But I beg you won't let any more such paragraphs appear. I happen to know that your correspondent is actuated by malevolence."

The cheery man again ran his eye over the cutting. "I shouldn't have judged that. People in politics are taking and giving knocks all the time—they're not mealy-mouthed. This seems perfectly innocuous as gossip goes."

Thus backhanded by the word 'thin-skinned' and 'mealy-mouthed,' Soames said testily:

"The whole thing's extremely petty."

"Well, sir, you know, I rather agree. Good morning!" and the cheery man blandly returned to his file.

The fellow was like an india-rubber ball! Soames clenched his top-hat. Now or never he must make him bound.

"If your correspondent thinks she can vent her spleen in print with impunity, she will find herself very much mistaken." He waited for the effect. There was absolutely none. "Good morning!" he said, and turned on his heel.

Somehow it had not been so friendly as he had expected. Michael's words "The Press is a sensitive plant" came into his mind. He shouldn't mention his visit.

Two days later, picking up 'The Evening Sun' at the

Connoisseurs, he saw the word "Foggartism." H'm! A leader!

"Of the panaceas rife among the young hopefuls in politics, perhaps the most absurd is one which goes by the name of Foggartism. We are in a position to explain the nature of this patent remedy for what is supposed to be the national ill-health before it has been put on the market. Based on Sir James Foggart's book, 'The Parlous State of England,' the main article of faith in this crazy creed would appear to be the depletion of British man-power. According to its prophets, we are to despatch to the ends of the Empire hundreds of thousands of our boys and girls as soon as they leave school. Quite apart from the rank impossibility of absorbing them into the life of the slowly developing Dominions, we are to lose this vital stream of labour and defensive material, in order that twenty years hence the demand from our Dominions may equal the supplying power of Great Britain. A crazier proposition was never conceived in woolly brains. Well does the word Foggartism characterise such a proposition. Alongside this emigration 'stunt'—for there is no other term which suits its sensational character—rises a feeble back-to-the-land propaganda. The keystone of the whole professes to be the doctrine that the standard of British wages and living now preclude us from any attempt to rival German production, or recover our trade with Europe. Such a turning of the tail on our industrial supremacy has probably never before been mooted in this country. The sooner these cheap-jack gerrymanders of British policy realise that the British voter will have nothing to do with so crack-brained a scheme, the sooner it will come to the still birth which is its inevitable fate."

Whatever attention Soames had given to 'The Parlous State of England,' he could not be accused of anything so rash as a faith in Foggartism. If Foggartism were killed to-morrow, he, with his inherent distrust of theories and ideas, his truly English pragmatism, could not help feeling that Michael would be well rid of a white elephant. What disquieted him, however, was the suspicion that he himself had inspired this article. Was this that too-cheery fellow's retort?

Decidedly, he should not mention his visit when he dined in South Square that evening.

The presence of a strange hat on the sarcophagus warned him of a fourth party. Mr. Blythe, in fact, with a cocktail in his hand, and an olive in his mouth, was talking to Fleur, who was curled up on a cushion by the fire.

"You know Mr. Blythe, Dad?"

Another Editor! Soames extended his hand with caution.

Mr. Blythe swallowed the olive. "It's of no importance," he said.

"Well," said Fleur, "*I* think you ought to put it all off, and let them feel they've made fools of themselves."

"Does Michael think that, Mrs. Mont?"

"No; Michael's got his shirt out!" And they all looked round at Michael, who was coming in.

He certainly had a somewhat headstrong air.

According to Michael, they must take it by the short hairs and give as good as they got, or they might as well put up the shutters. They were sent to Parliament to hold their own opinions, not those stuck into them by Fleet Street. If they genuinely believed the Foggart policy to be the only way to cure unemployment, and stem the steady drain into the towns, they must say so, and not be stampeded by every little newspaper attack that came along. Common-sense was on their side, and common-sense, if you aired it enough, won through in the end.

The opposition to Foggartism was really based on an intention to force lower wages and longer hours on Labour, only they daren't say so in so many words. Let the papers jump through their hoops as much as they liked. He would bet that when Foggartism had been six months before the public, they would be eating half their words, with an air of eating some one else's! And suddenly he turned to Soames:

"I suppose, sir, you didn't go down about that paragraph?"

Soames, privately, and as a business man, had always so conducted himself that, if cornered, he need never tell a direct untruth. Lies were not English, not even good form. Looking down his nose, he said slowly:

"Well, I let them know that I knew that woman's name."

Fleur frowned; Mr. Blythe reached out and took some salted almonds.

"What did I tell you, sir?" said Michael. "They always get back on you. The Press has a tremendous sense of dignity; and corns on both feet; eh, Mr. Blythe?"

Mr. Blythe said weightily: "It's a very human institution, young man. It prefers to criticise rather than to be criticised."

"I thought," said Fleur, icily, "that I was to be left to my own cudgels."

The discussion broke back to Foggartism, but Soames sat brooding. He would never again interfere in what didn't concern himself. Then, like all who love, he perceived the bitterness of his fate. He had only meddled with what *did* concern himself—her name, her happiness; and she resented it. Basket in which were all his eggs, to the end of his days he must go on walking gingerly, balancing her so that she was not upset, spilling his only treasure.

She left them over the wine that only Mr. Blythe was drinking. Soames heard an odd word now and then, gathered that this great frog-chap was going to burst next week in 'The Outpost,' gathered that Michael was to get on to his hind legs in the House at the first opportunity. It was all a muzz of words to him. When they rose, he said to Michael:

"I'll take myself off."

"We're going down to the House, sir; won't you stay with Fleur?"

"No," said Soames; "I must be getting back."

Michael looked at him closely.

"I'll just tell her you're going."

Soames had wrapped himself into his coat, and was opening the door when he smelled violet soap. A bare arm had come round his neck. He felt soft pressure against his back. "Sorry, Dad, for being such a pig."

Soames shook his head.

"No," said her voice; "you're not going like that."

She slipped between him and the door. Her clear eyes looked into his; her teeth gleamed, very white. "Say you forgive me!"

"There's no end to it," said Soames.

She thrust her lips against his nose. "There! Good night, ducky! I know I'm spoiled!"

Soames gave her body a convulsive little squeeze, opened the door and went out without a word.

Under Big Ben boys were calling—political news, he supposed. Those Labour chaps were going to fall—some Editor had got them into trouble. He would! Well—one down, t'other come on! It was all remote to him. She alone—she alone mattered.

CHAPTER XII

MICHAEL MUSES

MICHAEL and Mr. Blythe sought the Mother of Parliaments and found her in commotion. Liberalism had refused, and Labour was falling from its back. A considerable number of people were in Parliament Square contemplating Big Ben and hoping for sensation.

"I'm not going in," said Michael. "There won't be a division to-night. General Election's a foregone conclusion, now. I want to think."

"One will go up for a bit," said Mr. Blythe; and they parted, Michael returning to the streets. The night was clear, and he had a longing to hear the voice of his country. But—where? For his countrymen would be discussing this pro and that con, would be mentioning each his personal 'grief'—here the Income Tax, there the dole, the names of leaders, the word Communism. Nowhere would he catch the echo of the uneasiness in the hearts of all. The Tories—as Fleur had predicted—would come in now. The country would catch at the anodyne of 'strong stable government.' But could strong stable government remove the inherent canker, the lack of balance in the top-heavy realm? Could it still the gnawing ache which everybody felt, and nobody would express?

'Spoiled,' thought Michael, 'by our past prosperity. We shall never admit it,' he thought, 'never! And yet in our bones we feel it!'

England with the silver spoon in her mouth and no longer the teeth to hold it there, or the will to part with it! And her very qualities—the latent 'grit,' the power to take things smiling, the lack of nerves and imagination! Almost vices, now, perpetuating the rash belief that Eng-

land could still 'muddle through' without special effort,
although with every year there was less chance of recovering from shock, less time in which to exercise the British 'virtues.' 'Slow in the uptak',' thought Michael, 'it's
a ghastly fault in 1924.'

Thus musing, he turned East. Mid-theatre-hour, and
the 'Great Parasite'—as Sir James Foggart called it—was
lying inert, and bright. He walked the length of wakeful
Fleet Street into the City so delirious by day, so dead by
night. Here England's wealth was snoozing off the day's
debauch. Here were all the frame and filaments of English credit. And based on—what? On food and raw material from which England, undefended in the air, might
be cut off by a fresh war; on Labour, too big for European
boots. And yet that credit stood high still, soothing all
with its 'panache'—save, perhaps, receivers of the dole.
With her promise to pay, England could still purchase
anything, except a quiet heart.

And Michael walked on—through Whitechapel, busy
still and coloured—into Mile End. The houses had become low, as if to give the dwellers a better view of stars
they couldn't reach. He had crossed a frontier. Here
was a different race almost; another England, but as
happy-go-lucky and as hand-to-mouth as the England
of Fleet Street and the City. Aye, and more! For the
England in Mile End knew that whatever she felt could
have no effect on policy. Mile on mile, without an end,
the low grey streets stretched towards the ultimate deserted grass. Michael did not follow them, but coming
to a Cinema, turned in.

The show was far advanced. Bound and seated in front
of the bad cowboy on a bronco, the heroine was crossing
what Michael shrewdly suspected to be the Film Company's pet paddock. Every ten seconds she gave way
to John T. Bronson, Manager of the Tucsonville Copper

Mine, devouring the road in his 60 h. p. Dodge, to cut her off before she reached the Pima river. Michael contemplated his fellow gazers. Lapping it up! Strong stable government—not much! This was their anodyne and they could not have enough of it. He saw the bronco fall, dropped by a shot from John T. Bronson; and the screen disclose the words: "Hairy Pete grows desperate. . . . 'You shall not have her, Bronson.'" Quite! He was throwing her into the river instead, to the words: "John T. Bronson dives." There he goes! He has her by her flowing hair! But Hairy Pete is kneeling on the bank. The bullets chip the water. Through the heroine's fair perforated shoulder the landscape is almost visible. What is that sound? Yes! John T. Bronson is setting his teeth! He lands, he drags her out. From his cap he takes his automatic. Still dry—thank God!

"Look to yourself, Hairy Pete!" A puff of smoke. Pete squirms and bites the sand—he seems almost to absorb the desert. "Hairy Pete gets it for keeps!" Slow music, slower! John T. Bronson raises the reviving form. Upon the bank of the Pima river they stand embraced, and the sun sets. "At last, my dinky love!"

'Pom, pom! that's the stuff!' thought Michael, returning to the light of night: 'Back to the Land! "Plough the fields and scatter"—when they can get this? Not much!' And he turned West again, taking a seat on the top of a 'bus beside a man with grease-stains on his clothes. They travelled in silence till Michael said:

"What do you make of the political situation, sir?"

The possible plumber replied, without turning his head: "I should say they've overreached theirselves."

"Ought to have fought on Russia—oughtn't they?"

"Russia—that cock won't fight either. Nao—ought to 'ave 'eld on to the Spring, an' fought on a good stiff Budget."

"Real class issue?"

"Ah!"

"But do you think class politics can wipe out unemployment?"

The man's mouth moved under his moustache as if mumbling a new idea.

"Ah! I'm fed up with politics; in work to-day and out to-morrow—what's the good of politics that can't give you a permanent job?"

"That's it."

"Reparations," said his neighbour; "*we're* not goin' to benefit by reparations. The workin' classes ought to stand together in every country." And he looked at Michael to see how he liked *that*.

"A good many people thought so before the war; and see what happened."

"Ah!" said the man, "and what good's it done us?"

"Have you thought of emigrating to the Dominions?" The man shook his head.

"Don't like what I see of the Austrylians and Canydians."

"Confirmed Englishman—like myself."

"That's right," said the man. "So long, Mister," and he got off.

Michael travelled till the 'bus put him down under Big Ben, and it was nearly twelve. Another election! Could he stand a second time without showing his true colours? Not the faintest hope of making Foggartism clear to a rural constituency in three weeks! If he spoke from now till the day of the election, they would merely think he held rather extreme views on Imperial Preference, which, by the way, he did. He could never tell the electorate that he thought England was on the wrong tack—one might just as well not stand. He could never buttonhole the ordinary voter, and say to him: "Look here, you know,

there's no earthly hope of any real improvement for another ten years; in the meantime we must face the music,
and pay more for everything, so that twenty years hence
we may be safe from possible starvation, and self-support-
ing within the Empire." It wasn't done. Nor could he
say to his Committee: "My friends, I represent a policy
that no one else does, so far."

No! If he meant to stand again, he must just get the
old wheezes off his chest. But did he mean to stand
again? Few people had less conceit than Michael—he
knew himself for a lightweight. But he had got this bee
into his bonnet; the longer he lived the more it buzzed,
the more its buzz seemed the voice of one crying in the
wilderness, and that wilderness his country. To stop up
that buzzing in his ears; to turn his back on old Blythe;
to stifle his convictions, and remain in Parliament—he
could not! It was like the war over again. Once in, you
couldn't get out. And he was 'in'—committed to something deeper far than the top dressings of Party politics.
Foggartism had a definite solution of England's troubles
to work towards—an independent, balanced Empire; an
England safe in the air, and free from unemployment—
with Town and Country once more in some sort of due
proportion! Was it such a hopeless dream? Apparently!

'Well,' thought Michael, putting his latch-key in his
door, 'they may call me what kind of a bee fool they like
—I shan't budge.' He went up to his dressing-room and,
opening the window, leaned out.

The rumourous town still hummed; the sky was faintly
coloured by refraction from its million lights. A spire
was visible, some stars; the tree foliage in the Square
hung flat, unstirred by wind. Peaceful and almost warm
—the night. Michael remembered a May evening—the
last London air-raid of the war. From his convalescent
hospital he had watched it for three hours.

'What fools we all are not to drop fighting in the air,' he thought: 'Well, if we don't, I shall go all out for a great air force—all hangs, for us, on safety from air attack. Even the wise can understand that.'

Two men had stopped beneath his window, talking. One was his next-door neighbour.

"Mark my words," said his neighbour, "the election'll see a big turnover."

"Yes; and what are you going to do with it?" said the other.

"Let things alone; they'll right themselves. I'm sick of all this depressing twaddle. A shilling off the Income Tax, and you'll see."

"How are you going to deal with the Land?"

"Oh! damn the Land! Leave it to itself, that's all the farmers really want. The more you touch it, the worse it gets."

"Let the grass grow under your feet?"

The neighbour laughed. "That's about it. Well, what else *can* you do—the Country won't have it. Good night!"

Sounds of a door, of footsteps. A car drove by; a moth flew in Michael's face. "The Country won't have it!" Policies! What but mental yawns, long shrugs of the shoulders, trustings to Luck! What else could they be? *The Country wouldn't have it!* And Big Ben struck twelve.

CHAPTER XIII

INCEPTION OF THE CASE

THERE are people in every human hive born to focus talk; perhaps their magnetism draws the human tongue, or their lives are lived at an acute angle. Of such was Marjorie Ferrar—one of the most talked-of young women in London. Whatever happened to her was rumoured at once in that collection of the busy and the idle called Society. That she had been ejected from a drawing-room was swiftly known. Fleur's letters about her became current gossip. The reasons for ejectment varied from truth to a legend that she had lifted Michael from the arms of his wife.

The origins of lawsuits are seldom simple. And when Soames called it all 'a storm in a teacup,' he might have been right if Lord Charles Ferrar had not been so heavily in debt that he had withdrawn his daughter's allowance; if, too, a Member for a Scottish borough, Sir Alexander MacGown, had not for some time past been pursuing her with the idea of marriage. Wealth made out of jute, a rising Parliamentary repute, powerful physique, and a determined character, had not advanced Sir Alexander's claims in twelve months so much as the withdrawal of her allowance advanced them in a single night. Marjorie Ferrar was, indeed, of those who can always get money at a pinch, but even to such come moments when they have seriously to consider what kind of pinch. In proportion to her age and sex, she was 'dipped' as badly as her father, and the withdrawal of her allowance was in the nature of a last straw. In a moment of discouragement she consented to an engagement, not yet to be made public. When the incident at Fleur's came to Sir Alexander's ears, he went to his betrothed flaming. What could he do?

"Nothing, of course; don't be silly, Alec! Who cares?"

"The thing's monstrous. Let me go and exact an apology from this old blackguard."

"Father's been, and he wouldn't give it. He's got a chin you could hang a kettle on."

"Now, look here, Marjorie, you've got to make our engagement public, and let me get to work on him. I won't have this story going about."

Marjorie Ferrar shook her head.

"Oh! no, my dear. You're still on probation. I don't care a tuppenny ice about the story."

"Well, I do, and I'm going to that fellow to-morrow."

Marjorie Ferrar studied his face—its brown, burning eyes, its black, stiff hair, its iaw—shivered slightly, and had a brain-wave.

"You will do nothing of the kind, Alec, or you'll spill your ink. My father wants me to bring an action. He says I shall get swinging damages."

The Scotsman in MacGown applauded, the lover quailed.

"That may be very unpleasant for you," he muttered, "unless the brute settles out of Court."

"Of course he'll settle. I've got all his evidence in my vanity-bag."

MacGown gripped her by the shoulders and gave her a fierce kiss.

"If he doesn't, I'll break every bone in his body."

"My dear! He's nearly seventy, I should think."

"H'm! Isn't there a young man in the same boat with him?"

"Michael? Oh! Michael's a dear. I couldn't have his bones broken."

"Indeed!" said MacGown. "Wait till he launches this

precious Foggartism they talk of—dreary rot! I'll eat him!"

"Poor little Michael!"

"I heard something about an American boy, too."

"Oh!" said Marjorie Ferrar, releasing herself from his grip. "A bird of passage—don't bother about him."

"Have you got a lawyer?"

"Not yet."

"I'll send you mine. He'll make them sit up!"

She remained pensive after he had left her, distrusting her own brain-wave. If only she weren't so hard up! She had learned during this month of secret engagement that "Nothing for nothing and only fair value for sixpence" ruled North of the Tweed as well as South. He had taken a good many kisses and given her one trinket which she dared not take to 'her Uncle's.' It began to look as if she would have to marry him. The prospect was in some ways not repulsive—he was emphatically a man; her father would take care that she only married him on terms as liberal as his politics; and perhaps her motto 'Live dangerously' could be even better carried out with him than without. Resting inert in a long chair, she thought of Francis Wilmot. Hopeless as husband, he might be charming as lover, naïve, fresh, unknown in London, absurdly devoted, oddly attractive, with his lithe form, dark eyes, engaging smile. Too old-fashioned for words, he had made it clear already that he wanted to marry her. He was a baby. But until she was beyond his reach, she had begun to feel that he was beyond hers. After? Well, who knew? She lived in advance, dangerously, with Francis Wilmot. In the meantime this action for slander was a bore! And shaking the idea out of her head, she ordered her horse, changed her clothes, and repaired to the Row. After that she again changed her clothes, went to the Cosmopolis Hotel, and danced with her mask-faced partner, and Francis Wilmot. After that she changed her clothes once more, went to a first night, partook of supper afterwards with the principal actor and his party, and was in bed by two o'clock.

Like most reputations, that of Marjorie Ferrar received more than its deserts. If you avow a creed of indulgence, you will be indulged by the credulous. In truth she had only had two love-affairs passing the limits of decorum; had smoked opium once, and been sick over it; and had sniffed cocaine just to see what it was like. She gambled only with discretion, and chiefly on race-horses; drank with strict moderation and a good head; smoked of course, but the purest cigarettes she could get, and through a holder. If she had learned suggestive forms of dancing, she danced them but once in a blue moon. She rarely rode at a five-barred gate, and that only on horses whose powers she knew. To be in the know she read, of course, anything 'extreme,' but would not go out of her way to do so. She had flown, but just to Paris. She drove a car well, and of course fast, but never to the danger of herself, and seldom to the real danger of the public. She had splendid health, and took care of it in private. She could always sleep at ten minutes' notice, and when she sat up half the night, slept half the day. She was 'in' with the advanced theatre, but took it as it came. Her book of poems, which had received praise because they emanated from one of a class supposed to be unpoetic, was remarkable not so much for irregularity of thought as for irregularity of metre. She was, in sum, credited with a too strict observance of her expressed creed: 'Take life in both hands, and eat it.'

This was why Sir Alexander MacGown's lawyer sat on the edge of his chair in her studio the following morning, and gazed at her intently. He knew her renown better than Sir Alexander. Messrs. Settlewhite and Stark liked

to be on the right side of a matter before they took it up.
How far would this young lady, with her very attractive
appearance and her fast reputation, stand fire? For costs
—they had Sir Alexander's guarantee and the word
'traitress' was a good enough beginning; but in cases of
word against word, it was ill predicting.

Her physiognomy impressed Mr. Settlewhite favourably. She would not 'get rattled' in Court, if he was any
judge; nor had she the Aubrey Beardsley cast of feature,
he had been afraid of, that might alienate a Jury. No!
an upstanding young woman with a good blue eye and
popular hair. She would do, if her story were all right.

Marjorie Ferrar, in turn, scrutinised one, who looked
as if he might take things out of her hands. Long-faced,
with grey deep eyes under long dark lashes, all his hair,
and good clothes, he was as well preserved a man of sixty
as she had ever seen.

"What do you want me to tell you, Mr. Settlewhite?"

"The truth."

"Oh! but naturally. Well, I was just saying to Mr.
Quinsey that Mrs. Mont was very eager to form a 'salon,'
and had none of the right qualities, and the old person
who overheard me thought I was insulting her——"

"That all?"

"Well, I may have said she was fond of lions; and so
she is."

"Yes; but why did he call you a traitress?"

"Because she was his daughter and my hostess, I suppose."

"Will this Mr. Quinsey confirm you?"

"Philip Quinsey?—oh! rather! He's in my pocket."

"Did anybody else overhear you running her down?"

She hesitated a second. "No."

'First lie!' thought Mr. Settlewhite, with his peculiar
sweet-sarcastic smile. "What about an American?"

Marjorie Ferrar laughed. "He won't say so, anyway."

"An admirer?"

"No. He's going back to America."

'Second lie!' thought Mr. Settlewhite. 'But she tells them well.'

"You want an apology you can show to those who overheard the insult; and what we can get, I suppose?"

"Yes. The more the better."

'Speaking the truth there,' thought Mr. Settlewhite. "Are you hard up?"

"Couldn't well be harder."

Mr. Settlewhite put one hand on each knee, and reared his slim body.

"You don't want it to come into Court?"

"No; though I suppose it might be rather fun."

Mr. Settlewhite smiled again.

"That entirely depends on how many skeletons you have in your cupboard."

Marjorie Ferrar also smiled.

"I shall put everything in your hands," she said.

"Not *them*, my dear young lady. Well, we'll serve him and see how the cat jumps; but he's a man of means and a lawyer."

"I think he'll hate having anything about his daughter brought out in Court."

"Yes," said Mr. Settlewhite, drily. "So should I."

"And she *is* a little snob, you know."

"Ah! Did you happen to use that word?"

"N-no; I'm pretty sure I didn't."

'Third lie!' thought Mr. Settlewhite: 'not so well told.'

"It makes a difference. Quite sure?"

"Not quite."

"He says you did?"

"Well, I told him he was a liar."

"Oh! did you? And they heard you?"

"Rather!"

"That may be important."

"I don't believe he'll say I called her a snob in Court, anyway."

"That's very shrewd, Miss Ferrar," said Mr. Settlewhite. "I think we shall do."

And with a final look at her from under his long lashes, he stalked, thin and contained, to the door.

Three days later Soames received a legal letter. It demanded a formal apology, and concluded with the words "failing it, action will be taken." Twice in his life he had brought actions himself; once for breach of contract, once for divorce; and now to be sued for slander! In every case he had been the injured party, in his own opinion. He was certainly not going to apologise. Under the direct threat he felt much calmer. He had nothing to be ashamed of. He would call that 'baggage' a traitress to her face again to-morrow, and pay for the luxury, if need be. His mind roved back to when, in the early 'eighties, as a very young lawyer, he had handled his Uncle Swithin's defence against a fellow member of the Walpole Club. Swithin had called him in public "a little touting whipper-snapper of a parson." He remembered how he had whittled the charge down to the word 'whipper-snapper,' by proving the plaintiff's height to be five feet four, his profession the church, his habit the collection of money for the purpose of small-clothing the Fiji islanders. The Jury had assessed 'whipper-snapper' at ten pounds—Soames always believed the small clothes had done it. His Counsel had made great game of them—Bobstay, Q. C. There *were* Counsel in those days; the Q. C.'s had been better than the K. C.'s were. Bobstay would have gone clean through this 'baggage' and come out on the other side. Uncle Swithin had asked him to dinner afterwards and given him York ham with Madeira sauce, and his special Heidsieck. He had never given anybody anything else. Well! There must still be cross-examiners who could tear a reputation to tatters, especially if there wasn't one to tear. And one could always settle at the last moment if one wished. There was no possibility anyway of Fleur being dragged in as witness or anything of that sort.

He was thunder-struck, a week later, when Michael rang him up at Mapledurham to say that Fleur had been served with a writ for libel in letters containing among others the expressions 'a snake of the first water' and 'she hasn't a moral about her.'

Soames went cold all over. "I told you not to let her go about abusing that woman."

"I know; but she doesn't consult me every time she writes a letter to a friend."

"Pretty friend!" said Soames into the mouthpiece. "This is a nice pair of shoes!"

"Yes, sir; I'm very worried. She's absolutely spoiling for a fight—won't hear of an apology."

Soames grunted so deeply that Michael's ear tingled forty miles away.

"In the meantime, what shall we do?"

"Leave it to me," said Soames. "I'll come up to-night. Has she any evidence to support those words?"

"Well, she says——"

"No," said Soames, abruptly, "don't tell me over the 'phone." And he rang off. He went out on to the lawn. Women! Petted and spoiled—thought they could say what they liked! And so they could till they came up against another woman. He stopped by the boat-house and gazed at the river. The water was nice and clean, and there it was—flowing down to London to get all dirty! That feverish, quarrelsome business up there! Now he would have to set to and rake up all he could against this Ferrar woman, and frighten her off. It was distasteful.

But nothing else for it, if Fleur was to be kept out of Court! Terribly petty. Society lawsuits—who ever got anything out of them, save heart-burning and degradation? Like the war, you might win and regret it ever afterwards, or lose and regret it more. All temper! Jealousy and temper!

In the quiet autumn light, with the savour of smoke in his nostrils from his gardener's first leaf bonfire, Soames felt moral. Here was his son-in-law, wanting to do some useful work in Parliament, and make a name for the baby, and Fleur beginning to settle down and take a position; and now this had come along, and all the chatterers and busy mockers in Society would be gnashing on them with their teeth—if they had any! He looked at his shadow on the bank, grotesquely slanting towards the water as if wanting to drink. Everything was grotesque, if it came to that! In Society, England, Europe—shadows scrimmaging and sprawling; scuffling and posturing; the world just marking time before another Flood! H'm! He moved towards the river. There went his shadow, plunging in before him! They would all plunge into that mess of cold water if they didn't stop their squabblings. And, turning abruptly, he entered his kitchen-garden. Nothing unreal there, and most things running to seed—stalks, and so on! How to set about raking up the past of this young woman? Where was it? These young sparks and fly-by-nights! They all had pasts, no doubt; but the definite, the concrete bit of immorality alone was of use, and when it came to the point, was unobtainable, he shouldn't wonder. People didn't like giving chapter and verse! It was risky, and not the thing! Tales out of school!

And, among his artichokes, approving of those who did not tell tales, disapproving of any one who wanted them told, Soames resolved grimly that told they must be. The leaf-fire smouldered, and the artichokes smelled rank, the sun went down behind the high brick wall mellowed by fifty years of weather; all was peaceful and chilly, except in his heart. Often now, morning or evening, he would walk among his vegetables—they were real and restful, and you could eat them. They had better flavour than the green-grocer's and saved his bill—middlemen's profiteering and all that. Perhaps they represented atavistic instincts in this great-grandson of 'Superior Dosset's' father, last of a long line of Forsyte 'agriculturists.' He set more and more store by vegetables the older he grew. When Fleur was a little bit of a thing, he would find her when he came back from the City, seated among the sunflowers or black currants, nursing her doll. He had once taken a bee out of her hair, and the little brute had stung him. Best years he ever had, before she grew up and took to this gadabout Society business, associating with women who went behind her back. Apology! So she wouldn't hear of one? She was in the right. But to be in the right and have to go into Court because of it, was one of the most painful experiences that could be undergone. The Courts existed to penalise people who were in the right—in divorce, breach of promise, libel and the rest of it. Those who were in the wrong went to the South of France, or if they did appear, defaulted afterwards and left you to pay your costs. Had he not himself had to pay them in his action against Bosinney? And in his divorce suit had not Young Jolyon and Irene been in Italy when he brought it? And yet, he couldn't bear to think of Fleur eating humble-pie to that red-haired cat. Among the gathering shadows, his resolve hardened. Secure evidence that would frighten the baggage into dropping the whole thing like a hot potato—it was the only way!

CHAPTER XIV

FURTHER CONSIDERATION

THE Government had 'taken their toss' over the Editor—no one could say precisely why—and Michael sat down to compose his Address. How say enough without saying anything? And, having impetuously written: "Electors of Mid-Bucks," he remained for many moments still as a man who has had too good a dinner. "If"—he traced words slowly—"if you again return me as your representative, I shall do my best for the Country according to my lights. I consider the limitation of armaments, and, failing that, the security of Britain through the enlargement of our Air defences; the development of home agriculture; the elimination of unemployment through increased emigration to the Dominions; and the improvement of the national health particularly through the abatement of slums and smoke, to be the most pressing and immediate concerns of British policy. If I am returned, I shall endeavour to foster these ends with determination and coherence; and try not to abuse those whose opinions differ from my own. At my meetings I shall seek to give you some concrete idea of what is in my mind, and submit myself to your questioning."

Dared he leave it at that? Could one issue an address containing no disparagement of the other side, no panegyric of his own? Would his Committee allow it? Would the electors swallow it? Well, if his Committee didn't like it—they could turn it down, and himself with it; only—they wouldn't have time to get another candidate!

The Committee, indeed, did not like it, but they lumped it; and the Address went out with an effigy on it of Michael, looking, as he said, like a hair-dresser. Thereon he plunged into a fray, which, like every other, began in the general and ended in the particular.

During the first Sunday lull at Lippinghall, he developed his poultry scheme—by marking out sites, and deciding how water could be laid on. The bailiff was sulky. In his view it was throwing away money. "Fellers like that!" Who was going to teach them the job? He had no time, himself. It would run into hundreds, and might just as well be poured down the gutter. "The townsman's no mortial use on the land, Master Michael."

"So everybody says. But, look here, Tutfield, here are three 'down and outs,' two of them ex-Service, and you've got to help me put this through. You say yourself this land's all right for poultry—well, it's doing no good now. Bowman knows every last thing about chickens, set him on to it until these chaps get the hang. Be a good fellow and put your heart into it; you wouldn't like being 'down and out' yourself."

The bailiff had a weakness for Michael, whom he had known from his bottle up. He knew the result, but if Master Michael liked to throw his father's money away, it was no business of his. He even went so far as to mention that he knew "a feller" who had a hut for sale not ten miles away; and that there was "plenty of wood in the copse for the cuttin'."

On the Tuesday after the Government had fallen Michael went up to town and summoned a meeting of his 'down and outs.' They came at three the following day, and he placed them in chairs round the dining-table. Standing under the Goya, like a general about to detail a plan of attack which others would have to execute, he developed his proposal. The three faces expressed little, and that without conviction. Only Bergfeld had known anything of it, before, and his face was the most doubting.

"I don't know in the least," went on Michael, "what you think of it; but you all want jobs—two of you in the open, and you, Boddick, don't mind what it is, I think."

"That's right, sir," said Boddick, "I'm on."

Michael instantly put him down as the best man of the three.

The other two were silent till Bergfeld said:

"If I had my savings——"

Michael interrupted quickly:

"I'm putting in the capital; you three put in the brains and labour. It's probably not more than a bare living, but I hope it'll be a healthy one. What do *you* say, Mr. Swain?"

The hair-dresser, more shadow-stricken than ever, in the glow of Fleur's Spanish room, smiled.

"I'm sure it's very kind of you. I don't mind havin' a try—only, who's goin' to boss the show?"

"Co-operation, Mr. Swain."

"Ah!" said the hair-dresser; "thought so. But I've seen a lot of tries at that, and it always ends in one bloke swallerin' the rest."

"Very well," said Michael, suddenly, "I'll boss it. But if any of you crane at the job, say so at once, and have done with it. Otherwise I'll get that hut delivered and set up, and we'll start this day month."

Boddick got up, and said: "Right, sir. What about my children?"

"How old, Boddick?"

"Two little girls, four and five."

"Oh! yes!" Michael had forgotten this item. "We must see about that."

Boddick touched his forelock, shook Michael's hand, and went out. The other two remained standing.

"Good-bye, Mr. Bergfeld; good-bye, Mr. Swain!"

"If I might——"

"Could I speak to you for a minute?"

"Anything you have to say," said Michael, astutely, "had better be said in each other's presence."

"I've always been used to hair."

'Pity,' thought Michael, 'that Life didn't drop that "h" for him—poor beggar!' "Well, we'll get you a breed of birds that can be shingled," he said. The hairdresser smiled down one side of his face. "Beggars can't be choosers," he said.

"*I* wished to ask you," said Bergfeld, "what system we shall adopt?"

"That's got to be worked out. Here are two books on poultry-keeping; you'd better read one each, and swop."

He noted that Bergfeld took both without remonstrance on the part of Swain.

Seeing them out into the Square, he thought: 'Rum team! It won't work, but they've got their chance.'

A young man who had been standing on the pavement came forward.

"Mr. Michael Mont, M. P.?"

"Yes."

"Mrs. Michael Mont at home?"

"I think so. What do you want?"

"I must see her personally, please."

"Who are you from?"

"Messrs. Settlewhite and Stark—a suit."

"Dressmakers?"

The young man smiled.

"Come in," said Michael. "I'll see if she's at home." Fleur was in the 'parlour.'

"A young man from some dressmaker's for you, dear."

"Mrs. Michael Mont? In the suit of Ferrar against Mont—libel. Good day, madam."

Between those hours of four and eight when Soames arrived from Mapledurham, Michael suffered more than

Fleur. To sit and see a legal operation performed on her
with all the scientific skill of the British Bar, it was an
appalling prospect; and there would be no satisfaction in
Marjorie Ferrar's also being on the table, with her inside
exposed to the gaze of all! He was only disconcerted,
therefore, when Fleur said:

"All right; if she wants to be opened up, she shall be.
I know she flew to Paris with Walter Nazing last Novem-
ber; and I've always been told she was Bertie Curfew's
mistress for a year."

A Society case—cream for all the cats in Society, muck
for all the blow-flies in the streets—and Fleur the hub
of it! He waited for Soames with impatience. Though
Old Forsyte's indignation had started this, Michael
turned to him now, as to an anchor let go off a lee shore.
The 'old man' had experience, judgment, and a chin; he
would know what, except bearing it with a grin, could be
done. Gazing at a square foot of study wall which had
escaped a framed caricature, he reflected on the under-
lying savagery of life. He would be eating a lobster to-
night that had been slowly boiled alive! This study had
been cleaned out by a charwoman whose mother was
dying of cancer, whose son had lost a leg in the war, and
who looked so jolly tired that he felt quite bad whenever
he thought of her. The Bergfelds, Swains and Boddicks
of the world—the Camden Towns, and Mile Ends—the
devastated regions of France, the rock villages of Italy!
Over it all what a thin crust of gentility! Members of
Parliament, and ladies of fashion, like himself and Fleur,
simpering and sucking silver spoons, and now and then
dropping spoons and simper, and going for each other
like Kilkenny cats!

"What evidence has she got to support those words?"
Michael racked his memory. This was going to be a
game of bluff. That Walter Nazing and Marjorie Ferrar

had flown to Paris together appeared to him of next to
no importance. People could still fly in couples with impunity; and as to what had happened afterwards in the
great rabbit-warren Outre Manche—Pff! The Bertie
Curfew affair was different. Smoke of a year's duration
probably had fire behind it. He knew Bertie Curfew, the
enterprising Director of the 'Ne Plus Ultra Play Society,'
whose device was a stork swallowing a frog—a long young
man, with long young hair that shone and was brushed
back, and a long young record; a strange mixture of enthusiasm and contempt, from one to the other of which
he passed with extreme suddenness. His sister, of whom
he always spoke as 'Poor Norah,' in Michael's opinion
was worth ten of him. She ran a Children's House in
Bethnal Green, and had eyes from which meanness and
evil shrank away.

Big Ben thumped out eight strokes; the Dandie barked,
and Michael knew that Soames had come.

Very silent during dinner, Soames opened the discussion over a bottle of Lippinghall Madeira by asking to see
the writ.

When Fleur had brought it, he seemed to go into a
trance.

'The old boy,' thought Michael, 'is thinking of his past.
Wish he'd come to!'

"Well, Father?" said Fleur at last.

As if from long scrutiny of a ghostly Court of Justice,
Soames turned his eyes on his daughter's face.

"You won't eat your words, I suppose?"

Fleur tossed her now de-shingled head. "Do you want
me to?"

"Can you substantiate them? You mustn't rely on
what was told you—that isn't evidence."

"I know that Amabel Nazing came here and said that
she didn't mind Walter flying to Paris with Marjorie

Ferrar, but that she did object to not having been told
beforehand, so that she herself could have flown to Paris
with somebody else."

"We could subpœna that young woman," said Soames.

Fleur shook her head. "She'd never give Walter away
in Court."

"H'm! What else about this Miss Ferrar?"

"Everybody knows of her relationship with Bertie
Curfew."

"Yes," Michael put in, "and between 'everybody
knows' and 'somebody tells' is a great gap fixed."

Soames nodded.

"She just wants money out of us," cried Fleur; "she's
always hard up. As if she cared whether people thought
her moral or not! She despises morality—all her set
do."

"Ah! Her view of morality!" said Soames, deeply; he
was suddenly seeing a British Jury confronted by a bar-
rister describing the modern view of morals: "No need,
perhaps, to go into personal details."

Michael started up.

"By Jove, sir, you've hit it! If you can get her to admit that she's read certain books, seen or acted in certain
plays, danced certain dances, worn certain clothes—"
He fell back again into his chair; what if the other side
started asking Fleur the same questions? Was it not the
fashion to keep abreast of certain things, however moral
one might really be? Who could stand up and profess to
be shocked, to-day?

"Well?" said Soames.

"Only that one's own point of view isn't quite a British Jury's, sir. Even yours and ours, I expect, don't precisely tally."

Soames looked at his daughter. He understood. Loose
talk—afraid of being out of the fashion—evil communi-

cations corrupting all profession of good manners! Still,
no Jury could look at her face without—who could resist
the sudden raising of those white lids? Besides, she was
a mother, and the other woman wasn't; or if she was—
she shouldn't be! No, he held to his idea. A clever fellow
at the Bar could turn the whole thing into an indictment
of the fast set and modern morality, and save all the in-
vidiousness of exposing a woman's private life.

"You give me the names of her set and those books
and plays and dancing clubs and things," he said. "I'll
have the best man at the Bar."

Michael rose from the little conference somewhat eased
in mind. If the matter could be shifted from the particular to the general; if, instead of attacking Marjorie Ferrar's practice, the defence could attack her theory, it
would not be so dreadful. Soames took him apart in the
hall.

"I shall want all the information I can get about that
young man and her."

Michael's face fell.

"You can't get it from me, sir, I haven't got it."

"She must be frightened," said Soames. "If I can
frighten her, I can probably settle it out of Court without
an apology."

"I see; use the information out of Court, but not in."

Soames nodded. "I shall tell them that we shall justify. Give me the young man's address."

"Macbeth Chambers, Bloomsbury. It's close to the
British Museum. But do remember, sir, that to air Miss
Ferrar's linen in Court will be as bad for us as for her."

Again Soames nodded.

When Fleur and her father had gone up, Michael lit a
cigarette, and passed back into the 'parlour.' He sat
down at the clavichord. The instrument made very little
noise—so he could strum on it without fear of waking the

eleventh baronet. From a Spanish tune picked up three years ago on his honeymoon, whose savagery always soothed him, his fingers wandered on: "I got a crown, you got a crown—all God's chillun got a crown! Ev'y-body talkin' 'bout heav'n ain't goin' dere. All God's chillun got a crown."

Glass lustres on the walls gleamed out at him. As a child he had loved the colours of his aunt Pamela's glass chandeliers in the panelled rooms at Brook Street; but when he knew what was what, he and every one had laughed at them. And now lustres had come in again; and Aunt Pamela had gone out! "She had a crown—he had a crown—" Confound that tune! "*Auprès de ma blonde—il fait bon—fait bon—fait bon; Auprès de ma blonde, il fait bon dormir.*"

His 'blonde'—not so very blonde, either—would be in bed by now. Time to go up! But still he strummed on, and his mind wandered in and out—of poultry and politics, Old Forsyte, Fleur, Foggartism, and the Ferrar girl —like a man in a maelstrom whirling round with his head just above water. Who was it said the landing-place for modernity was a change of heart; the rebirth of a belief that life was worth while, and better life attainable? 'Better life?' Prerogative of priests? Not now. Humanity had got to save itself! To save itself—what was that, after all, but expression of 'the will to live'? But did humanity will to live as much as it used? That was the point. Michael stopped strumming and listened to the silence. Not even a clock ticking—time was inhospitable in 'parlours'; and England asleep outside. Was the English 'will to live' as strong as ever; or had they all become so spoiled, so sensitive to life, that they had weakened on it? Had they sucked their silver spoon so long that, threatened with a spoon of bone, they preferred to get down from table? 'I don't believe it,' thought Michael,

'I won't believe it. Only where are we going? Where am I going? Where are all God's children going?' To bed, it seemed.

Big Ben struck: One.

PART II

CHAPTER I

MICHAEL MAKES HIS SPEECH

WHEN in the new Parliament Michael rose to deliver his maiden effort towards the close of the debate on the King's Speech, he had some notes in his hand and not an idea in his head. His heart was beating and his knees felt weak. The policy he was charged to express, if not precisely new in concept, was in reach and method so much beyond current opinion, that he awaited nothing but laughter. His would be a stray wind carrying the seed of a new herb into a garden, so serried and so full that no corner would welcome its growth. There was a plant called Chinese weed which having got hold never let go, and spread till it covered everything. Michael desired for Foggartism the career of Chinese weed; but all he expected was the like of what he had seen at Monterey on his tour round the world after the war. Chance had once brought to that Californian shore the seeds of the Japanese yew. In thick formation the little dark trees had fought their way inland to a distance of some miles. That battalion would never get farther now that native vegetation had been consciously roused against it; but its thicket stood—a curious and strong invader.

His first period had been so rehearsed that neither vacant mind nor dry mouth could quite prevent delivery. Straightening his waistcoat, and jerking his head back, he regretted that the Speech from the throne foreshadowed no coherent and substantial policy such as might hope to free the country from its present plague of underemployment, and overpopulation. Economically speaking, any foreseeing interpretation of the course of affairs must now place Britain definitely in the orbit of the overseas world. . . . ("*Oh! oh!*") Ironical laughter so soon and sudden cleared Michael's mind, and relaxed his lips; and, with the grin that gave his face a certain charm, he resumed:

Speakers on all sides of the House, dwelling on the grave nature of the Unemployment problem, had pinned their faith to the full recapture of European trade, some in one way, some in another. August as they were, he wished very humbly to remark that they could not eat cake and have it. (*Laughter.*) Did they contend that wages in Britain must come down and working hours be lengthened; or did they assert that European wages must go up, and European working hours be shortened? No, they had not had the temerity. Britain, which was to rid itself of unemployment in the ways suggested, was the only important country in the world which had to buy about seven-tenths of its food, and of whose population well-nigh six-sevenths lived in Towns. It employed those six-sevenths in producing articles in some cases too dearly for European countries to buy, and yet it had to sell a sufficient surplus above the normal exchanges of trade, to pay for seven-tenths of the wherewithal to keep its producers alive. (*A laugh.*) If this was a joke, it was a grim one. (*A voice: "You have forgotten the carrying trade."*) He accepted the honourable Member's correction, and hoped that he felt happy about the future of that trade. It was, he feared, a somewhat shrinking asset.

At this moment in his speech Michael himself became a somewhat shrinking asset, overwhelmed by a sudden desire to drop Foggartism, and sit down. The cool attention, the faint smiles, the expression on the face of a past Prime Minister, seemed conspiring towards his subsidence. 'How young—oh! how young you are!' they seemed to say. 'We sat here before you were breeched.' And he agreed with them completely. Still there was nothing for it but to go on—with Fleur in the Ladies' Gallery, old Blythe in the Distinguished Strangers'; yes, and something stubborn in his heart! Clenching the notes in his hand, therefore, he proceeded:

In spite of the war, and because of the war, the population of their Island had increased by 2,000,000. Emigration had fallen from 300,000 to 100,000. And this state of things was to be remedied by the mere process of recapturing to the full European trade which, quite obviously, had no intention of being so recaptured. What alternative, then, was there? Some honourable Members, he was afraid not many, would be familiar with the treatise of Sir James Foggart, entitled 'The Parlous State of England.' (*"Hear, hear!" from a back Labour bench.*) He remembered to have read in a certain organ, or perhaps he should say harmonium, of the Press, for it was not a very deep-voiced instrument—(*laughter*) that no such crack-brained policy had ever been devised for British consumption. (*"Hear, hear!"*) Certainly Foggartism was mad enough to look ahead, to be fundamental, and to ask the country to face its own position and the music into the bargain. . . .

About to go over 'the top'—with public confession of his faith trembling behind his lips—Michael was choked by the sudden thought: 'Is it all right—is it what I think it, or am I an ignorant fool?' He swallowed vigorously, and staring straight before him, went on:

"Foggartism deprecates surface measures for a people in our position; it asks the country to fix its mind on a date—say twenty years hence—a minute in a nation's life—and to work steadily and coherently up to that date. It demands recognition of the need to make the British Empire, with its immense resources mostly latent, a self-sufficing unit. Imperialists will ask: What is there new in that? The novelty lies in degree and in method. Foggartism urges that the British people should be familiarised with the Empire by organised tours and propaganda on a great scale. It urges a vast increase—based on this familiarisation—of controlled and equipped emigration from these shores. But it has been found impossible, as honourable members well know, to send out suitable grown folk in any adequate quantity, because confirmed town-dwellers with their town tastes and habits, and their physique already impaired by town life, are of little use in the Dominions, while the few still on the English land cannot be spared. Foggartism, therefore, would send out boys and girls, between the ages of fourteen, or perhaps fifteen, and eighteen, in great numbers. The House is aware that experiments in this direction have already been made, with conspicuous success, but such experiments are but a drop in the bucket. This is a matter which can only be tackled in the way that things were tackled during the war. Development of child emigration is wanted, in fact, on the same scale and with the same energy as was manifested in Munitions after a certain most honourable Member had put his shoulder to that wheel—multiplication a hundredfold. Although the idea must naturally prove abortive without the utmost goodwill and co-operating energy on the part of the Dominions, I submit that this co-operation is not beyond the bounds of hope. The present hostility of people in the Dominions towards British immigrants is due to their very reasonable distrust of the usefulness of adult immigrants from this country. Once they have malleable youth to deal with, that drawback vanishes. In fact, the opening up of these vast new countries is like the progress of a rolling snowball, each little bit of 'all right'—I beg the House's pardon—picks up another little bit; and there is no limit to the cumulative possibilities if a start is made at the right end and the scheme pushed and controlled by the right people." Some one behind him said: "Talking through his hat." Michael paused, disconcerted; then, snatching at his bitt, went on: "A job of this sort half done is better left alone, but in the war, when something was found necessary, it *was* done, and men were always available for the doing of it. I put it to the House that the condition of our country now demands efforts almost as great as then."

He could see that some members were actually listening to him with attention, and, taking a deep breath, he went on:

"Leaving out Ireland—" (*A voice: "Why?"*) "I prefer not to touch on anything that does not like to be touched—" (*laughter*) "the present ratio of white population between Britain and the rest of the Empire is roughly in the nature of five to two. Child Emigration on a great scale will go far to equalise this ratio within twenty years; the British character of the British Empire will be established for ever, and supply and demand between the Mother Country and the Dominions will be levelled up." (*A voice: "The Dominions will then supply themselves."*) "The honourable member will forgive me if I doubt that for some time to come. We have the start in the machinery of manufacture. It may, of course, be five, seven, ten years before unemployment here comes down even to the prewar rate, but can you point to any other plan which will really decrease it? I am all for good wages and moderate working hours. I believe the standard in Britain and the new countries, though so much higher than the European, is only a decent minimum, and in some cases does not reach it; I want better wages, even more moderate working hours; and the want is common among working men wherever the British flag flies." (*"Hear, hear!"*) "They are not going back

He sat down, after speaking for thirteen minutes. Off his chest! An honourable Member rose.

"I must congratulate the Member for Mid-Bucks on what, despite its acquaintanceship with the clouds, and its Lewis Carrollian appeal for less bread, more taxes, we must all admit to be a lively and well-delivered first effort. The Member for Tyne and Tees, earlier in the Debate, made an allusion to the Party to which I have the honour to belong, which—er——"

'Exactly!' thought Michael, and after waiting for the next speech, which contained no allusion whatever to his own, he left the House.

CHAPTER II

RESULTS

HE walked home, lighter in head and heart. That was the trouble—a light weight! No serious attention would be paid to him. He recollected the maiden speech of the Member for Cornmarket. At least he had stopped, to-day, as soon as the House began to fidget. He felt hot, and hungry. Opera-singers grew fat through their voices, Members of Parliament thin. He would have a bath.

He was half clothed again when Fleur came in.

"You did splendidly, Michael. That beast!"

"Which?"

"His name's MacGown."

"Sir Alexander MacGown? What about him?"

"You'll see to-morrow. He insinuated that you were interested in the sale of the Foggart book, as one of its publishers."

"That's rather the limit."

"And all the rest of his speech was a cut-up; horrid tone about the whole thing. Do you know him?"

"MacGown? No. He's Member for some Scottish borough."

"Well, he's an enemy. Blythe is awfully pleased with you, and wild about MacGown; and so is Bart. I've never seen him so angry. You'll have to write to 'The Times' and explain that you've had no interest in Danby & Winter's since before you were elected. Bart and your mother are coming to dinner. Did you know she was with me?"

"Mother? She abhors politics."

"All she said was: 'I wish dear Michael would brush his hair back before speaking. I like to see his forehead.' And when MacGown sat down, she said: 'My dear, the back of that man's head is perfectly straight. D'you think he's a Prussian? And he's got thick lobes to his ears. I shouldn't like to be married to him!' She had her opera-glasses."

Sir Lawrence and Lady Mont were already in the 'parlour' when they went down, standing opposite each other like two storks, if not precisely on one leg, still very distinguished. Pushing Michael's hair up, Lady Mont pecked his forehead, and her dove-like eyes gazed at the top of his head from under their arched brows. She was altogether a little Norman in her curves; she even arched her words. She was considered "a deah; but not too frightfully all there."

"How did you manage to stick it, Mother?"

"My dear boy, I was thrilled; except for that person in jute. I thought the shape of his head insufferable. Where did you get all that knowledge? It was so sensible."

Michael grinned. "How did it strike you, sir?"

Sir Lawrence grimaced.

"You played the *enfant terrible*, my dear. Half the party won't like it because they've never thought of it; and the other half won't like it because they *have*."

"What! Foggartists at heart?"

"Of course; but in Office. You mustn't support your real convictions in Office—it's not done."

"This nice room," murmured Lady Mont. "When I was last here it was Chinese. And where's the monkey?"

"In Michael's study, Mother. We got tired of him. Would you like to see Kit before dinner?"

Left alone, Michael and his father stared at the same object, a Louis Quinze snuff-box picked up by Soames.

"Would you take any notice of MacGown's insinuation, Dad?"

"Is that his name—the hairy haberdasher! I should."

"How?"

"Give him the lie."

"In private, in the Press, or in the House?"

"All three. In private I should merely call him a liar. In the Press you should use the words: 'Reckless disregard for truth.' And in Parliament—that you regret he 'should have been so misinformed.' To complete the crescendo you might add that men's noses have been pulled for less."

"But you don't suppose," said Michael, "that people would believe a thing like that?"

"They will believe anything, my dear, that suggests corruption in public life. It's one of the strongest traits in human nature. Anxiety about the integrity of public men would be admirable, if it wasn't so usually felt by those who have so little integrity themselves that they can't give others credit for it." Sir Lawrence grimaced, thinking of the P. P. R. S. "And talking of that—why wasn't Old Forsyte in the House to-day?"

"I offered him a seat, but he said: He hadn't been in the House since Gladstone moved the Home Rule Bill, and then only because he was afraid his father would have a fit."

Sir Lawrence screwed his eyeglass in.

"That's not clear to me," he said.

"His father had a pass, and didn't like to waste it."

"I see. That was noble of Old Forsyte."

"He said that Gladstone had been very windy."

"Ah! They were even longer in those days. You covered your ground very quickly, Michael. I should say with practice you would do. I've a bit of news for Old Forsyte. Shropshire doesn't speak to Charlie Ferrar because the third time the old man paid his debts to prevent his being posted, he made that a condition, for fear of being asked again. It's not so lurid as I'd hoped. How's the action?"

"The last I heard was something about administering what they call interrogatories."

"Ah! I know. They answer you in a way nobody can make head or tail of, and that without prejudice. Then they administer them to you, and you answer in the same way; it all helps the lawyers. What is there for dinner?"

"Fleur said we'd kill the fatted calf when I'd got my speech off."

Sir Lawrence sighed.

"I'm glad. Your mother has Vitamins again rather badly; we eat little but carrots, generally raw. French blood in a family is an excellent thing—prevents faddiness about food. Ah! here they come! . . ."

It has often been remarked that the breakfast-tables of people who avow themselves indifferent to what the Press may say of them are garnished by all the newspapers on the morning when there is anything to say. In Michael's case this was a waste of almost a shilling. The only allusions to his speech were contained in four out of thirteen dailies. 'The Times' reported it (including the laughter) with condensed and considered accuracy. 'The Morning Post' picked out three imperial bits, prefaced by the words: 'In a promising speech.' 'The Daily Telegraph' remarked: "Among the other speakers were Mr. Michael Mont." And 'The Manchester Guardian' observed: "The Member for Mid-Bucks in a maiden speech advocated the introduction of children into the Dominions."

Sir Alexander MacGown's speech received the added attention demanded by his extra years of Parliamentary service, but there was no allusion to the insinuation. Michael turned to Hansard. His own speech seemed more coherent than he had hoped. When Fleur came down he was still reading MacGown's.

"Give me some coffee, old thing."

Fleur gave him the coffee and leaned over his shoulder.

"This MacGown is after Marjorie Ferrar," she said; "I remember now."

Michael stirred his cup. "Dash it all! The House is free from that sort of pettiness."

"No. I remember Alison telling me—I didn't connect him up yesterday. Isn't it a disgusting speech?"

"Might be worse," said Michael, with a grin.

"'As a member of the firm who published this singular production, he is doubtless interested in pressing it on the public, so that we may safely discount the enthusiasm displayed.' Doesn't that make your blood boil?"

Michael shrugged his shoulders.

"Don't you ever feel angry, Michael?"

"My dear, I was through the war. Now for 'The Times.' What shall I say?

"'SIR,

"'May I trespass upon your valuable space' (that's quite safe), 'in the interests of public life—' (that keeps it impersonal) 'to—' er— Well?"

"To say that Sir Alexander MacGown in his speech yesterday told a lie when he suggested that I was interested in the sale of Sir James Foggart's book."

"Straight," said Michael, "but they wouldn't put it in. How's this?

"'To draw attention to a misstatement in Sir Alexander MacGown's speech of yesterday afternoon. As a matter of fact' (always useful) 'I ceased to have any interest whatever in the firm which published Sir James

Foggart's book, "The Parlous State of England," even
before I became a member of the late Parliament; and am
therefore in no way interested, as Sir Alexander Mac-
Gown suggested, in pressing it on the Public. I hesitate
to assume that he meant to impugn my honour' (must
get in 'honour') 'but his words might bear that construction. My interest in the book is simply my interest in
what is truly the "parlous state of England."

'Faithfully, etc.'

That do?"

"Much too mild. Besides, I shouldn't say that you
really believe the state of England is parlous. It's all
nonsense, you know. I mean it's exaggerated."

"Very well," said Michael, "I'll put the State of the
Country, instead. In the House I suppose I rise to a
point of order. And in the Lobby to a point of disorder,
probably. I wonder what 'The Evening Sun' will say?"

'The Evening Sun,' which Michael bought on his way
to the House, gave him a leader, headed: "Foggartism
again," beginning as follows: "Young Hopeful, in the
person of the Member for Mid-Bucks, roused the laughter
of the House yesterday by his championship of the insane
policy called Foggartism, to which we have already alluded in these columns"; and so on for twenty lines of
vivid disparagement. Michael gave it to the door-keeper.

In the House, after noting that MacGown was present,
he rose at the first possible moment.

"Mr. Speaker, I rise to correct a statement in yesterday's debate reflecting on my personal honour. The
honourable Member for Greengow in his speech said—"
He then read the paragraph from Hansard. "It is true
that I was a member of the firm which published Sir
James Foggart's book in August, 1923, but I retired from
all connection with that firm in October, 1923, before

ever I entered this House. I have therefore no pecuniary or other interest whatever in pressing the claims of the book, beyond my great desire to see its principles adopted."

He sat down to some applause; and Sir Alexander Mac-Gown rose. Michael recognised the face with the un-political expression he had noticed during his speech.

"I believe," he said, "that the honourable Member for Mid-Bucks was not sufficiently interested in his own speech to be present when I made my reply to it yesterday. I cannot admit that my words bear the construction which he has put on them. I said, and I still say, that one of the publishers of a book must necessarily be interested in having the judgment which induced him to publish it vindicated by the Public. The honourable Member has placed on his head a cap which I did not intend for it." His face came round towards Michael, grim, red, provocative.

Michael rose again.

"I am glad the honourable Member has removed a construction which others besides myself had put on his words."

A few minutes later, with a certain unanimity, both left the House.

The papers not infrequently contain accounts of how Mr. Swash, the honourable Member for Topcliffe, called Mr. Buckler, the honourable Member for Pooting, something unparliamentary. ("*Order!*") And of how Mr. Buckler retorted that Mr. Swash was something worse. ("*Hear, hear!*" and "*Order!*") And of how Mr. Swash waved his fists (*uproar*), and Mr. Buckler threw himself upon the Chair, or threw some papers. ("*Order! order! order!*") And of how there was great confusion, and Mr. Swash, or Mr. Buckler, was suspended, and led vociferous out of the Mother of Parliaments by the Serjeant-at-

Arms, with other edifying details. The little affair between Michael and Sir Alexander went off in other wise.
With an instinct of common decency, they both made
for the lavatory; nor till they reached those marble halls
did either take the slightest notice of the other. In front
of a roller towel Michael said:

"Now, sir, perhaps you'll tell me why you behaved like
a dirty dog. You knew perfectly well the construction
that would be placed on your words."

Sir Alexander turned from a hair-brush.

"Take that!" he said, and gave Michael a swinging
box on the ear. Staggering, Michael came up wildly with
his right, and caught Sir Alexander on the nose. Their
movements then became intensive. Michael was limber,
Sir Alexander stocky; neither was overproficient with his
fists. The affair was cut short by the honourable Member for Washbason, who had been in retirement. Coming
hastily out of a door, he received simultaneously a black
eye, and a blow on the diaphragm, which caused him to
collapse. The speaker, now, was the Member for Washbason, in language stronger than those who knew the
honourable gentleman would have supposed possible.

"I'm frightfully sorry, sir," said Michael. "It's always
the innocent party who comes off worst."

"I'll dam' well have you both suspended," gasped the
Member for Washbason.

Michael grinned, and Sir Alexander said: "To hell!"

"You're a couple of brawling cads!" said the Member
for Washbason. "How the devil am I to speak this afternoon?"

"If you went in bandaged," said Michael, dabbing the
damaged eye with cold water, "and apologised for a
motor accident, you would get special hearing, and a good
Press. Shall I take the silver lining out of my tie for a
bandage?"

"Leave my eye alone," bellowed the Member for Washbason, "and get out, before I lose my temper!"

Michael buttoned the top of his waistcoat, loosened by Sir Alexander's grip, observed in the glass that his ear was very red, his cuff bloodstained, and his opponent still bleeding from the nose, and went out.

'Some scrap!' he thought, entering the fresher air of Westminster. 'Jolly lucky we were tucked away in there! I don't think I'll mention it!' His ear was singing, and he felt rather sick, physically and mentally. The salvational splendour of Foggartism already reduced to a brawl in a lavatory! It made one doubt one's vocation. Not even the Member for Washbason, however, had come off with dignity, so that the affair was not likely to get into the papers.

Crossing the road towards home, he sighted Francis Wilmot walking West.

"Hallo!"

Francis Wilmot looked up, and seemed to hesitate. His face was thinner, his eyes deeper set; he had lost his smile.

"How is Mrs. Mont?"

"Very well, thanks. And you?"

"Fine," said Francis Wilmot. "Will you tell her I've had a letter from her cousin Jon. They're in great shape. He was mighty glad to hear I'd seen her, and sent his love."

"Thanks," said Michael drily. "Come and have tea with us."

The young man shook his head.

"Have you cut your hand?"

Michael laughed. "No, somebody's nose."

Francis Wilmot smiled wanly. "I'm wanting to do that all the time. Whose was it?"

"A man called MacGown's."

Francis Wilmot seized Michael's hand. "It's the very nose!" Then, apparently disconcerted by his frankness, he turned on his heel and made off, leaving Michael putting one and one together.

Next morning's papers contained no allusion to the blood-letting of the day before, except a paragraph to the effect that the Member for Washbason was confined to his house by a bad cold. The Tory journals preserved a discreet silence about Foggartism; but in two organs— one Liberal and one Labour—were little leaders, which Michael read with some attention.

The Liberal screed ran thus: "The debate on the King's speech produced one effort which at least merits passing notice. The policy alluded to by the Member for Mid-Bucks under the label of Foggartism, because it emanates from that veteran Sir James Foggart, has a certain speciousness in these unsettled times, when every one is looking for quack specifics. Nothing which departs so fundamentally from all that Liberalism stands for will command for a moment the support of any truly Liberal vote. The risk lies in its appeal to backwoodism in the Tory ranks. Loose thought and talk of a pessimistic nature always attracts a certain type of mind. The state of England is not really parlous. It in no way justifies any unsound or hysterical departure from our traditional policy. But there is no disguising the fact that certain so-called thinkers have been playing for some time past with the idea of reviving a 'splendid isolation,' based (whether they admit it or not) on the destruction of Free Trade. The young Member for Mid-Bucks in his speech handled for a moment that corner-stone of Liberalism, and then let it drop; perhaps he thought it too weighty for him. But reduced to its elements, Foggartism is a plea for the abandonment of Free Trade, and a blow in the face of the League of Nations."

Michael sighed and turned to the Labour article, which was signed, and struck a more human note:

"And so we are to have our children carted off to the Antipodes as soon as they can read and write, in order that the capitalist class may be relieved of the menace lurking in Unemployment. I know nothing of Sir James Foggart, but if he was correctly quoted in Parliament yesterday by a member for an agricultural constituency, I smell Prussianism about that old gentleman. I wonder what the working man is saying over his breakfast-table? I fear the words: 'To hell!' are not altogether absent from his discourse. No, Sir James Foggart, English Labour intends to call its own hand; and with all the old country's drawbacks, still prefers it for itself and its children. We are not taking any, Sir James Foggart."

'There it is naked,' thought Michael. 'The policy ought never to have been intrusted to me. Blythe ought to have found a Labour townsman.'

Foggartism, whittled to a ghost by jealousy and class-hatred, by shibboleth, section and Party—he had a vision of it slinking through the purlieus of the House and the corridors of the Press, never admitted to the Presence, nor accepted as flesh and blood!

"Never mind," he muttered; "I'll stick it. If one's a fool, one may as well be a blazing fool. Eh, Dan?"

The Dandie, raising his head from his paws, gave him a lustrous glance.

CHAPTER III

MARJORIE FERRAR AT HOME

FRANCIS WILMOT went on his way to Chelsea. He had a rendezvous with Life. Over head and ears in love, and old-fashioned to the point of marriage, he spent his days at the tail of a petticoat as often absent as not. His simple fervour had wrung from Marjorie Ferrar confession of her engagement. She had put it bluntly: She was in debt, she wanted shekels and she could not live in the backwoods.

He had promptly offered her all his shekels. She had refused them with the words:

"My poor dear, I'm not so far gone as that."

Often on the point of saying 'Wait until I'm married,' the look on his face had always deterred her. He was primitive; would never understand her ideal: Perfection, as wife, mistress, and mother, all at once. She kept him only by dangling the hope that she would throw Mac-Gown over; taking care to have him present when Mac-Gown was absent, and absent when MacGown was present. She had failed to keep them apart on two occasions, painful and productive of more lying than she was at all accustomed to. For she was really taken with this young man; he was a new flavour. She 'loved' his dark 'slinky' eyes, his grace, the way his 'back-chat' grew, dark and fine, on his slim comely neck. She 'loved' his voice and his old-fashioned way of talking. And, rather oddly, she 'loved' his loyalty. Twice she had urged him to find out whether Fleur wasn't going to 'climb down' and 'pay up.' Twice he had refused, saying: "They were mighty nice to me; and I'd never tell you what they said, even if I did go and find out."

She was painting his portrait, so that a prepared canvas with a little paint on it chaperoned their almost daily interviews, which took place between three and four when the light had already failed. It was an hour devoted by MacGown to duty in the House. A low and open collar suited Francis Wilmot's looks. She liked him to sit lissom on a divan with his eyes following her; she liked to come close to him, and see the tremor of his fingers touching her skirt or sleeve, the glow in his eyes, the change in his face when she moved away. His faith in her was inconvenient. P's and Q's were letters she despised. And yet, to have to mind them before him gave her a sort of pleasure, made her feel good. One did not shock children!

That day, since she expected MacGown at five, she had become uneasy, before the young man came in, saying:

"I met Michael Mont; his cuff was bloody. Guess whose blood!"

"Not Alec's?"

Francis Wilmot dropped her hands.

"Don't call that man 'Alec' to me."

"My dear child, you're too sensitive. I thought they'd have a row—I read their speeches. Hadn't Michael a black eye? No? Tt—tt! Al—er—'that man' will be awfully upset. Was the blood fresh?"

"Yes," said Francis Wilmot, grimly.

"Then he won't come. Sit down, and let's do some serious work for once."

But throwing himself on his knees, he clasped his hands behind her waist.

"Marjorie, Marjorie!"

Disciple of Joy, in the forefront of modern mockery, she was yet conscious of pity, for him and for herself. It was hard not to be able to tell him to run out, get licence and ring, or whatever he set store by, and have done with it! Not even that she was ready to have done with it without ring or licence! For one must keep one's head. She had watched one lover growing tired, kept her head, and dismissed him before he knew it; grown tired of another, kept her head, and gone on till he was tired too. She had watched favourites she had backed go down, kept her head and backed one that didn't; had seen cards turn against her, and left off playing before her pile was gone. Time and again she had earned the good mark of Modernity.

So she kissed the top of his head, unclasped his hands, and told him to be good; and, in murmuring it, felt that she had passed her prime.

"Amuse me while I paint," she said. "I feel rotten."

And Francis Wilmot, like a dark ghost, amused her.

Some believe that a nose from which blood has been drawn by a blow swells less in the first hour than it does later. This was why Sir Alexander MacGown arrived at half past four to say that he could not come at five. He had driven straight from the House with a little bag of ice held to it. Having been led to understand that the young American was 'now in Paris,' he stood stock still, staring at one whose tie was off and whose collar was unbuttoned. Francis Wilmot rose from the divan, no less silent. Marjorie Ferrar put a touch on the canvas.

"Come and look, Alec; it's only just begun."

"No, thanks," said MacGown.

Crumpling his tie into his pocket, Francis Wilmot bowed and moved towards the door.

"Won't you stay for tea, Mr. Wilmot?"

"I believe not, thank you."

When he was gone Marjorie Ferrar fixed her eyes on the nose of her betrothed. Strong and hard, it was, as yet, little differentiated from the normal.

"Now," said MacGown, "why did you lie about that young blighter? You said he was in Paris. Are you playing fast and loose with me, Marjorie?"

"Of course! Why not?"

MacGown advanced to within reach of her.

"Put down that brush."

Marjorie Ferrar raised it; and suddenly it hit the wall opposite.

"You'll stop that picture, and you'll not see that fellow again; he's in love with you."

He had taken her wrists.

Her face, quite as angry as his own, reined back.

"Let go! I don't know if you call yourself a gentleman?"

"No, a plain man."

"Strong and silent—out of a dull novel. Sit down, and don't be unpleasant."

The duel of their eyes, brown and burning, blue and icy, endured for quite a minute. Then he did let go.

"Pick up that brush and give it to me."

"I'm damned if I will!"

"Then our engagement is off. If you're old-fashioned, I'm not. You want a young woman who'll give you a whip for a wedding-present."

MacGown put his hands up to his head.

"I want you too badly to be sane."

"Then pick up the brush."

MacGown picked it up.

"What have you done to your nose?"

MacGown put his hand to it.

"Ran it against a door."

Marjorie Ferrar laughed. "Poor door!"

MacGown gazed at her in genuine astonishment.

"You're the hardest woman I ever came across; and why I love you, I don't know."

"It hasn't improved your looks or your temper, my dear. You were rash to come here to-day."

MacGown uttered a sort of groan. "I can't keep away, and you know it."

Marjorie Ferrar turned the canvas face to the wall, and leaned there beside it.

"I don't know what you think of the prospects of our happiness, Alec; but I think they're pretty poor. Will you have a whisky and soda? It's in that cupboard. Tea, then? Nothing? We'd better understand each other. If I marry you, which is very doubtful, I'm not going into purdah. I shall see what friends I choose. And until I marry you, I shall also see them. If you don't like it, you can leave it."

She watched his clenching hands, and her wrists tingled. To be perfect wife to him would 'take a bit of doing!' If only she knew of a real 'good thing' instead, and had a 'shirt to put on it!' If only Francis Wilmot had money and did not live where the cotton came from, and darkies crooned in the fields; where rivers ran red, Florida moss festooned the swamps, and the sun shone; where grapefruit grew—or didn't?—and mocking-birds sang sweeter than the nightingale. South Carolina, described to her with such enthusiasm by Francis Wilmot! A world that was not her world stared straight into the eyes of Marjorie Ferrar. South Carolina! Impossible! It was like being asked to be ancient!

MacGown came up to her. "I'm sorry," he said. "Forgive me, Marjorie."

On her shrugging shoulders he put his hands, kissed her lips, and went away.

And she sat down in her favourite chair, listless, swinging her foot. The sand had run out of her dolly—life was a bore! It was like driving tandem, when the leader would keep turning round; or the croquet party in

'Alice in Wonderland,' read in the buttercup-fields at High Marshes not twenty years ago that felt like twenty centuries!

What did she want? Just a rest from men and bills? or that fluffy something called 'real love'? Whatever it was, she hadn't got it! And so! Dress, and go out, and dance; and later dress again, and go out and dine; and the dresses not paid for!

Well! Nothing like an egg-nog for 'the hump'!

Ringing for the ingredients, she made one with plenty of brandy, capped it with nutmeg, and drank it down.

CHAPTER IV

FONS ET ORIGO

TWO mornings later Michael received two letters. The first, which bore an Australian post-mark, ran thus:

"DEAR SIR,

"I hope you are well and the lady. I thought perhaps you'd like to know how we are. Well, Sir, we're not much to speak of out here after a year and a half. I consider there's too much gilt on the ginger-bread as regards Australia. The climate's all right when it isn't too dry or too wet—it suits my wife fine, but Sir when they talk about making your fortune all I can say is tell it to the marines. The people here are a funny lot they don't seem to have any use for us and I don't seem to have any use for them. They call us Pommies and treat us as if we'd took a liberty in coming to their blooming country. You'd say they wanted a few more out here, but they don't seem to think so. I often wish I was back in the old Country. My wife says we're better off here, but I don't know. Anyway they tell a lot of lies as regards emigration.

"Well, Sir, I've not forgotten your kindness. My wife says please to remember her to you and the lady.

Yours faithfully,
ANTHONY BICKET."

With that letter in his hand, Michael, like some psychometric medium, could see again the writer, his thin face, prominent eyes, large ears, a shadowy figure of the London streets behind his coloured balloons. Poor little snipe —square peg in round hole wherever he might be; and all those other pegs—thousands upon thousands, that would never fit in. Pommies! Well! He wasn't recommending emigration for them; he was recommending it for those who could be shaped before their wood had set. Surely they wouldn't put that stigma on to children! He opened the other letter.

> "Roll Manor,
> Nr. Huntingdon.

"MY DEAR SIR,

"The disappointment I have felt since the appearance of my book was somewhat mitigated by your kind allusions to it in Parliament, and your championship of its thesis. I am an old man, and do not come to London now, but it would give me pleasure to meet you. If you are ever in this neighbourhood, I should be happy if you would lunch with me, or stay the night, as suits you best.

"With kind regards,

> Faithfully yours,
> JAS. FOGGART."

He showed it to Fleur.

"If you go, my dear, you'll be bored to tears."

"I must go," said Michael; "Fons et Origo!"

He wrote that he would come to lunch the following day.

He was met at the station by a horse drawing a vehicle of a shape he had never before beheld. The green-liveried man to whose side he climbed introduced it with the words: "Sir James thought, sir, you'd like to see about you; so 'e sent the T cart."

It was one of those grey late autumn days, very still, when the few leaves that are left hang listless, waiting to be windswept. The puddled road smelled of rain; rooks rose from the stubbles as if in surprise at the sound of horses' hoofs; and the turned earth of ploughed fields had the sheen that betokened clay. To the flat landscape poplars gave a certain spirituality; and the russet-tiled farmhouse roofs a certain homeliness.

"That's the manor, sir," said the driver, pointing with his whip. Between an orchard and a group of elms, where was obviously a rookery, Michael saw a long low house of deeply weathered brick covered by Virginia creeper whose leaves had fallen. At a little distance were barns, out-houses, and the wall of a kitchen-garden. The T cart turned into an avenue of limes and came suddenly on the house unprotected by a gate. Michael pulled an old iron bell. Its lingering clang produced a lingering man, who, puckering his face, said: "Mr. Mont? Sir James is ex-pecting you. This way, sir."

Through an old low hall smelling pleasantly of wood-smoke, Michael reached a door which the puckered man closed in his face.

Sir James Foggart! Some gaitered old countryman with little grey whiskers, neat, weathered and firm-featured; or one of those short-necked John Bulls, still extant, square and weighty, with a flat top to his head, and a flat white topper on it!

The puckered man reopened the door, and said:

"Sir James will see you, sir."

Before the fire in a large room with a large hearth and many books was a huge old man, grey-bearded and grey-locked, like a superannuated British lion, in an old velvet coat with whitened seams.

He appeared to be trying to rise.

"Please don't, sir," said Michael.

"If you'll excuse me, I won't. Pleasant journey?"

"Very."

"Sit down. Much touched by your speech. First speech, I think?"

Michael bowed.

"Not the last, I hope."

The voice was deep and booming; the eyes looked up keenly, as if out of thickets, so bushy were the eyebrows, and the beard grew so high on the cheeks. The thick grey hair waved across the forehead and fell on to the coat collar. A primeval old man in a high state of cultivation. Michael was deeply impressed.

"I've looked forward to this honour, sir," he said, "ever since we published your book."

"I'm a recluse—never get out now. Tell you the truth, don't want to—see too many things I dislike. I write, and smoke my pipe. Ring the bell, and we'll have lunch. Who's this Sir Alexander MacGown?—his head wants punching!"

"No longer, sir," said Michael.

Sir James Foggart leaned back and laughed. His laugh was long, deep, slightly hollow, like a laugh in a trombone.

"Capital! And how did those fellows take your speech? Used to know a lot of 'em at one time—fathers of these fellows, grandfathers, perhaps."

"How do you know so well what England wants, sir," said Michael, suavely, "now that you never leave home?"

Sir James Foggart pointed with a large thin hand covered with hair to a table piled with books and magazines.

"Read," he said; "read everything—eyes as good as ever—seen a good deal in my day." And he was silent, as if seeing it again.

"Are you following your book up?"

"Mm! Something for 'em to read when I'm gone. Eighty-four, you know."

"I wonder," said Michael, "that you haven't had the Press down."

"Have—had 'em yesterday; three by different trains; very polite young men; but I could see they couldn't make head or tail of the old creature—too far gone, eh?"

At this moment the door was opened, and the puckered man came in, followed by a maid and three cats. They put a tray on Sir James' knees and another on a small table before Michael. On each tray was a partridge with chipped potatoes, spinach and bread sauce. The puckered man filled Sir James' glass with barley-water, Michael's with claret, and retired. The three cats, all tortoise-shells, began rubbing themselves against Sir James' trousers, purring loudly.

"Don't mind cats, I hope? No fish to-day, pussies!"

Michael was hungry and finished his bird. Sir James gave most of his to the cats. They were then served with fruit salad, cheese, coffee and cigars, and everything removed, except the cats, who lay replete before the fire, curled up in a triangle.

Michael gazed through the smoke of two cigars at the fount and origin, eager, but in doubt whether it would stand pumping—it seemed so very old! Well! anyway, he must have a shot!

"You know Blythe, sir, of 'The Outpost'? He's your great supporter; I'm only a mouthpiece."

"Know his paper—best of the weeklies; but too clever by half."

"Now that I've got the chance," said Michael, "would you mind if I asked you one or two questions?"

Sir James Foggart looked at the lighted end of his cigar. "Fire ahead."

"Well, sir, can England really stand apart from Europe?"

"Can she stand with Europe? Alliances based on promise of assistance that won't be forthcoming—worse than useless."

"But suppose Belgium were invaded again, or Holland?"

"The one case, perhaps. Let that be understood.

Knowledge in Europe, young man, of what England will or will not do in given cases is most important. And they've never had it. *Perfide Albion!* Heh! We always wait till the last moment to declare our policy. Great mistake. Gives the impression that we serve Time— which, with our democratic system, by the way, we generally do."

"I like that, sir," said Michael, who did not. "About wheat? How would you stabilise the price so as to encourage our growth of it?"

"Ha! My pet lamb. We want a wheat loan, Mr. Mont, and Government control. Every year the Government should buy in advance all the surplus we need and store it; then fix a price for the home farmers that gives them a good profit; and sell to the public at the average between the two prices. You'd soon see plenty of wheat grown here, and a general revival of agriculture."

"But wouldn't it raise the price of bread, sir?"

"Not it."

"And need an army of officials?"

"No. Use the present machinery properly organised."

"State trading, sir?" said Michael, with diffidence.

Sir James Foggart's voice boomed out. "Exceptional case—basic case—why not?"

"I quite agree," said Michael, hastily. "I never thought of it, but why not? . . . Now as to the opposition to child emigration in this country. Do you think it comes from the affection of parents for their children?"

"More from dislike of losing the children's wages."

"Still, you know," murmured Michael, "one might well kick against losing one's children for good at fifteen!"

"One might; human nature's selfish, young man. Hang on to 'em and see 'em rot before one's eyes, or grow up to worse chances than one's own—as you say, that's human nature."

Michael, who had not said it, felt somewhat stunned.

"The child emigration scheme will want an awful lot of money, and organisation."

Sir James stirred the cats with his slippered foot.

"Money! There's still a mint of money—misapplied. Another hundred million loan—four and a half millions a year in the Budget; and a hundred thousand children sent out every year. In five years at least we should save the lot in unemployment dole." He waved his cigar, and its ash spattered on his velvet coat.

'Thought it would,' said Michael to himself, knocking his own off into a coffee-cup. "But can children sent out wholesale like that be properly looked after, and given a real chance, sir?"

"Start gradually; where there's a will there's a way."

"And won't they just swell the big towns out there?"

"Teach 'em to want land, and give it 'em."

"I don't know if it's enough," said Michael, boldly; "the lure of the towns is terrific."

Sir James nodded. "A town's no bad thing till it's overdone, as they are here. Those that go to the towns will increase the demand for our supplies."

'Well,' thought Michael, 'I'm getting on. What shall I ask him next?' And he contemplated the cats, who were stirring uneasily. A peculiar rumbling noise had taken possession of the silence. Michael looked up. Sir James Foggart was asleep! In repose he was more tremendous than ever—perhaps rather too tremendous; for his snoring seemed to shake the room. The cats tucked their heads farther in. There was a slight smell of burning. Michael picked a fallen cigar from the carpet. What should he do now? Wait for a revival, or clear out? Poor old boy! Foggartism had never seemed to Michael a more forlorn hope than in this sanctum of its fount and origin. Covering his ears, he sat quite still. One by one

the cats got up. Michael looked at his watch. 'I shall
lose my train,' he thought, and tiptoed to the door behind a procession of deserting cats. It was as though Foggartism were snoring the little of its life away! "Good-
bye, sir!" he said softly, and went out. He walked to
the station very thoughtful. Foggartism! That vast if
simple programme seemed based on the supposition that
human beings could see two inches before their noses.
But was that supposition justified; if so, would England
be so town-ridden and overpopulated? For one man
capable of taking a far and comprehensive view and going to sleep on it, there were nine—if not nine-and-ninety
—who could take near and partial views and remain wide
awake. Practical politics! The answer to all wisdom,
however you might boom it out. "Oh! Ah! Young
Mont—not a practical politician!" It was public death
to be so labelled. And Michael, in his railway-carrriage,
with his eyes on the English grass, felt like a man on
whom every one was heaping earth. Had pelicans crying
in the wilderness a sense of humour? If not, their time
was poor. Grass, grass, grass! Grass and the towns!
And, nestling his chin into his heavy coat, he was soon
faster asleep than Sir James Foggart.

CHAPTER V

PROGRESS OF THE CASE

WHEN Soames said: "Leave it to me," he meant it, of course; but it was really very trying that whenever anything went wrong, he, and not somebody else, had to set it right!

To look more closely into the matter he was staying with his sister Winifred Dartie in Green Street. Finding his nephew Val at dinner there the first night, he took the opportunity of asking him whether he knew anything of Lord Charles Ferrar.

"What do you want to know, Uncle Soames?"

"Anything unsatisfactory. I'm told his father doesn't speak to him."

"Well," said Val, "it's generally thought he'll win the Lincolnshire with a horse that didn't win the Cambridgeshire."

"I don't see the connection."

Val Dartie looked at him through his lashes. He was not going to enter for the slander stakes. "Well, he's got to bring off a *coup* soon, or go under."

"Is that all?"

"Except that he's one of those chaps who are pleasant to you when you can be of use, and unpleasant when you can't."

"So I gathered from his looks," said Soames. "Have you had any business dealings with him?"

"Yes; I sold him a yearling by Torpedo out of Banshee."

"Did he pay you?"

"Yes," said Val, with a grin; "and she turned out no good."

"H'm! I suppose he was unpleasant afterwards? That all you know?"

Val nodded. He knew more, if gossip can be called 'more'; but what was puffed so freely with the smoke of racing-men's cigars was hardly suited to the ears of lawyers.

For so old a man of the world Soames was singularly unaware how in that desirable sphere, called Society, every one is slandered daily, and no bones broken; slanderers and slandered dining and playing cards together with the utmost good feeling and the intention of reslandering each other the moment they are round the corner. Such genial and hair-raising reports reach no outside ears, and Soames really did not know where to begin investigation.

"Can you ask this Mr. Curfew to tea?" he said to Fleur.

"What for, Father?"

"So that I can pump him."

"I thought there were detectives for all that sort of thing."

Soames went a special colour. Since his employment of Mr. Polteed, who had caught him visiting his own wife's bedroom in Paris, at the beginning of the century, the word detective produced a pain in his diaphragm. He dropped the subject. And yet, without detectives, what was he to do?

One night, Winifred having gone to the theatre, he sat down with a cigar, to think. He had been provided by Michael with a list of 'advanced' books and plays which 'modern' people were reading, attending and discussing. He had even been supplied with one of the books: "Canthar," by Perceval Calvin. He fetched it from his bedroom, and, turning up a lamp, opened the volume. After reading the first few pages, in which he could see nothing, he turned to the end and read backwards. In this way he could skip better, and each erotic passage, to which he very soon came, led him insensibly on to the one before it. He had reached the middle of the novel, before he had resort in wonder to the title-pages. How was it that the publisher and author were at large? Ah! The imprint was of a foreign nature. Soames breathed more freely. Though sixty-nine, and neither Judge, juryman, nor otherwise professionally compelled to be shocked, he was shaken. If women were reading this sort of thing, then there really was no distinction between men and women nowadays. He took up the book again, and read steadily on to the beginning. The erotic passages alone interested him. The rest seemed rambling, disconnected stuff. He rested again. What was this novel written for? To make money, of course. But was there another purpose? Was the author one of these 'artist' fellows who thought that to give you 'life'—wasn't that the phrase?—they must put down every visit to a bedroom, and some besides? 'Art for Art's sake,' 'realism'—what did they call it? In Soames' comparatively bleak experience 'life' did not consist wholly of visiting bedrooms, so that he was unable to admit that this book was life, the whole of life, and nothing but life. "Calvin's a crank, sir," Michael had said, when he handed him the novel. "He thinks people can't become continent except through being excessively incontinent; so he shows his hero and heroine arriving gradually at continence." 'At Bedlam,' thought Soames. They would see what a British Jury had to say to that, anyway. But how elicit a confession that this woman and her set had read it with gusto? And then an idea occurred to him, so brilliant that he had to ponder deeply before he could feel any confidence in it. These 'advanced' young people had any amount of conceit; every one who didn't share their views was a 'dud,'

or a 'grundy.' Suppose the book were attacked in the
Press, wouldn't it draw their fire? And if their fire could
be drawn in print, could it not be used afterwards as
evidence of their views on morality? H'm! This would
want very nice handling. And first of all, how was he to
prove that Marjorie Ferrar had read this book? Thus
casting about him, Soames was rewarded by another
brilliant thought: Young Butterfield—who had helped
him to prove the guilt of Elderson in that matter of the
P. P. R. S. and owed his place at Danby & Winter's, the
publishers, to Soames' recommendation! Why not make
use of him? Michael always said the young man was
grateful. And obscuring the title of the book against his
flank, in case he should meet a servant, Soames sought
his own bedroom.

His last thought that night was almost diagnostic.

'In my young days we read that sort of book if we
could get hold of it, and didn't say so; now, it seems, they
make a splash of reading it, and pretend it does them
good!'

Next morning from the Connoisseurs' he telephoned
to Danby & Winter's, and asked to speak to Mr. Butterfield.

"Yes?"

"Mr. Forsyte speaking. Do you remember me?"

"Yes, indeed, sir."

"Can you step round to the Connoisseurs' Club this
morning some time?"

"Certainly, sir. Will twelve thirty suit you?"

Secretive and fastidious in matters connected with sex,
Soames very much disliked having to speak to a young
man about an 'immoral' book. He saw no other way of
it, however, and, on his visitor's arrival, shook hands and
began at once.

"This is confidential, Mr. Butterfield."

Butterfield, whose dog-like eyes had glowed over the handshake, answered:

"Yes, sir. I've not forgotten what you did for me, sir."

Soames held out the book.

"Do you know that novel?"

Butterfield smiled slightly.

"Yes, sir. It's printed in Brussels. They're paying five pounds a copy for it."

"Have you read it?"

The young man shook his head. "It's not come my way, sir."

Soames was relieved. "Well, don't! But just attend a moment. Can you buy ten copies of it, at my expense, and post them to ten people whose names I'll give you? They're all more or less connected with literature. You can put in slips to say the copies are complimentary, or whatever you call it. But mention no names."

The young man Butterfield said deprecatingly:

"The price is rising all the time, sir. It'll cost you well on sixty pounds."

"Never mind that."

"You wish the book boomed, sir?"

"Good Gad—no! I have my reasons, but we needn't go into them."

"I see, sir. And you want the copies to come—as if— as if from heaven?"

"That's it," said Soames. "I take it that publishers often send doubtful books to people they think will support them. There's just one other thing. Can you call a week later on one of the people to whom you've sent the books, and offer to sell another copy as if you were an agent for it? I want to make quite sure it's already reached that person, and been read. You won't give your name, of course. Will you do this for me?"

The eyes of the young man Butterfield again glowed:

"Yes, sir. I owe you a great deal, sir."

Soames averted his eyes; he disliked all expression of gratitude.

"Here's the list of names, then, with their addresses. I've underlined the one you call on. I'll write you a cheque to go on with; and you can let me know later if there's anything more to pay."

He sat down, while the young man Butterfield scrutinised the list.

"I see it's a lady, sir, that I'm to call on."

"Yes; does that make any difference to you?"

"Not at all, sir. Advanced literature is written for ladies nowadays."

"H'm!" said Soames. "I hope you're doing well?"

"Splendidly, sir. I was very sorry that Mr. Mont left us; we've been doing better ever since."

Soames lifted an eyebrow. The statement confirmed many an old suspicion. When the young man had gone, he took up "Canthar." Was he capable of writing an attack on it in the Press, over the signature 'Paterfamilias'? He was not. The job required some one used to that sort of thing. Besides, a real signature would be needed to draw fire. It would not do to ask Michael to suggest one; but Old Mont might know some fogey at the 'Parthenæum' who carried metal. Sending for a bit of brown paper, he disguised the cover with it, put the volume in his overcoat pocket, and set out for 'Snooks.'

He found Sir Lawrence about to lunch, and they sat down together. Making sure that the waiter was not looking over his shoulder, Soames, who had brought the book in with him, pushed it over, and said:

"Have you read that?"

Sir Lawrence whinnied.

"My dear Forsyte, why this morbid curiosity? Everybody's reading it. They say the thing's unspeakable."

"Then you haven't?" said Soames, keeping him to the point.

"Not yet, but if you'll lend it me, I will. I'm tired of people who've enjoyed it asking me if I've read 'that most disgusting book.' It's not fair, Forsyte. Did *you* enjoy it?"

"I skimmed it," said Soames, looking round his nose. "I had a reason. When you've read it, I'll tell you."

Sir Lawrence brought it back to him at 'the Connoisseurs' two days later.

"Here you are, my dear Forsyte," he said. "I never was more glad to get rid of a book! I've been in a continual stew for fear of being overseen with it! Perceval Calvin—*quel sale Monsieur!*"

"Exactly!" said Soames. "Now, I want to get that book attacked."

"You! Is Saul also among the prophets? Why this sudden zest?"

"It's rather roundabout," said Soames, sitting on the book. He detailed the reason, and ended with:

"Don't say anything to Michael, or Fleur."

Sir Lawrence listened with his twisting smile.

"I see," he said, "I see. Very cunning, Forsyte. You want me to get some one whose name will act like a red rag. It mustn't be a novelist, or they'll say he's jealous —which he probably is—the book's selling like hot cakes —I believe that's the expression. Ah! I think—I rather think, Forsyte, that I have the woman."

"Woman!" said Soames. "They won't pay any attention to that."

Sir Lawrence cocked his loose eyebrow. "I believe you're right—the only women they pay attention to nowadays are those who go one better than themselves. Shall I do it myself, and sign 'Outraged Parent'?"

"I believe it wants a real name."

"Again right, Forsyte; it does. I'll drop into the 'Parthenæum,' and see if any one's alive."

Two days later Soames received a note.

> "Snooks' Club,
> Friday.
>
> "My dear Forsyte,
>
> "I've got the man—the Editor of 'The Protagonist'; and he'll do it under his own name. What's more, I've put him onto the right line. We had a spirited argument. He wanted to treat it *de haut en bas* as the work of a dirty child. I said: 'No. This thing is symptomatic. Treat it seriously; show that it represents a school of thought, a deliberate literary attitude; and make it a plea for censorship.' Without the word censorship, Forsyte, they will never rise. So he's leaving his wife and taking it into the country for the week-end. I admire your conduct of the defence, my dear Forsyte; it's very subtle. But if you'll forgive me for saying so, it's more important to prevent the case coming into Court than to get a verdict if it does.
>
> Sincerely yours,
>
> Lawrence Mont."

With which sentiment Soames so entirely agreed, that he went down to Mapledurham, and spent the next two afternoons going round and round with a man he didn't like, hitting a ball, to quiet his mind.

CHAPTER VI

MICHAEL VISITS BETHNAL GREEN

THE feeling of depression with which Michael had come back from the fount and origin was somewhat mitigated by letters he was receiving from people of varying classes, nearly all young. They were so nice and earnest. They made him wonder whether after all practical politicians were not too light-hearted, like the managers of music-halls who protected the Public carefully from their more tasteful selves. They made him feel that there might be a spirit in the country that was not really represented in the House, or even in the Press. Among these letters was one which ran:

> "Sunshine House,
> Bethnal Green.

"DEAR MR. MONT,

"I was so awfully glad to read your speech in 'The Times.' I instantly got Sir James Foggart's book. I think the whole policy is simply splendid. You've no idea how heart-breaking it is for us who try to do things for children, to know that whatever we do is bound to be snowed under by the life they go to when school age ends. We have a good opportunity here of seeing the realities of child life in London. It's wonderful to see the fondness of the mothers for the little ones, in spite of their own hard lives—though not all, of course, by any means; but we often notice, and I think it's common experience, that when the children get beyond ten or twelve, the fondness for them begins to assume another form. I suppose it's really the commercial possibilities of the child making themselves felt. When money comes in at the door, disinterested love seems to move towards the window. I suppose it's natural, but it's awfully sad, because the commercial possibilities are generally so miserable; and the children's after-life is often half ruined for the sake of the few shillings they earn. I do fervently hope something will come of your appeal; only—things move so slowly, don't they? I wish you would come down and see our House here. The children are adorable, and we try to give them sunshine.

Sincerely yours,

NORAH CURFEW."

Bertie Curfew's sister! But surely that case would not really come to anything! Grateful for encouragement, and seeking light on Foggartism, he decided to go. Perhaps Norah Curfew would take the little Boddicks! He suggested to Fleur that she should accompany him, but she was afraid of picking up something unsuitable to the eleventh baronet, so he went alone.

The house, facing the wintry space called Bethnal Green, consisted of three small houses converted into one, with their three small back yards, trellised round and gravelled, for a playground. Over the door were the words: SUNSHINE HOUSE, in gold capitals. The walls were cream-coloured, the woodwork dark, and the curtains of gay chintz. Michael was received in the entrance-lobby by Norah Curfew herself. Tall, slim and straight, with dark hair brushed back from a pale face, she had brown eyes, clear, straight and glowing.

'Gosh!' thought Michael, as she wrung his hand. 'She *is* swept and garnished. No basement in her soul!'

"It *was* good of you to come, Mr. Mont. Let me take you over the house. This is the playroom."

Michael entered a room of spotless character, which had evidently been formed from several knocked into one. Six small children dressed in blue linen were seated

on the floor, playing games. They embraced the knees
of Norah Curfew when she came within reach. With the
exception of one little girl Michael thought them rather
ugly.

"These are our residents. The others only come out of
school hours. We have to limit them to fifty, and that's
a pretty good squeeze. We want funds to take the next
two houses."

"How many of you are working here?"

"Six. Two of us do the cooking; one the accounts; and
the rest washing, mending, games, singing, dancing, and
general chores. Two of us live in."

"I don't see your harps and crowns."

Norah Curfew smiled.

"Pawned," she said.

"What do you do about religion?" asked Michael,
thinking of the eleventh baronet's future.

"Well, on the whole we don't. You see, they're none
of them more than twelve; and the religious age, when it
begins at all, begins with sex about fourteen. We just
try to teach kindness and cheerfulness. I had my brother
down the other day. He's always laughed at me; but
he's going to do a matinée for us, and give us the pro-
ceeds."

"What play?"

"I think it's called 'The Plain Dealer.' He says he's
always wanted to do it for a good object."

Michael stared. "Do you know 'The Plain Dealer'?"

"No; it's by one of the Restoration people, isn't it?"

"Wycherley."

"Oh! yes!" Her eyes remaining clearer than the dawn,
Michael thought: 'Poor dear! It's not my business to
queer the pitch of her money-getting; but Master Bertie
likes his little joke!'

"I must bring my wife down here," he said; "she'd

love your walls and curtains. And I wanted to ask you—
You haven't room, have you, for two more little girls, if
we pay for them? Their father's down and out, and I'm
starting him in the country—no mother."

Norah Curfew wrinkled her straight brows, and on her
face came the look Michael always connected with haloes,
an anxious longing to stretch good-will beyond power and
pocket.

"Oh! we must!" she said. "I'll manage somehow.
What are their names?"

"Boddick—Christian, I don't know. I call them by
their ages—Four and Five."

"Give me the address. I'll go and see them myself; if
they haven't got anything catching, they shall come."

"You really are an angel," said Michael, simply.

Norah Curfew coloured, and opened a door. "That's
silly," she said, still more simply. "This is our mess-
room."

It was not large, and contained a girl working a typewriter, who stopped with her hands on the keys and
looked round; another girl beating up eggs in a bowl, who
stopped reading a book of poetry; and a third, who seemed
practising a physical exercise, and stopped with her arms
extended.

"This is Mr. Mont," said Norah Curfew, "who made
that splendid speech in the House. Miss Betts, Miss La
Fontaine, Miss Beeston."

The girls bowed, and the one who continued to beat
the eggs, said: "It was bully."

Michael also bowed. "Beating the air, I'm afraid."

"Oh! but, Mr. Mont, it must have an effect. It said
what so many people are really thinking."

"Ah!" said Michael, "but their thoughts are so deep,
you know."

"Do sit down."

Michael sat on the end of a peacock-blue divan.

"I was born in South Africa," said the egg-beater, "and I know what's waiting."

"My father was in the House," said the girl whose arms had come down to her splendid sides. "He was very much struck. Anyway, we're jolly grateful."

Michael looked from one to the other.

"I suppose if you didn't all believe in things, you wouldn't be doing this? *You* don't think the shutters are up in England, anyway?"

"Good Lord, no!" said the girl at the typewriter; "you've only to live among the poor to know that."

"The poor haven't got every virtue, and the rich haven't got every vice—that's nonsense!" broke in the physical exerciser.

Michael murmured soothingly.

"I wasn't thinking of that. I was wondering whether something doesn't hang over our heads too much?"

"D'you mean poison-gas?"

"Partly; and town blight, and a feeling that Progress has been found out."

"Well, I don't know," replied the egg-beater, who was dark and pretty. "I used to think so in the war. But Europe isn't the world. Europe isn't even very important, really. The sun hardly shines there, anyway."

Michael nodded. "After all, if the Millennium comes and we do blot each other out, in Europe, it'll only mean another desert about the size of the Sahara, and the loss of a lot of people obviously too ill-conditioned to be fit to live. It'd be a jolly good lesson to the rest of the world, wouldn't it? Luckily the other continents are far off each other."

"Cheerful!" exclaimed Norah Curfew.

Michael grinned.

"Well, one can't help catching the atmosphere of this

place. I admire you all frightfully, you know, giving up everything, to come and do this."

"That's tosh," said the girl at the typewriter. "What is there to give up—bunny-hugging? One got used to doing things, in the war."

"If it comes to that," said the egg-beater, "we admire you much more, for not giving up Parliament."

Again Michael grinned.

"Miss La Fontaine—wanted in the kitchen!"

The egg-beater went towards the door.

"Can you beat eggs? D'you mind—shan't be a minute." Handing Michael the bowl and fork, she vanished.

"What a shame!" said Norah Curfew. "Let me!"

"No," said Michael; "I can beat eggs with anybody. What do you all feel about cutting children adrift at fourteen?"

"Well, of course, it'll be bitterly opposed," said the girl at the typewriter. "They'll call it inhuman, and all that. It's much more inhuman really to keep them here."

"The real trouble," said Norah Curfew, "apart from the shillings earned, is the class-interference idea. Besides, Imperialism isn't popular."

"I should jolly well think it isn't," muttered the physical exerciser.

"Ah!" said the typist, "but this isn't Imperialism, is it, Mr. Mont? It's all on the lines of making the Dominions the equal of the Mother Country."

Michael nodded. "Commonwealth."

"That won't prevent their camouflaging their objection to losing the children's wages," said the physical exerciser.

A close discussion ensued between the three young women as to the exact effect of children's wages on the working-class budget. Michael beat his eggs and listened. It was, he knew, a point of the utmost importance. The general conclusion seemed to be that children earned on the whole rather more than their keep, but that it was "very short-sighted in the long run," because it fostered surplus population and unemployment, and a "great shame" to spoil the children's chances for the sake of the parents.

The re-entrance of the egg-beater put a stop to it.

"They're beginning to come in, Norah."

The physical exerciser slipped out, and Norah Curfew said:

"Now, Mr. Mont, would you like to see them?"

Michael followed her. He was thinking: 'I wish Fleur had come!' These girls seemed really to believe in things.

Down-stairs the children were trickling in from school. He stood and watched them. They seemed a queer blend of anæmia and vitality, of effervescence and obedience. Unselfconscious as puppies, but old beyond their years; and yet, looking as if they never thought ahead. Each movement, each action was as if it were their last. They were very quick. Most of them carried something to eat in a paper bag, or a bit of grease-paper. They chattered, and didn't laugh. Their accent struck Michael as deplorable. Six or seven at most were nice to look at; but nearly all looked good-tempered, and none seemed to be selfish. Their movements were jerky. They mobbed Norah Curfew and the physical exerciser; obeyed without question, ate without appetite, and grabbed at the house-cat. Michael was fascinated.

With them came four or five mothers, who had questions to ask, or bottles to fill. They too were on perfect terms with the young women. Class did not exist in this house; only personality was present. He noticed that the children responded to his grin, that the women didn't, though they smiled at Norah Curfew and the physical exerciser; he wondered if they would give him a bit of their minds if they knew of his speech.

Norah Curfew accompanied him to the door.

"Aren't they ducks?"

"If I saw much of them, I'm afraid I should give up Foggartism."

"Oh! but why?"

"Well, you see it designs to make them men and women of property."

"You mean that would spoil them?"

Michael grinned. "There's something dangerous about silver spoons. Here's my initiation fee." He handed her all his money.

"Oh! Mr. Mont, we didn't——!"

"Well, give me back sixpence, otherwise I shall have to walk home."

"It's frightfully kind of you. Do come again; and please don't give up Foggartism."

He walked to the train thinking of her eyes; and, on reaching home, said to Fleur:

"You absolutely must come and see that place. It's quite clean, and the spirit's topping. It's bucked me up like anything. Norah Curfew's perfectly splendid."

Fleur looked at him between her lashes.

"Oh!" she said. "I will."

CHAPTER VII

THE land beyond the coppice at Lippinghall was a ten-acre bit of poor grass, chalk and gravel, fenced round, to show that it was property. Except for one experiment with goats, abandoned because nobody would drink their milk in a country that did not demean itself by growing food, nothing had been done with it. By December this poor relation of Sir Lawrence Mont's estate was being actively exploited. Close to the coppice the hut had been erected, and at least an acre converted into a sea of mud. The coppice itself presented an incised and draggled appearance, owing to the ravages of Henry Boddick and another man, who had cut and stacked a quantity of timber, which a contractor was gradually rejecting for the fowl-house and granary. The incubator-house was at present in the nature of a prophecy. Progress, in fact, was somewhat slow, but it was hoped that fowls might be asked to begin their operations soon after the New Year. In the meantime Michael had decided that the colony had better get the worst over and go into residence. Scraping the Manor House for furniture, and sending in a store of groceries, oil-lamps, and soap, he installed Boddick on the left, earmarked the centre for the Bergfelds, and the right hand for Swain. He was present when the Manor car brought them from the station. The murky day was turning cold, the trees dripped, the car-wheels splashed up the surface water. From the doorway of the hut Michael watched them get out, and thought he had never seen three more untimely creatures. Bergfeld came first; having only one suit, he had put it on, and looked what he was—an actor out of a job. Mrs. Bergfeld came second, and having no outdoor coat, looked what she was—nearly frozen. Swain came last. On his shadowy face was nothing quite so spirited as a sneer; but he gazed about him, and seemed to say: 'My hat!'

Boddick, with a sort of prescience, was absent in the coppice. 'He,' thought Michael, 'is my only joy!'

Taking them into the kitchen messroom of the hut, he deployed a thermos of hot coffee, a cake, and a bottle of rum.

"Awfully sorry things look so dishevelled; but I think the hut's dry, and there are plenty of blankets. These oil-lamps smell rather. You were in the war, Mr. Swain; you'll feel at home in no time. Mrs. Bergfeld, you look so cold, do put some rum into your coffee; we always do when we go over the top."

They all put rum into their coffee, which had a marked effect. Mrs. Bergfeld's cheeks grew pink, and her eyes darkened. Swain remarked that the hut was a 'bit of all right'; Bergfeld began making a speech. Michael checked him. "Boddick knows all the ropes. I'm afraid I've got to catch a train; I've only just time to show you round."

While whirling back to town afterwards he felt that he had, indeed, abandoned his platoon just as it was going over the top. That night he would be dining in Society; there would be light and warmth, jewels and pictures, wine and talk; the dinner would cost the board of his 'down and outs' for a quarter at least; and nobody would give them and their like a thought. If he ventured to draw Fleur's attention to the contrast, she would say:

"My dear boy, that's like a book by Gurdon Minho; you're getting sentimental." And he would feel a fool. Or would he? Would he not, perhaps, look at her small distinguished head, and think: 'Too easy a way out, my dear; those who take it have little heads!' And, then, his eyes, straying farther down to that white throat and all the dainty loveliness below, would convey a warmth to his blood and a warning to his brain not to give way to blasphemy, lest it end by disturbing bliss. For what with Foggartism, poultry, and the rest of it, Michael had serious thoughts sometimes that Fleur had none; and with wisdom born of love, he knew that if she hadn't, she never would have, and he must get used to it. She was what she was, and could be converted only in popular fiction. Excellent business for the self-centred heroine to turn from interest in her own belongings to interest in people who had none; but in life it wasn't done. Fleur at least camouflaged her self-concentration gracefully; and with Kit—! Ah! but Kit was herself!

So he did not mention his 'down and outs' on their way to dinner in Eaton Square. He took instead a lesson in the royal Personage named on their invitation card, and marvelled at Fleur's knowledge. "She's interested in social matters. And do remember, Michael, not to sit down till she asks you to, and not to get up before her, and to say 'ma'am.'"

Michael grinned. "I suppose they'll all be nobs, or sn—er—why the deuce did they ask us?"

But Fleur was silent, thinking of her curtsey.

Royalty was affable, the dinner short but superb, served and eaten off gold plate, at a rate which suited the impression that there really wasn't a moment to spare. Fleur took a mental note of this new necessity. She knew personally five of the twenty-four diners, and the rest as in an illustrated paper, darkly. She had seen them all there at one time or another, stepping hideously in paddocks, photographed with their offspring or their dogs, about to reply for the Colonies, or 'taking a lunar' at a flying grouse. Her quick instinct apprehended almost at once the reason why she and Michael had been invited.

His speech! Like some new specimen at the Zoo, he was an object of curiosity, a stunt. She saw people nodding in the direction of him, seated opposite her between two ladies covered with flesh and pearls. Excited and very pretty, she flirted with the Admiral on her right, and defended Michael with spirit from the Under-Secretary on her left. The Admiral grew warm, the Under-Secretary, too young for emotion, cold.

"A little knowledge, Mrs. Mont," he said at the end of his short second innings, "is a dangerous thing."

"Now where have I heard that?" said Fleur. "Is it in the Bible?"

The Under-Secretary tilted his chin.

"We who have to work Departments know too much, perhaps; but your husband certainly doesn't know enough. Foggartism is an amusing idea, but there it stops."

"We shall see!" said Fleur. "What do you say, Admiral?"

"Foggartism! What's that—new kind of death ray? I saw a fellow yesterday, Mrs. Mont—give you my word! —who's got a ray that goes through three bullocks, a nine-inch brick wall, and gives a shock to a donkey on the other side; and only at quarter strength."

Fleur flashed a look round towards the Under-Secretary, who had turned his shoulder, and, leaning towards the Admiral, murmured:

"I wish you'd give a shock to the donkey on *my* other side; he wants it, and I'm not nine inches thick."

But before the Admiral could shoot his death ray, Royalty had risen.

In the apartment to which Fleur was withdrawn, she had been saying little for some minutes, and noticing much, when her hostess came up and said:

"My dear, Her Royal Highness——"

Fleur followed, retaining every wit.

A frank and simple hand patted the sofa beside her. Fleur sat down. A frank and simple voice said:

"What an interesting speech your husband made! It was so refreshing, I thought."

"Yes, ma'am," said Fleur; "but there it will stop, I am told."

A faint smile curled lips guiltless of colouring matter.

"Well, perhaps. Has he been long in Parliament?"

"Only a year."

"Ah! I liked his taking up the cudgels for the children."

"Some people think he's proposing a new kind of child slavery."

"Oh! really! Have you any children?"

"One," said Fleur, and added honestly: "And I must say I wouldn't part with him at fourteen."

"Ah! And have you been long married?"

"Four years."

At this moment the royal lady saw some one else she wished to speak to, and was compelled to break off the conversation, which she did very graciously, leaving Fleur with the feeling that she had been disappointed with the rate of production.

In the cab trailing its way home through the foggy night, she felt warm and excited, and as if Michael wasn't.

"What's the matter, Michael?"

His hand came down on her knee at once.

"Sorry, old thing! Only, really—when you think of it —eh?"

"Of what? You were quite a li— object of interest."

"The whole thing's a game. Anything for novelty!"

"The Princess was very nice about you."

"Ah! Poor thing! But I suppose you get used to anything!"

Fleur laughed. Michael went on:

"Any new idea gets seized and talked out of existence. It never gets farther than the brain, and the brain gets bored; and there it is, already a back number!"

"That can't be true, Michael. What about Free Trade, or Woman Suffrage?"

Michael squeezed her knee. "All the women say to me: 'But how interesting, Mr. Mont; I think it's most thrilling!' And the men say: 'Good stunt, Mont! But not practical politics, of course.' And I've only one answer: 'Things as big got done in the war.' By George, it's foggy!"

They were going, indeed, at a snail's pace, and through the windows could see nothing but the faint glow of the street-lamps emerging slowly, high up, one by one. Michael let down a window, and leaned out.

"Where are we?"

"Gawd knows, sir."

Michael coughed, put up the window again, and resumed his clutch of Fleur.

"By the way, Wastwater asked me if I'd read 'Canthar.' He says there's a snorting cut-up of it in 'The Philosopher.' It'll have the usual effect—send sales up."

"They say it's very clever."

"Horribly out of drawing—not fit for children, and tells adults nothing they don't know. I don't see how it can be justified."

"Genius, my dear. If it's attacked, it'll be defended."

"Sib Swan won't have it—he says it's muck."

"Oh! yes; but Sib's getting a back number."

"That's very true," said Michael, thoughtfully. "By Jove! how fast things move, except in politics, and fog."

Their cab had come to a standstill. Michael let down the window again.

"I'm fair lost, sir," said the driver's hoarse voice. "Ought to be near the Embankment, but for the life of me I can't find the turning." Michael buttoned his coat, put up the window again, and got out on the near side.

The night was smothered, alive only with the continual hootings of creeping cars. The black vapour, acrid and cold, surged into Michael's lungs.

"I'll walk beside you; we're against the curb; creep on till we strike the river, or a bobby."

The cab crept on, and Michael walked beside it, feeling with his foot for the curb.

The refined voice of an invisible man said: "This is sanguinary!"

"It is," said Michael. "Where are we?"

"In the twentieth century, and the heart of civilisation."

Michael laughed, and regretted it; the fog tasted of filth.

"Think of the police!" said the voice, "having to be out in this all night!"

"Splendid force, the police!" replied Michael. "Where are you, sir?"

"Here, sir. Where are you?"

It was the exact position. The blurred moon of a lamp glowed suddenly above Michael's head. The cab ceased to move.

"If I could only smell the 'Ouses of Parliament," said the cabman. "They'll be 'avin' supper there be now."

"Listen!" said Michael—Big Ben was striking. "That was to our left."

"At our back," said the cabman.

"Can't be, or we should be in the river; unless you've turned right round!"

"Gawd knows where I've turned," said the cabman, sneezing. "Never saw such a night!"

"There's only one thing for it—drive on until we hit something. Gently does it."

The cabman started the cab, and Michael, with his hand on it, continued to feel for the curb with his foot.

"Steady!" he said, suddenly. "Car in front." There was a slight bump.

"Nah then!" said a voice. "Where yer comin'? Cawn't yer see?"

Michael moved up alongside of what seemed to be another taxi.

"Comin' along at that pice!" said its driver; "and full moon, too!"

"Awfully sorry," said Michael. "No harm done. You got any sense of direction left?"

"The pubs are all closed—worse luck! There's a bloomin' car in front o' me that I've hit three times. Can't make any impression on it. The driver's dead, I think. Would yer go and look, Guv'nor?"

Michael moved towards the loom in front. But at that moment it gave way to the more universal blackness. He ran four steps to hail the driver, stumbled off the curb, fell, picked himself up and spun round. He moved along the curb to his right, felt he was going wrong, stopped, and called: "Hallo!" A faint "Hallo!" replied from—where? He moved what he thought was back, and called again. No answer! Fleur would be frightened! He shouted. Half a dozen faint hallos replied to him; and some one at his elbow said: "Don't cher know where y'are?"

"No; do you?"

"What do you think? Lost anything?"

"Yes; my cab."

"Left anything in it?"

"My wife."

"Lawd! You won't get 'er back to-night." A hoarse laugh, ghostly and obscene, floated by. A bit of darkness loomed for a moment, and faded out. Michael stood

still. 'Keep your head!' he thought. 'Here's the curb—
either they're in front, or they're behind; or else I've
turned a corner.' He stepped forward along the curb.
Nothing! He stepped back. Nothing! "What the blazes
have I done?" he muttered; "or have they moved on?"
Sweat poured down him in spite of the cold. Fleur would
be really scared! And the words of his election address
sprang from his lips: "Chiefly by the elimination of
smoke!"

"Ah!" said a voice, "got a cigarette, Guv'nor?"

"I'll give you all I've got and half a crown, if you'll
find a cab close by with a lady in it. What street's this?"

"Don't arst me! The streets 'ave gone mad, I think."

"Listen!" said Michael sharply.

"That's right, 'Some one callin' so sweet.'"

"Hallo!" cried Michael.   "Fleur!"

"Here! Here!"

It sounded to his right, to his left, behind him, in front.
Then came the steady blowing of a cab's horn.

"Now we've got 'em," said the bit of darkness. "This
way, Guv'nor, step slow, and mind my corns!"

Michael yielded to a tugging at his coat.

"It's like No-Man's Land in a smoke barrage!" said
his guide.

"You're right. Hallo! Coming!"

The horn sounded a yard off. A voice said: "Oh!
Michael!"

His face touched Fleur's in the window of the cab.

"Just a second, darling. There you are, my friend, and
thanks awfully! Hope you'll get home!"

"I've 'ad worse nights out than this. Thank you, Cap-
tain! Wish you and the lady luck." There was a sound
of feet shuffling on, and the fog sighed out: "So long!"

"All right, sir," said the hoarse voice of Michael's cabman. "I know where I am now. First on the left, second

on the right. I'll bump the curb till I get there. Thought you was swallered up, sir!"

Michael got into the cab, and clasped Fleur close. She uttered a long sigh, and sat quite still.

"Nothing more scaring than a fog!" he said.

"I thought you'd been run over!"

Michael was profoundly touched.

"Awfully sorry, darling. And you've got all that beastly fog down your throat. We'll drown it out when we get in. That poor chap was an ex-Service man. Wonderful the way the English keep their humour and don't lose their heads."

"I lost mine!"

"Well, you've got it back," said Michael, pressing it against his own to hide the emotion he was feeling. "Fog's our sheet-anchor, after all. So long as we have fog, England will survive." He felt Fleur's lips against his.

He belonged to her, and she couldn't afford to have him straying about in fogs or Foggartism! Was that the—? And then he yielded to the thrill.

The cabman was standing by the opened door. "Now, sir, I'm in your Square. P'r'aps you know your own 'ouse."

Wrenched from the kiss, Michael stammered: "Righto!" The fog was thinner here; he could consult the shape of trees. "On and to your right, third house."

There it was—desirable—with its bay-trees in its tubs and its fanlight shining. He put his latch-key in the door.

"A drink?" he said.

The cabman coughed: "I won't say no, sir."

Michael brought the drink.

"Far to go?"

"Near Putney Bridge. Your 'ealth, sir!"

Michael watched his pinched face drinking.

"Sorry you've got to plough into that again!"

The cabman handed back the glass.

"Thank'ee, sir; I shall be all right now; keep along the river, and down the Fulham Road. Thought they couldn't lose me in London. Where I went wrong was trying for a short cut instead of takin' the straight road round. 'Ope the young lady's none the worse, sir. She was properly scared while you was out there in the dark. These fogs ain't fit for 'uman bein's. They ought to do somethin' about 'em in Parliament."

"They ought!" said Michael, handing him a pound note. "Good night, and good luck!"

"It's an ill wind!" said the cabman, starting his cab. "Good night, sir, and thank you kindly."

"Thank *you!*" said Michael.

The cab ground slowly away, and was lost to sight.

Michael went in to the Spanish room. Fleur, beneath the Goya, was boiling a silver kettle, and burning pastilles. What a contrast to the world outside—its black malodorous cold reek, its risk and fear! In this pretty glowing room, with this pretty glowing woman, why think of its tangle, lost shapes, and straying cries?

Lighting his cigarette, he took his drink from her by its silver handle, and put it to his lips.

"I really think we ought to have a car, Michael!"

CHAPTER VIII

COLLECTING EVIDENCE

THE Editor of 'The Protagonist' had so evidently enjoyed himself that he caused a number of other people to do the same.

"There's no more popular sight in the East, Forsyte," said Sir Lawrence, "than a boy being spanked; and the only difference between East and West is that in the East the boy at once offers himself again at so much a spank. I don't see Mr. Percival Calvin doing that."

"If he defends himself," said Soames, gloomily, "other people won't."

They waited, reading daily denunciations signed: 'A Mother of Three'; 'Roger: Northampton'; 'Victorian'; 'Alys St. Maurice'; 'Plus Fours'; 'Arthur Whiffkin'; 'Sportsman if not Gentleman'; and 'Pro Patriâ'; which practically all contained the words: 'I cannot say that I have read the book through, but I have read enough to——'

It was five days before the defence fired a shot. But first came a letter above the signature: 'Swishing Block,' which, after commenting on the fact that a whole school of so-called literature had been indicted by the Editor of 'The Protagonist' in his able letter of the 14th inst., noted with satisfaction that the said school had grace enough to take its swishing without a murmur. Not even an anonymous squeak had been heard from the whole apostolic body.

"Forsyte," said Sir Lawrence, handing it to Soames, "that's my very own mite, and if it doesn't draw them —nothing will!"

But it did. The next issue of the interested journal in which the correspondence was appearing contained a letter from the greater novelist L. S. D. which restored every one to his place. This book might or might not be Art, he hadn't read it; but the Editor of 'The Protagonist' wrote like a pedagogue, and there was an end of him. As to the claim that literature must always wear a flannel petticoat, it was 'piffle,' and that was that. From under the skirts of this letter the defence, to what of exultation Soames ever permitted himself, moved out in force. Among the defenders were as many as four of the selected ten associates to whom young Butterfield had purveyed copies. They wrote over their own names that 'Canthar' was distinctly LITERATURE; they were sorry for people who thought in these days that LITERATURE had any business with morals. The work must be approached æsthetically or not at all. ART was ART, and morality was morality, and never the twain could, would, or should meet. It was monstrous that a work of this sort should have to appear with a foreign imprint. When would England recognise genius when she saw it?

Soames cut the letters out one after the other, and pasted them in a book. He had got what he wanted, and the rest of the discussion interested him no more. He had received, too, a communication from young Butterfield.

"SIR,

"I called on the lady last Monday, and was fortunately able to see her in person. She seemed rather annoyed when I offered her the book. 'That book,' she said: 'I read it weeks ago.' 'It's exciting a great deal of interest, Madam,' I said. 'I know,' she said. 'Then you won't take a copy; the price is rising steadily, it'll be very valuable in time?' 'I've got one,' she said. That's what you told me to find out, sir; so I didn't pursue the matter. I hope I have done what you wanted. But if there is anything more, I shall be most happy. I consider that I owe my present position entirely to you."

Soames didn't know about that, but as to his future position—he might have to put the young man into the box. The question of a play remained. He consulted Michael.

"Does that young woman still act in the advanced theatre place you gave me the name of?"

Michael winced. "I don't know, sir; but I could find out."

Inquiry revealed that she was cast for the part of Olivia in Bertie Curfew's matinée of 'The Plain Dealer.'

"'The Plain Dealer'?" said Soames. "Is that an advanced play?"

"Yes, sir, two hundred and fifty years old."

"Ah!" said Soames; "they were a coarse lot in those days. How is it she goes on there if she and the young man have split?"

"Oh! well, they're very cool hands. I do hope you're going to keep things out of Court, sir?"

"I can't tell. When's this performance?"

"January the seventh."

Soames went to his Club library and took down 'Wycherley.' He was disappointed with the early portions of 'The Plain Dealer,' but it improved as it went on, and he spent some time making a list of what George Forsyte would have called the 'nubbly bits.' He understood that at that theatre they did not bowdlerise. Excellent! There were passages that should raise hair on any British Jury. Between 'Canthar' and this play, he felt as if he had a complete answer to any claim by the young woman and her set to having 'morals about them.' Old professional instincts were rising within him. He had retained Sir James Foskisson, K. C., not because he admired him personally, but because if he didn't, the other side might. As junior he was employing very young Nicholas Forsyte; he had no great opinion of him, but it was as well to keep the matter in the family, especially if it wasn't to come into Court.

A conversation with Fleur that evening contributed to his intention that it should not.

"What's happened to that young American?" he said.

Fleur smiled acidly. "Francis Wilmot? Oh! he's 'fallen for' Marjorie Ferrar."

"'Fallen for her'?" said Soames. "What an expression!"

"Yes, dear; it's American."

"'For' her? It means nothing, so far as I can see."

"Let's hope not, for his sake! She's going to marry Sir Alexander MacGown, I'm told."

"Oh!"

"Did Michael tell you that he hit him on the nose?"

"Which—who?" said Soames testily. "Whose nose?"

"MacGown's, dear; and it bled like anything."

"Why on earth did he do that?"

"Didn't you read his speech about Michael?"

"Oh!" said Soames. "Parliamentary fuss—that's nothing. They're always behaving like children, there. And so she's going to marry him. Has he been putting her up to all this?"

"No; *she's* been putting him."

Soames discounted the information with a sniff; he scented the hostility of woman for woman. Still, chicken and egg—political feeling and social feeling, who could say which first prompted which? In any case, this made a difference. Going to be married—was she? He debated the matter for some time, and then decided that he would go and see Settlewhite and Stark. If they had been a firm of poor repute or the kind always employed in 'causes célèbres,' he wouldn't have dreamed of it; but, as a fact, they stood high, were solid family people, with an aristocratic connection and all that.

He did not write, but took his hat and went over from 'the Connoisseurs' to their offices in King Street, St. James's. The journey recalled old days—to how many such negotiatory meetings had he not gone or caused his adversaries to come! He had never cared to take things into Court if they could be settled out of it. And always he had approached negotiation with the impersonality of one passionless about to meet another of the same kidney —two calculating machines, making their livings out of human nature. He did not feel like that to-day; and, aware of this handicap, stopped to stare into the print and picture shop next door. Ah! There were those first proofs of the Roussel engravings of the Prince Consort Exhibition of '51, that Old Mont had spoken of—he had an eye for an engraving, Old Mont. Ah! and there was a Fred Walker, quite a good one! Mason, and Walker— they weren't done for yet by any means. And the sensation that a man feels hearing a blackbird sing on a tree just coming into blossom, stirred beneath Soames' ribs. Long—long since he had bought a picture! Let him but get this confounded case out of the way, and he could enjoy himself again. Riving his glance from the window, he took a long breath, and walked into Settlewhite and Stark's.

The chief partner's room was on the first floor, and the chief partner standing where chief partners stand.

"How do you do, Mr. Forsyte? I've not met you since 'Bobbin against the L. & S. W.' That must have been 1900!"

"1899," said Soames. "You were for the Company."

Mr. Settlewhite pointed to a chair.

Soames sat down and glanced up at the figure before the fire. H'm! A long-lipped, long-eyelashed, long-chinned face; a man of his own calibre, education, and probity! He would not beat about the bush.

"This action," he said, "is a very petty business. What can we do about it?"

Mr. Settlewhite frowned.

"That depends, Mr. Forsyte, on what you have to propose? My client has been very grossly libelled."

Soames smiled sourly.

"She began it. And what is she relying on—private letters to personal friends of my daughter's, written in very natural anger! I'm surprised that a firm of your standing——"

Mr. Settlewhite smiled.

"Don't trouble to compliment my firm! I'm surprised myself that you're acting for your daughter. You can hardly see all round the matter. Have you come to offer an apology?"

"That!" said Soames. "I should have thought it was for your client to apologise."

"If such is your view, I'm afraid it's no use continuing this discussion."

Soames regarded him fixedly.

"How do you think you're going to prove damage? She belongs to the fast set."

Mr. Settlewhite continued to smile.

"I understand she's going to marry Sir Alexander Mac-Gown," said Soames.

Mr. Settlewhite's lips tightened.

"Really, Mr. Forsyte, if you have come to offer an apology and a substantial sum in settlement, we can talk. Otherwise——"

"As a sensible man," said Soames, "you know that

these Society scandals are always dead-sea fruit—nothing but costs and vexation, and a feast for all the gossips about town. I'm prepared to offer you a thousand pounds to settle the whole thing, but an apology I can't look at. A mutual expression of regret—perhaps; but an apology's out of the question."

"Fifteen hundred I mig!.+ accept—the insults have had wide currency. But an apology is essential."

Soames sat silent, chewing the injustice of it all. Fifteen hundred! Monstrous! Still he would pay even that to keep Fleur out of Court. But humble-pie! She wouldn't eat it, and he couldn't make her, and he didn't know that he wanted to. He got up.

"Look here, Mr. Settlewhite, if you take this into Court, you will find yourself up against more than you think. But the whole thing is so offensive to me, that I'm prepared to meet you over the money, though I tell you frankly I don't believe a Jury would award a penny piece. As to an apology, a 'formula' could be found, perhaps"—why the deuce was the fellow smiling?—"something like this: 'We regret that we have said hasty things about each other,' to be signed by both parties."

Mr. Settlewhite caressed his chin.

"Well, I'll put your proposition before my client. I join with you in wishing to see the matter settled, not because I'm afraid of the result"—'Oh, no!' thought Soames—"but because these cases, as you say, are not edifying." He held out his hand.

Soames gave it a cold touch.

"You understand that this is entirely 'without prejudice,'" he said, and went out. 'She'll take it!' he thought. Fifteen hundred pounds of his money thrown away on that baggage, just because for once she had been labelled what she was; and all his trouble to get evidence wasted! For a moment he resented his devotion to Fleur. Really

it was fatuous to be so fond as that! Then his heart re-
bounded. Thank God! He had settled it.

Christmas was at hand. It did not alarm him, therefore, that he received no answering communication. Fleur
and Michael were at Lippinghall with the ninth and
eleventh baronets. He and Annette had Winifred and
the Cardigans down at 'The Shelter.' Not till the 6th of
January did he receive a letter from Messrs. Settlewhite
and Stark.

"DEAR SIR,

"In reference to your call of the 17th ultimo, your
proposition was duly placed before our client, and we are
instructed to say that she will accept the sum of £1,500
—fifteen hundred pounds—and an apology, duly signed
by your client, copy of which we enclose.

We are, dear Sir,

Faithfully yours,

SETTLEWHITE AND STARK."

Soames turned to the enclosure. It ran thus:

"I, Mrs. Michael Mont, withdraw the words concerning Miss Marjorie Ferrar contained in my letters to Mrs.
Ralph Ppynrryn and Mrs. Edward Maltese of October
4th last, and hereby tender a full and free apology for
having written them.

(Signed)"

Pushing back the breakfast-table, so violently that it
groaned, Soames got up.

"What is it, Soames?" said Annette. "Have you
broken your plate again? You should not bite so hard."

"Read that!"

Annette read.

"You would give that woman fifteen hundred pounds?

I think you are mad, Soames. I would not give her fifteen hundred pence! Pay this woman, and she tells her friends. That is fifteen hundred apologies in all their minds. Really, Soames—I am surprised. A man of business, a clever man! Do you not know the world better than that? With every pound you pay, Fleur eats her words!"

Soames flushed. It was so French, and yet somehow it was so true. He walked to the window. The French—they had no sense of compromise, and every sense of money!

"Well," he said, "that ends it anyway. She won't sign. And I shall withdraw my offer."

"I should hope so. Fleur has a good head. She will look very pretty in Court. I think that woman will be sorry she ever lived! Why don't you have her what you call shadowed? It is no good to be delicate with women like that."

In a weak moment he had told Annette about the book and the play; for, unable to speak of them to Fleur and Michael, he had really had to tell some one; indeed, he had shown her 'Canthar,' with the words: "I don't advise you to read it; it's very French."

Annette had returned it to him two days later, saying: "It is not French at all; it is disgusting. You English are so coarse. It has no wit. It is only nasty. A serious nasty book—that is the limit. You are so old-fashioned, Soames. Why do you say this book is French?"

Soames, who didn't really know why, had muttered:

"Well, they can't get it printed in England." And with the words: "Bruxelles, Bruxelles, you call Bruxelles —" buzzing about his ears, had left the room. He had never known any people so touchy as the French!

Her remark about 'shadowing,' however, was not easily forgotten. Why be squeamish, when all depended on frightening this woman? And on arriving in London he visited an office that was not Mr. Polteed's, and gave instructions for the shadowing of Marjorie Ferrar's past, present, and future.

His answer to Settlewhite and Stark, too, was brief, determined, and written on the paper of his own firm.

"Jan. 6th, 1924.
"Dear Sirs,

"I have your letter of yesterday's date, and note that your client has rejected my proposition, which, as you know, was made entirely without prejudice, and is now withdrawn in toto.
                                        Yours faithfully,
                                            Soames Forsyte."

If he did not mistake, they would be sorry. And he gazed at the words 'in toto'; somehow they looked funny. In toto! And now for 'The Plain Dealer'!

The theatre of the 'Ne Plus Ultra' Play-producing Society had a dingy exterior, a death-mask of Congreve in the hall, a peculiar smell, and an apron stage. There was no music. They hit something three times before the curtain went up. There were no footlights. The scenery was peculiar—Soames could not take his eyes off it till, in the first Entr'acte, its principle was revealed to him by the conversation of two people sitting just behind.

"The point of the scenery here is that no one need look at it, you see. They go farther than anything yet done."

"They've gone farther in Moscow."

"I believe not. Curfew went over there. He came back raving about the way they speak their lines."

"Does he know Russian?"

"No. You don't need to. It's the timbre. I think he's doing pretty well here with that. You couldn't give a play like this if you took the words in."

Soames, who had been trying to take the words in— it was, indeed, what he had come for—squinted round at the speakers. They were pale and young and went on with a strange unconcern.

"Curfew's doing great work. He's shaking them up."

"I see they've got Marjorie Ferrar as Olivia."

"Don't know why he keeps on an amateur like that."

"Box office, my dear boy; she brings the smart people. She's painful, I think."

"She did one good thing—the dumb girl in that Russian play. But she can't speak for nuts; you're following the sense of her words all the time. She doesn't rhythmatise you a little bit."

"She's got looks."

"M'yes."

At this moment the curtain went up again. Since Marjorie Ferrar had not yet appeared, Soames was obliged to keep awake; indeed, whether because she couldn't 'speak for nuts,' or merely from duty, he was always awake while she was on the stage, and whenever she had anything outrageous to say he noted it carefully; otherwise he passed an excellent afternoon, and went away much rested. In his cab he mentally rehearsed Sir James Foskisson in the part of cross-examiner:

"I think, madam, you played Olivia in a production of 'The Plain Dealer' by the 'Ne Plus Ultra' Play-producing Society? . . . Would it be correct to say that the part was that of a modest woman? . . . Precisely. And did it contain the following lines? (Quotation of nubbly bits.) . . . Did that convey anything to your mind, madam? . . . I suppose that you would not say it was an immoral passage? . . . No? Nor calculated to offend the ears and debase the morals of a decent-minded audience? . . . No. In fact, you don't take the same view of morality that I, or I venture to think, the Jury do? . . . No. The dark scene—you did not remonstrate with the producer for not omitting that scene? . . .

Quite. Mr. Curfew, I think, was the producer? Yes. Are you on such terms with that gentleman as would have made a remonstrance easy? . . . Ah! Now, madam, I put it to you that throughout 1923 you were seeing this gentleman nearly every day. . . . Well, say three or four times a week. And yet you say that you were not on such terms as would have made it possible for you to represent to him that no modest young woman should be asked to play a scene like that. . . . Indeed! The Jury will form their own opinion of your answer. You are not a professional actress, dependent for your living on doing what you are told to do? . . . No. And yet you have the face to come here and ask for substantial damages because of the allegation in a private letter that you haven't a moral about you? . . . Have you? . . ." And so on, and so on. Oh! no. Damages! She wouldn't get a farthing.

CHAPTER IX

VOLTE FACE

KEEPING Sir Alexander MacGown and Francis Wilmot in the air, fulfilling her week-end and other en-
gagements, playing much Bridge in the hope of making
her daily expenses, getting a day's hunting when she
could, and rehearsing the part of Olivia, Marjorie Ferrar
had almost forgotten the action, when the offer of fifteen
hundred pounds and the formula were put before her by
Messrs. Settlewhite and Stark. She almost jumped at it.
The money would wipe out her more pressing debts; she
would be able to breathe, and reconsider her future.

She received their letter on the Friday before Christmas,
just as she was about to go down to her father's, near
Newmarket, and wrote hastily to say she would call at
their office on her way home on Monday. The following
evening she consulted her father. Lord Charles was of
opinion that if this attorney fellow would go as far as
fifteen hundred, he must be dead keen on settling, and
she had only to press for the apology to get it. Anyway
she should let them stew in their juice for a bit. On
Monday he wanted to show her his yearlings. She did
not, therefore, return to Town till the 23d, and found
the office closed for Christmas. It had never occurred to
her that solicitors had holidays. On Christmas Eve she
herself went away for ten days; so that it was January
the 4th before she was again able to call. Mr. Settlewhite was still in the South of France, but Mr. Stark
would see her. Mr. Stark knew little about the matter,
but thought Lord Charles' advice probably sound; he
proposed to write accepting the fifteen hundred pounds
if a formal apology were tendered; they could fall back

185

on the formula if necessary, but it was always wise to get as much as you could. With some misgiving Marjorie Ferrar agreed.

Returning from the matinée on January 7th, tired and elated by applause, by Bertie Curfew's words: "You did quite well, darling," and almost the old look on his face, she got into a hot bath, and was just out when her maid announced Mr. Wilmot.

"Keep him, Fanny; say I'll be with him in twenty minutes."

Feverish and soft, as if approaching a crisis, she dressed hastily, put essence of orange-blossom on her neck and hands, and went to the studio. She entered without noise. The young man, back to the door, in the centre of the room, evidently did not hear her. Approaching within a few feet, she waited for the effect on him of orange-blossom. He was standing like some Eastern donkey, that with drooped ears patiently awaits the fresh burdening of a sore back. And suddenly he spoke: "I'm all in."

"Francis!"

The young man turned.

"Oh! Marjorie!" he said, "I never heard." And taking her hands, he buried his face in them.

She was hampered at that moment. To convert his mouth from despairing kissing of her hands to triumphal flame upon her lips would have been so easy if he had been modern, if his old-fashioned love had not complimented her so subtly; if, too, she were not feeling for him something more—or was it less?—than passion. Was she to know at last the sensations of the simple—a young girl's idyll—something she had missed? She led him to the divan, sat down by his side, and looked into his eyes. Fabled sweetness, as of a Spring morning—Francis and she, children in the wood, with the world well lost! She surrendered to the innocence of it; deliberately grasped something delicious, new. Poor boy! How delightful to feel him happy at last—to promise marriage and mean to perform it! When? Oh! when he liked— Soon, quite soon; the sooner the better! Almost unconscious that she was 'playing' a young girl, she was carried away by his amazement and his joy. He was on fire, on air; yet he remained delicate—he was wonderful! For an hour they sat—a fragrant hour for memory to sniff—before she remembered that she was dining out at half past eight. She put her lips to his, and closed her eyes. And thought ran riot. Should she spoil it, and make sure of him in modern fashion? What was his image of her but a phlizz, but a fraud? She saw his eyes grow troubled, felt his hands grow fevered. Something seemed drowning before her eyes. She stood up.

"Now, my darling, you must fly!"

When he had flown, she threw off her dress and brushed out her hair that in the mirror seemed to have more gold than red. . . . Some letters on her dressing-table caught her eye. The first was a bill, the second a bill; the third ran thus:

"DEAR MADAM,

"We regret to say that Cuthcott Kingson & Forsyte have refused to give the apology we asked for, and withdrawn their verbal offer in toto. We presume, therefore, that the action must go forward. We have every hope, however, that they may reconsider the matter before it comes into Court.

Your obedient servants,
SETTLEWHITE AND STARK."

She dropped it and sat very still, staring at a little hard line on the right side of her mouth and a little hard line on the left. . . .

Francis Wilmot, flying, thought of steamship-lines and
staterooms, of registrars and rings. An hour ago he had
despaired; now it seemed he had always known she was
"too fine not to give up this Congressman whom she
didn't love." He would make her the queen of South
Carolina—ah! he would! But if she didn't like it out
there, he would sell the 'old home,' and they would go
and live where she wished—in Venice; he had heard her
say Venice was wonderful; or New York, or Sicily; with
her he wouldn't care! And London in the cold dry wind
seemed beautiful, no longer a grey maze of unreality and
shadows, but a city where you could buy rings and steam-
ship passages. The wind cut him like a knife and he did
not feel it. That poor devil of a 'Congressman'! He
hated the sight, the thought of him, and yet felt sorry,
thinking of him with the cup dashed from his lips. And
all the days, weeks, months himself had spent circling
round the flame, his wings scorched and drooping, seemed
now but the natural progress of the soul towards Para-
dise. Twenty-four—his age and hers; an eternity of bliss!
He pictured her on the porch at home. Horses! A better
car than the old Ford! The darkies would adore her—
kind of grand, and so white! To walk with her among
the azaleas in the Spring, he could smell them already;
no—it was his hands where he had touched her! He
shivered, and resumed his flight under the bare trees,
well-nigh alone in the East wind; the stars of a bitter
night shining.

A card was handed to him as he entered his Hotel.

"Mr. Wilmot, a gentleman to see you."

MacGown was seated in a corner of the Lounge,
with a crush hat in his hand. He rose and came towards
Francis Wilmot, grim and square.

"I've been meaning to call on you for some time, Mr.
Wilmot."

"Yes, sir. May I offer you a cocktail, or a glass of sherry?"

"No, thank you. You are aware of my engagement to Miss Ferrar?"

"I was, sir."

This red aggressive face, with its stiff moustache and burning eyes, revived his hatred; so that he no longer felt sorry.

"You know that I very much object to your constant visits to that young lady. In this country it is not the part of a gentleman to pursue an engaged young woman."

"That," said Francis Wilmot, coolly, "is for Miss Ferrar herself to say."

MacGown's face grew even redder.

"If you hadn't been an American, I should have warned you to keep clear a long time ago."

Francis Wilmot bowed.

"Well! Are you going to?"

"Permit me to decline an answer."

MacGown thrust forward his face.

"I've told you," he said. "If you trespass any more, look out for yourself."

"Thank you; I will," said Francis Wilmot, softly.

MacGown stood for a moment swaying slightly. Was he going to hit out? Francis Wilmot put his hands into his trouser pockets.

"You've had your warning," said MacGown, and turned on his heel.

"Good night!" said Francis Wilmot to that square receding back. He had been gentle, he had been polite, but he hated the fellow, yes, indeed! Save for the triumphal glow within him, there would have been a fuss!

CHAPTER X

PHOTOGRAPHY

SUMMONED to the annual Christmas covert-shooting at Lippinghall, Michael found there two practical politicians, and one member of the Government.

In the mullion-windowed smoking-room, where men retired, and women too sometimes, into chairs old, soft, leathery, the ball of talk was lightly tossed, and naught so devastating as Foggartism mentioned. But in odd minutes and half-hours Michael gained insight into political realities, and respect for practical politicians. Even on this holiday they sat up late, got up early, wrote letters, examined petitions, dipped into Blue Books. They were robust, ate heartily, took their liquor like men, never seemed fatigued. They shaved clean, looked healthy, and shot badly with enjoyment. The member of the Government played golf instead, and Fleur went round with him. Michael learned the lesson: Have so much on your mind that you have practically nothing in it; no time to pet your schemes, fancies, feelings. Carry on, and be careful that you don't know to what end.

As for Foggartism, they didn't—*à la* 'Evening Sun'—pooh-pooh it; they merely asked, as Michael had often asked himself: "Yes, but how are you going to work it? Your scheme might be very good, if it didn't hit people's pockets. Any addition to the price of living is out of the question—the country's taxed up to the hilt. Your Foggartism's going to need money in every direction. You may swear till you're blue in the face that ten or twenty years hence it'll bring fivefold return; nobody will listen. You may say: 'Without it we're all going to the devil'; but we're accustomed to that—some people think we're there already, and they resent its being said. Others, especially manufacturers, believe what they want to. They can't bear any one who cries 'stinking fish,' whatever his object. Talk about reviving trade, and less taxation, or offer more wages and talk of a capital levy, and, according to Party, we shall believe you've done the trick—until we find you haven't. But you're talking of less trade and more taxation in the present with a view to a better future. Great Scott! In politics you can shuffle the cards, but you mustn't add or subtract. People only react to immediate benefit, or, as in the war, to imminent danger. You must cut out sensationalism."

In short, they were intelligent, and completely fatalistic.

After these quiet talks, Michael understood much better than before, the profession of politics. He was greatly attracted by the member of the Government; his personality was modest, his manner pleasant, he had Departmental ideas, and was doing his best with his own job according to those ideas; if he had others he kept them to himself. He seemed to admire Fleur, and he listened better than the other two. He said, too, some things they hadn't. "Of course, what we're able to do may be found so inadequate that there'll be a great journalistic outcry, and under cover of it we may bring in some sweeping measures that people will swallow before they know what they're in for."

"The Press," said Michael, "I don't see them helping."

"Well! It's the only voice there is. If you could get real hold of the vociferous papers, you might even put your Foggartism over. What you're really up against is the slow town growth of the last hundred and fifty years, an ingrained state of mind which can only see England in terms of industrialism and the carrying trade. And in the town-mind, of course, hope springs eternal. They don't like calamity talk. Some genuinely think we can go on indefinitely on the old lines, and get more and more prosperous into the bargain. Personally, I don't. It's possible that much of what old Foggart advocates may be adopted bit by bit, even child emigration, from sheer practical necessity; but it won't be called Foggartism. Inventor's luck! *He'll* get no credit for being the first to see it. And," added the Minister, gloomily, "by the time it's adopted, it'll probably be too late."

Receiving the same day a request for an interview from a Press Syndicate whose representative would come down to suit his convenience, Michael made the appointment, and prepared an elaborate exposition of his faith. The representative, however, turned out to be a camera, and a photograph entitled: 'The Member for Mid-Bucks expounding Foggartism to our Representative,' became the only record of it. The camera was active. It took a family group in front of the porch: 'Right to Left, Mr. Michael Mont, M. P., Lady Mont, Mrs. Michael Mont, Sir Lawrence Mont, Bt.' It took Fleur: 'Mrs. Michael Mont, with Kit and Dandie.' It took the Jacobean wing. It took the Minister, with his pipe, 'enjoying a Christmas rest.' It took a corner of the walled garden: 'In the grounds.' It then had lunch. After lunch it took the whole house-party: 'At Sir Lawrence Mont's, Lippinghall Manor, Bucks'; with the Minister on Lady Mont's right and the Minister's wife on Sir Lawrence's left. This photograph would have turned out better, if the Dandie, inadvertently left out, had not made a sudden onslaught on the camera's legs. It took a photograph of Fleur alone: 'Mrs. Michael Mont—a charming young Society hostess.' It understood that Michael was making an interesting practical experiment—could it take Foggartism in action? Michael grinned and said: Yes, if it would take a walk, too.

They departed for the coppice. The colony was in its normal state—Boddick, with two of the contractor's men cheering him on, was working at the construction of the incubator-house; Swain, smoking a cigarette, was reading 'The Daily Mail'; Bergfeld was sitting with his head in his hands, and Mrs. Bergfeld was washing up.

The camera took three photographs. Michael, who had noted that Bergfeld had begun shaking, suggested to the camera that it would miss its train. It at once took a final photograph of Michael in front of the hut, two cups of tea at the Manor, and its departure.

As Michael was going up-stairs that night, the butler came to him.

"The man Boddick's in the pantry, Mr. Michael; I'm afraid something's happened, sir."

"Oh!" said Michael, blankly.

Where Michael had spent many happy hours, when he was young, was Boddick, his pale face running with sweat, and his dark eyes very alive.

"The German's gone, sir."

"Gone?"

"Hanged hisself. The woman's in an awful state. I cut him down, and sent Swain to the village."

"Good God! Hanged! But why?"

"He's been very funny these last three days; and that camera upset him properly. Will you come, sir?"

They set out with a lantern, Boddick telling his tale.

"As soon as ever you was gone this afternoon he started to shake and carry on about having been made game of. I told 'im not to be a fool, and went out to get on with it. But when I came in to tea, he was still shakin', and talkin' about his honour and his savin's; Swain had got fed-up and was jeerin' at him, and Mrs. Bergfeld was as white as a ghost in the corner. I told Swain to shut his head; and Fritz simmered down after a bit, and sat humped up as he does for hours together. Mrs. Bergfeld got our tea. I had some chores to finish, so I went out after. When I come in at seven, they was at it again hammer and tongs, and Mrs. Bergfeld cryin' fit to bust her heart. 'Can't you see,' I said, 'how you're upsettin' your wife?' 'Henry Boddick,' he said, 'I've nothing against *you*, you've always been decent to me. But this Swain,' he said, "'is name is Swine!' and he took up the bread-knife. I got it away from him, and spoke him calm. 'Ah!' he said, 'but *you've* no pride.' Swain was lookin' at him with that sort o' droop in his mouth he's got. 'Pride,' he says, 'you silly blighter, what call 'ave *you* to 'ave any pride?' Well, I see that while we was there he wasn't goin' to get any better, so I took Swain off for a glass at the pub. When we came back at ten o'clock, Swain went straight to bed, and I went into the mess-room, where I found his wife alone. 'Has he gone to bed?' I said. 'No,' she said, 'he's gone out to cool his head. Oh! Henry Boddick,' she said, 'I don't know what to do with him!' We sat there a bit, she tellin' me about 'im brooding, and all that—nice woman she is, too; till suddenly she said: 'Henry Boddick,' she said, 'I'm frightened. Why don't he come?' We went out to look for him, and where d'you think he was, sir? You know that big tree we're just goin' to have down? There's a ladder against it, and the guidin' rope all fixed. He'd climbed up that ladder in the moonlight, put the rope round his neck, and jumped off; and there he was, six feet from the ground, dead as a duck. I roused up Swain, and we got him in, and— Well, we 'ad a proper time! Poor woman, I'm sorry for her, sir—though really I think it's just as well he's gone—he couldn't get upsides with it anyhow. That camera chap would have given something for a shot at what we saw there in the moonlight."

'Foggartism in action!' thought Michael, bitterly. 'So endeth the First Lesson!'

The hut looked lonely in the threading moonlight and

the bitter wind. Inside, Mrs. Bergfeld was kneeling beside the body placed on the deal table, with a handker-
chief over its face. Michael put a hand on her shoulder.
She gave him a wild look, bowed her head again, and her
lips began moving. 'Prayer!' thought Michael. 'Catholic
—of course!' He took Boddick aside. "Don't let her see
Swain. I'll talk to him."

When the police and the doctor came in, he button-
holed the hair-dresser, whose shadowy face looked ghastly
in the moonlight. He seemed much upset.

"You'd better come down to the house for the night,
Swain."

"All right, sir. I never meant to hurt the poor beggar.
But he did carry on so, and I've got my own trouble. I
couldn't stand 'im monopolisin' misfortune the way he
does. When the inquest's over, I'm off. If I can't get
some sun soon, I'll be as dead as 'im."

Michael was relieved. Boddick would be left alone.

When at last he got back to the house with Swain,
Fleur was asleep. He did not wake her to tell her the
news, but lay a long time trying to get warm, and thinking of that great obstacle to all salvation—the human
element. And, mingled with his visions of the woman
beside that still, cold body were longings for the warmth
of the young body close to him.

The photographs were providential. For three days no
paper could be taken up which did not contain some allusion, illustrated, to "The Tragedy on a Buckinghamshire
Estate"; "German actor hangs himself"; "The drama
at Lippinghall"; "Tragic end of an experiment"; "Right
to Left: Mr. Michael Mont, Member for Mid-Bucks;
Bergfeld, the German actor who hanged himself. Mrs.
Bergfeld."

'The Evening Sun' wrote more in sorrow than in anger:
"The suicide of a German actor on Sir Lawrence

Mont's estate at Lippinghall has in it a touch of the grotesquely moral. The unfortunate man seems to have been
one of three 'out-of-works' selected by the young Member
for Mid-Bucks, recently conspicuous for his speech on
'Foggartism,' for a practical experiment in that peculiar
movement. Why he should have chosen a German to as-
sist the English people to return to the Land is not perhaps very clear; but, largely speaking, the incident illus-
trates the utter unsuitability of all amateur attempts to
solve this problem, and the futility of pretending to deal
with the unemployment crisis while we still tolerate
among us numbers of aliens who take the bread out of
the mouths of our own people." The same issue contained a short leader entitled: "The Alien in our Midst."
The inquest was well attended. It was common knowledge that three men and one woman lived in the hut, and
sensational developments were expected. A good deal of
disappointment was felt that the evidence disclosed
nothing at all of a sexual character.

Fleur, with the eleventh baronet, returned to town
after it was over. Michael remained for the funeral—in
a Catholic cemetery some miles away. He walked with
Henry Boddick behind Mrs. Bergfeld. A little sleet was
drifting out of a sky the colour of the gravestones, and
against that whitish sky the yew-trees looked very stark.
He had ordered a big wreath laid on the grave, and when
he saw it thus offered up, he thought: 'First human beings,
then rams, now flowers! Progress!'

Having arranged that Norah Curfew should take Mrs.
Bergfeld as cook in Bethnal Green, he drove her up to
London in the Manor car. During that long drive he
experienced again feelings that he had not had since the
war. Human hearts, dressed-up to the nines in circumstance, interests, manners, accents, race, and class, when
stripped by grief, by love, by hate, by laughter were one

and the same heart. But how seldom were they stripped! Life was a clothed affair! A good thing too, perhaps— the strain of nakedness was too considerable! He was, in fact, infinitely relieved to see the face of Norah Curfew, and hear her cheerful words to Mrs. Bergfeld:

"Come in, my dear, and have some tea!" She was the sort who stripped to the heart without strain or shame.

Fleur was in the drawing-room when he got home, furred up to her cheeks, which were bright as if she had just come in from the cold.

"Been out, my child?"

"Yes. I—" She stopped, looked at him rather queer-ly, and said: "Well, have you finished with that busi-ness?"

"Yes; thank God. I've dropped the poor creature on Norah Curfew."

Fleur smiled. "Ah! Yes, Norah Curfew! *She* lives for everybody but herself, doesn't she?"

"She does," said Michael, rather sharply.

"The new woman. One's getting clean out of fashion." Michael took her cheeks between his hands.

"What's the matter, Fleur?"

"Nothing."

"There is."

"Well, one gets a bit fed up with being left out, as if one were fit for nothing but Kit, and looking appetising."

Michael dropped his hands, hurt and puzzled. Cer-tainly he had not consulted her about his 'down and outs'; had felt sure it would only bore or make her laugh— No future in it! And had there been?

"Any time you like to go shares in any mortal thing, Fleur, you've only to say so."

"Oh! I don't want to poke into your affairs. I've got my own. Have you had tea?"

"Do tell me what's the matter?"

"My dear boy, you've already asked me that, and I've already told you—nothing."

"Won't you kiss me?"

"Of course. And there's Kit's bath—would you like to go up?"

Each short stab went in a little farther. This was a spiritual crisis, and he did not know in the least how to handle it. Didn't she want him to admire her, to desire her? What did she want? Recognition that she was as interested as he in—in the state of the Country? Of course! Only—was she?

"Well," she said, "*I* want tea, anyway. Is the new woman dramatic?"

Jealousy? The notion was absurd. He said quietly:

"I don't quite follow you."

Fleur looked up at him with very clear eyes.

"Good God!" said Michael, and left the room.

He went up-stairs and sat down before 'The White Monkey.' In that strategic position he better perceived the core of his domestic moment. Fleur had to be first— had to take precedence. No object in her collection must live a life of its own! He was appalled by the bitterness of that thought. No, no! It was only that she had a complex—a silver spoon, and it had become natural in her mouth. She resented his having interests in which she was not first; or, rather, perhaps, resented the fact that they were not her interests too. And that was to her credit, when you came to think of it. She was vexed with herself for being egocentric. Poor child! 'I've got to mind my eye,' thought Michael, 'or I shall make some modern-novel mess of this in three parts.' And his mind strayed naturally to the science of dishing up symptoms as if they were roots—ha! He remembered his nursery governess locking him in; he had dreaded being penned

Photography

up ever since. The psychoanalysts would say that was due to the action of his governess. It wasn't—many small boys wouldn't have cared a hang; it was due to a nature that existed before that action. He took up the photograph of Fleur that stood on his desk. He loved the face, he would always love it. If she had limitations—well! So had he—lots! This was comedy, one mustn't make it into tragedy! Surely she had a sense of humour, too! Had she? Had she not? And Michael searched the face he held in his hands. . . .

But, as is usual with husbands, he had diagnosed without knowledge of all the facts.

Fleur had been bored at Lippinghall, even collection of the Minister had tried her. She had concealed her boredom from Michael. But self-sacrifice takes its revenge. She reached home in a mood of definite antagonism to public affairs. Hoping to feel better if she bought a hat or two, she set out for Bond Street. At the corner of Burlington Street, a young man bared his head.

"Fleur!"

Wilfrid Desert! Very lean and very brown!

"You!"

"Yes. I'm just back. How's Michael?"

"Very well. Only he's in Parliament."

"Great Scott! And how are you?"

"As you see. Did you have a good time?"

"Yes. I'm only perching. The East has got me!"

"Are you coming to see us?"

"I think not. The burnt child, you know."

"Yes; you *are* brown!"

"Well, good-bye, Fleur! You look just the same, only more so. I'll see Michael somewhere."

"Good-bye!" She walked on without looking back, and then regretted not having found out whether Wilfrid had done the same.

She had given Wilfrid up for—well, for Michael, who—who had forgotten it! Really she was too self-sacrificing! And then at three o'clock a note was brought her:

"By hand, ma'am; answer waiting."

She opened an envelope, stamped 'Cosmopolis Hotel.'

"MADAM,

"We apologise for troubling you, but are in some perplexity. Mr. Francis Wilmot, a young American gentleman, who has been staying in this hotel since early October, has, we are sorry to say, contracted pneumonia. The doctor reports unfavourably on his condition. In these circumstances we thought it right to examine his effects, in order that we might communicate with his friends; but the only indication we can find is a card of yours. I venture to ask you if you can help us in the matter.

Believe me to be, Madam,
Your faithful servant,
(for the Management)."

Fleur stared at an illegible signature, and her thoughts were bitter. Jon had dumped Francis on her as a herald of his happiness; her enemy had lifted him! Then, why didn't that Cat look after him herself? Oh! well, poor boy! Ill in a great hotel—without a soul!

"Call me a taxi, Coaker."

On her way to the Hotel she felt slight excitement of the 'ministering angel' order.

Giving her name at the bureau, she was taken up to Room 209. A chambermaid was there. The doctor, she said, had ordered a nurse, who had not yet come.

Francis Wilmot, very flushed, was lying back, propped up; his eyes were closed.

"How long has he been ill like this?"

"I've noticed him looking queer, ma'am; but we didn't know how bad he was until to-day. I think he's just neglected it. The doctor says he's got to be packed. Poor gentleman, it's very sad. You see, he's hardly there!"

Francis Wilmot's lips were moving; he was evidently on the verge of delirium.

"Go and make some lemon tea in a jug as weak and hot as you can; quick!"

When the maid had gone, she went up and put her cool hand to his forehead.

"It's all right, Francis. Much pain?"

Francis Wilmot's lips ceased to move; he looked up at her and his eyes seemed to burn.

"If you cure me," he said, "I'll hate you. I just want to get out, quick!"

She changed her hand on his forehead, whose heat seemed to scorch the skin of her palm. His lips resumed their almost soundless movement. The meaningless, meaningful whispering frightened her, but she stood her ground, constantly changing her hand till the maid came back with the tea.

"The nurse has come, miss; she'll be up in a minute."

"Pour out the tea. Now, Francis, drink!"

His lips sucked, chattered, sucked. Fleur handed back the cup, and stood away. His eyes had closed again.

"Oh! ma'am," whispered the maid, "he *is* bad! Such a nice young gentleman, too."

"What was his temperature; do you know?"

"I did hear the doctor say nearly 105. Here is the nurse, ma'am."

Fleur went to her in the doorway.

"It's not just ordinary, nurse—he *wants* to go. I think a love-affair's gone wrong. Shall I stop and help you pack him?"

When the pneumonia jacket had been put on, she lingered, looking down at him. His eyelashes lay close and dark against his cheeks, long and innocent, like a little boy's.

Outside the door, the maid touched her arm.

"I found this letter, ma'am; ought I to show it to the doctor?"

Fleur read:

"MY POOR DEAR BOY,

"We were crazy yesterday. It isn't any good, you know. Well, I haven't got a breakable heart; nor have you really, though you may think so when you get this. Just go back to your sunshine and your darkies, and put me out of your thoughts. I couldn't stay the course. I couldn't possibly stand being poor. I must just go through it with my 'Congressman,' and travel the appointed road. What is the good of thinking we can play at children in the wood, when one of them is

Your miserable (at the moment)

MARJORIE.

"I mean this—I mean it. Don't come and see me any more, and make it worse for yourself."

"Exactly!" said Fleur. "I've told the nurse. Keep it, and give it him back if he gets well. If he doesn't, burn it. I shall come to-morrow." And, looking at the maid with a faint smile, she added: "*I* am not that lady!"

"Oh! no, ma'am—miss—no, I'm sure! Poor young gentleman! Isn't there nothing to be done?"

"I don't know. I should think not. . . ."

She had kept all these facts from Michael with a sudden retaliatory feeling. He couldn't have private—or was it public—life all to himself!

After he had gone out with his 'Good God!' she went to the window. Queer to have seen Wilfrid again! Her heart had not fluttered, but it tantalised her not to know whether she could attract him back. Out in the square it was as dark as when last she had seen him before he fled to the East—a face pressed to this window that she was touching with her fingers. 'The burnt child!' No! She didn't want to reduce him to that state again; to copy Marjorie Ferrar, who had copied her. If, instead of going East, Wilfrid had chosen to have pneumonia like poor Francis! What would she have done? Let him die for want of her? And what ought she to do about Francis, having seen that letter? Tell Michael? No, he thought her frivolous and irresponsible. Well! She would show him! And that sister—who had married Jon? Ought she to be cabled to? But this would have a rapid crisis, the nurse had said, and to get over from America in time would be impossible! Fleur went back to the fire. What kind of girl was this wife of Jon's? Another in the new fashion—like Norah Curfew; or just one of those Americans out for her own way and the best of everything? But they would have the new fashion in America, too—even though it didn't come from Paris. Anne Forsyte!—Fleur gave a little shiver in front of the hot fire.

She went up-stairs, took off her hat, and scrutinised her image. Her face was coloured and rounded, her eyes were clear, her brow unlined, her hair rather flattened. She fluffed it out, and went across into the nursery.

The eleventh baronet, asleep, was living his private life with a very determined expression on his face; at the foot of his cot lay the Dandie, with his chin pressed to the floor, and at the table the nurse was sewing. In front of her lay an illustrated paper with the photograph inscribed: "Mrs. Michael Mont, with Kit and Dandie."

"What do you think of it, nurse?"

"I think it's horrible, ma'am; it makes Kit look as if he hadn't any sense—giving him a stare like that!"

Fleur took up the paper; her quick eyes had seen that it concealed another. There on the table was a second effigy of herself: "Mrs. Michael Mont, the pretty young London hostess, who, rumour says, will shortly be defendant in a Society lawsuit." And, above, yet another effigy inscribed: "Miss Marjorie Ferrar, the brilliant granddaughter of the Marquis of Shropshire, whose engagement to Sir Alexander MacGown, M. P., is announced."

Fleur dropped paper back on paper.

CHAPTER XI

SHADOWS

THE dinner, which Marjorie Ferrar had so suddenly recollected, was MacGown's, and when she reached the appointed restaurant, he was waiting in the hall.

"Where are the others, Alec?"

"There are no others," said MacGown.

Marjorie Ferrar reined back. "I can't dine with you alone in a place like this!"

"I had the Ppynrryns, but they fell through."

"Then I shall go to my Club."

"For God's sake, no, Marjorie. We'll have a private room. Go and wait in there, while I arrange it."

With a shrug she passed into a little 'lounge.' A young woman whose face seemed familiar idled in, looked at her, and idled out again, the ormolu clock ticked, the walls of striped pale grey stared blankly in the brilliant light, and Marjorie Ferrar stared blankly back—she was still seeing Francis Wilmot's ecstatic face.

"Now!" said MacGown. "Up those stairs, and third on the right. I'll follow in a minute."

She had acted in a play, she had passed an emotional hour, and she was hungry. At least she could dine before making the necessary scene. And while she drank the best champagne MacGown could buy, she talked and watched the burning eyes of her adorer. That red-brown visage, square, stiff-haired head, and powerful frame—what a contrast to the pale, slim face and form of Francis! This was a man, and when he liked, agreeable. With him she would have everything she wanted except—what Francis could give her. And it was one or the other—not both, as she had thought it might be. She had once crossed the 'striding edge' on Helvellyn, with a precipice on one side and a precipice on the other, and herself, doubting down which to fall, in the middle. She hadn't fallen, and—she supposed—she wouldn't now! One didn't, if one kept one's head!

Coffee was brought; and she sat, smoking, on the sofa. Her knowledge of private rooms taught her that she was now as alone with her betrothed as money could make them. How would he behave?

He threw his cigar away, and sat down by her side. This was the moment to rise and tell him that he was no longer her betrothed. His arm went round her, his lips sought her face. "Mind my dress; it's the only decent one I've got."

And, suddenly, not because she heard a noise, but because her senses were not absorbed like his, she perceived a figure in the open doorway. A woman's voice said: "Oh! I beg your pardon; I thought—" Gone!

Marjorie Ferrar started up.

"Did you see that young woman?"

"Yes. Damn her!"

"She's shadowing me."

"What?"

"I don't know her, and yet I know her perfectly. She had a good look at me down-stairs, when I was waiting."

MacGown dashed to the door and flung it open. Nobody was there! He shut it, and came back.

"By heaven! Those people! I'll— Well, that ends it! Marjorie, I shall send our engagement to the papers to-morrow."

Marjorie Ferrar, leaning her elbows on the mantelpiece, stared at her own face in the glass above it. 'Not a moral about her!' What did it matter? If only she could decide to marry Francis out of hand, slide away

from them all—debts, lawyers, Alec! And then the 'You
be damned' spirit in her blood revolted. The impudence
of it! Shadowing her! No! She was not going to leave
Miss Fleur triumphant—the little snob; and that old party
with the chin!

MacGown raised her hand to his lips; and, somehow,
the caress touched her.

"Oh! well," she said, "I suppose you'd better."

"Thank God!"

"Do you really think that to get me is a cause for
gratitude?"

"I would go through Hell to get you."

"And after? Well, as we're public property, let's go
down and dance."

For an hour she danced. She would not let him take
her home, and in her cab she cried. She wrote to Francis
when she got in. She went out again to post it. The bitter stars, the bitter wind, the bitter night! At the little
slurred thump of her letter dropping, she laughed. To
have played at children! It was too funny! So that was
done with! 'On with the dance!'

Extraordinary, the effect of a little paragraph in the
papers! Credit, like new-struck oil, spurted sky-high.
Her post contained, not bills for dresses, but solicitations
to feed, frizz, fur, flower, feather, furbelow, and photograph her. London offered itself. To escape that cynical
avalanche she borrowed a hundred pounds and flew to
Paris. There, every night, she went to the theatre. She
had her hair done in a new style, she ordered dresses, ate
at places known to the few—living up to Michael's nick-
name for her; and her heart was heavy.

She returned after a week, and burned the avalanche
—fortunately all letters of congratulation contained the
phrase 'of course you won't think of answering this.'
She didn't. The weather was mild; she rode in the Row;

she prepared to hunt. On the eve of departure, she received an anonymous communication.

"Francis Wilmot is very ill with pneumonia at the Cosmopolis Hotel. He is not expected to live."

Her heart flurried round within her breast and flumped; her knees felt weak; her hand holding the note shook; only her head stayed steady. The handwriting was 'that little snob's.' Had Francis caused that message to be sent? Was it his appeal? Poor boy! And must she go and see him if he were going to die? She so hated death. Did this mean that it was up to her to save him? What did it mean? But indecision was not her strong point. In ten minutes she was in a cab, in twenty at the Hotel. Handing her card, she said:

"You have a Mr. Wilmot here—a relative of mine. I've just heard of his serious illness. Can I go up and see the nurse?"

The Management looked at the card, inquisitively at her face, touched a bell, and said:

"Certainly, madam. . . . Here, you—take this lady up to Room—er—209."

Led by what poor Francis called a 'bell-boy' into the lift she walked behind his buttons along a pale-grey river of corridor carpet, between pale-grey walls, past cream-coloured after cream-coloured door in the bright electric light, with her head a little down.

The 'bell-boy' knocked ruthlessly on a door.

It was opened, and in the lobby of the suite stood Fleur. . . .

CHAPTER XII

DEEPENING

HOWEVER untypically American, according to Soames, Francis Wilmot seemed to have the national passion for short cuts.

In two days from Fleur's first visit he had reached the crisis, hurrying towards it like a man to his bride. Yet, compared with the instinct to live, the human will is limited, so that he failed to die. Fleur, summoned by telephone, went home cheered by the doctor's words: "He'll do now, if we can coax a little strength into him." That, however, was the trouble. For three afternoons she watched his exhausted indifference seeming to increase. And she was haunted by cruel anxiety. On the fourth day she had been sitting for more than an hour when his eyes opened.

"Yes, Francis?"

"I'm going to quit all right, after all."

"Don't talk like that—it's not American. Of course you're not going to quit."

He smiled, and shut his eyes. She made up her mind then.

Next day he was about the same, more dead than alive. But her mind was at rest; her messenger had brought back word that Miss Ferrar would be in at four o'clock. She would have had the note by now; but would she come? How little one knew of other people, even when they were enemies!

He was drowsing, white and strengthless, when she heard the 'bell-boy's' knock. Passing into the lobby, she closed the door softly behind her, and opened the outer door. So she *had* come!

If this meeting of two declared enemies had in it something dramatic, neither perceived it at the moment. It was just intensely unpleasant to them both. They stood for a moment looking at each other's chins. Then Fleur said:

"He's extremely weak. Will you sit down while I tell him you're here?"

Having seen her settled where Francis Wilmot put his clothes out to be valeted in days when he had worn them, Fleur passed back into the bedroom, and again closed the door.

"Francis," she said, "some one is waiting to see you."

Francis Wilmot did not stir, but his eyes opened and cleared strangely. To Fleur they seemed suddenly the eyes she had known; as if all these days they had been 'out,' and some one had again put a match to them.

"You understand what I mean?"

The words came clear and feeble: "Yes; but if I wasn't good enough for her before, I surely am not now. Tell her I'm through with that fool business."

A lump rose in Fleur's throat.

"Thank her for coming!" said Francis Wilmot, and closed his eyes again.

Fleur went back into the lobby. Marjorie Ferrar was standing against the wall with an unlighted cigarette between her lips.

"He thanks you for coming; but he doesn't want to see you. I'm sorry I brought you down."

Marjorie Ferrar took out the cigarette. Fleur could see her lips quivering. "Will he get well?"

"I don't know. I think so—now. He says he's 'through with that fool business.'"

Marjorie Ferrar's lips tightened. She opened the outer door, turned suddenly, and said:

"Will you make it up?"

"No," said Fleur.

There was a moment of complete stillness; then Marjorie Ferrar gave a little laugh, and slipped out.

Fleur went back. He was asleep. Next day he was stronger. Three days later Fleur ceased her visits; he was on the road to recovery. She had become conscious, moreover, that she had a little lamb which, wherever Mary went, was sure to go. She was being shadowed! How amusing! And what a bore that she couldn't tell Michael; because she had not yet begun again to tell him anything.

On the day that she ceased her visits he came in while she was dressing for dinner, with 'a weekly' in his hand.

"Listen to this," he said:

'When to God's fondouk the donkeys are taken—
    Donkeys of Africa, Sicily, Spain—
If, peradventure, the Deity waken,
    He shall not easily slumber again.

Where in the sweet of God's straw they have laid them,
    Broken and dead of their burdens and sores,
He, for a change, shall remember He made them—
    One of the best of His numerous chores—

Order from some one a sigh of repentance—
    Donkeys of Araby, Syria, Greece—
Over the fondouk distemper the sentence:
    "God's own forsaken—the stable of Peace."'

"Who's that by?"

"It sounds like Wilfrid."

"It is by Wilfrid," said Michael, and did not look at her. "I met him at the Hotch-Potch."

"And how is he?"

"Very fit."

"Have you asked him here?"

"No. He's going East again soon."

Was he fishing? Did he know that she had seen him? And she said:

"I'm going down to father's, Michael. He's written twice."

Michael put her hand to his lips.

"All right, darling."

Fleur reddened; her strangled confidences seemed knotted in her throat. She went next day with Kit and Dandie. The 'little lamb' would hardly follow to 'The Shelter.'

Annette had gone with her mother to Cannes for a month; and Soames was alone with the English winter. He was paying little attention to it, for the 'case' was in the list, and might be reached in a few weeks' time. Deprived of French influence, he was again wavering towards compromise. The announcement of Marjorie Ferrar's engagement to MacGown had materially changed the complexion of affairs. In the eyes of a British Jury, the character of a fast young lady, and the character of the same young lady publicly engaged to a Member of Parliament, with wealth and a handle to his name, would not be at all the same thing. They were now virtually dealing with Lady MacGown, and nothing, Soames knew, was so fierce as a man about to be married. To libel his betrothed was like approaching a mad dog.

He looked very grave when Fleur told him of her 'little lamb.' It was precisely the retaliation he had feared; nor could he tell her that he had 'told her so,' because he hadn't. He had certainly urged her to come down to him, but delicacy had forbidden him to give her the reason. So far as he could tell through catechism, there had been nothing 'suspect' in her movements since Lippinghall, except those visits to the Cosmopolis Hotel. But they were bad enough. Who was going to believe that she went to this sick young man out of pure kindness?

Such a motive was not current in a Court of Law. He was staggered when she told him that Michael didn't know of them. Why not?

"I didn't feel like telling him."

"Feel? Don't you see what a position you've put yourself in? Here you are, running to a young man's bedside, without your husband's knowledge."

"Yes, darling; but he was terribly ill."

"I dare say," said Soames; "so are lots of people."

"Besides, he was over head and ears in love with *her*."

"D'you think he's going to admit that, even if we could call him?"

Fleur was silent, thinking of Francis Wilmot's face.

"Oh! I don't know," she said at last. "How horrid it all is!"

"Of course it's horrid," said Soames. "Have you had a quarrel with Michael?"

"No; not a quarrel. Only he doesn't tell *me* things."

"What things?"

"How should I know, dear?"

Soames grunted. "Would he have minded your going?"

"Of course not. He'd have minded if I hadn't. He likes that boy."

"Well, then," said Soames, "either you or he, or both, will have to tell a lie, and say that he did know. I shall go up and talk to him. Thank goodness we can prove the illness. If I catch anybody coming down here after you——!"

He went up the following afternoon. Parliament being in recess, he sought the Hotch-Potch Club. He did not like a place always connected in his mind with his dead cousin, that fellow young Jolyon, and said to Michael at once: "Can we go somewhere else?"

"Yes, sir; where would you like?"

"To your place, if you can put me up for the night. I want to have a talk with you."

Michael looked at him askance.

"Now," said Soames, after dinner, "what's this about Fleur—she says you don't tell her things?"

Michael gazed into his glass of port.

"Well, sir," he said, slowly, "I'd be only too glad to, of course, but I don't think they really interest her. She doesn't feel that public things matter."

"Public! I meant private."

"There aren't any private things. D'you mean that she thinks there are?"

Soames dropped his scrutiny.

"I don't know—she said 'things.'"

"Well, you can put that out of your head, and hers."

"H'm! Anyway, the result's been that she's been visiting that young American with pneumonia at the Cosmopolis Hotel, without letting you know. It's a mercy she hasn't picked it up."

"Francis Wilmot?"

"Yes. He's out of the wood, now. That's not the point. She's been shadowed."

"Good God!" said Michael.

"Exactly! This is what comes of not talking to your wife. Wives are funny—they don't like it."

Michael grinned.

"Put yourself in my place, sir. It's my profession, now, to fuss about the state of the Country, and all that; and you know how it is—one gets keen. But to Fleur, it's all a stunt. I quite understand that; but, you see, the keener I get, the more I'm afraid of boring her, and the less I feel I can talk to her about it. In a sort of way she's jealous."

Soames rubbed his chin. The state of the Country was a curious sort of corespondent. He himself was often worried by the state of the Country, but as a source of division between husband and wife it seemed to him cold-blooded; he had known other sources in his time!

"Well, you mustn't let it go on," he said. "It's trivial."

Michael got up.

"Trivial! Well, sir, I don't know, but it seems to me very much the sort of thing that happened when the war came. Men had to leave their wives then."

"Wives put up with that," said Soames, "the Country was in danger."

"Isn't it in danger now?"

With his inveterate distrust of words, it seemed to Soames almost indecent for a young man to talk like that. Michael was a politician, of course; but politicians were there to keep the Country quiet, not to go raising scares and talking through their hats.

"When you've lived a little longer," he said, "you'll know that there's always something to fuss about if you like to fuss. There's nothing in it really; the pound's going up. Besides, it doesn't matter what you tell Fleur, so long as you tell her something."

"She's intelligent, sir," said Michael.

Soames was taken aback. He could not deny the fact, and answered:

"Well, national affairs are too remote; you can't expect a woman to be interested in them."

"Quite a lot of women are."

"Blue-stockings."

"No, sir; they nearly all wear 'nude.'"

"H'm! Those! As to interest in national affairs—put a tax on stockings, and see what happens!"

Michael grinned.

"I'll suggest it, sir."

"If you expect," said Soames, "that people—women or not—are going to put themselves out of the way for any scheme like this—this Foggartism of yours, you'll be very much disappointed."

"So everybody tells me. It's just because I don't like cold water at home as well as abroad, that I've given up worrying Fleur."

"Well, if you take my advice, you'll take up something practical—the state of the traffic, or penny postage. Drop pessimism; people who talk at large like that, never get trusted in this country. In any case you'll have to say you knew about her visits to that young man."

"Certainly, sir, wife and husband are one. But you don't really mean to let them make a circus of it in Court?"

Soames was silent. He did not *mean* them to; but what if they did?

"I can't tell," he said, at last. "The fellow's a Scotch-man. What did you go hitting him on the nose for?"

"He gave me a thick ear first. I know it was an excellent opportunity for turning the other cheek, but I didn't think of it in time."

"You must have called him something."

"Only a dirty dog. As you know, he suggested a low motive for my speech."

Soames stared. In his opinion this young man was taking himself much too seriously.

"Your speech! You've got to get it out of your mind," he said, "that anything you can say or do will make any difference."

"Then what's the good of my being in Parliament?"

"Well, you're in the same boat with everybody else. The Country's like a tree; you can keep it in order, but you can't go taking it up by the roots to look at them."

Michael looked at him, impressed.

"In public matters," said Soames, "the thing is to keep a level head, and do no more than you're obliged."

"And what's to govern one's view of necessity?"

"Common-sense. One can't have everything."

And rising, he began scrutinising the Goya.

"Are you going to buy another Goya, sir?"

"No; if I buy any more pictures, I shall go back to the English School."

"Patriotism?"

Soames gave him a sharp look.

"There's no patriotism," he said, "in fussing. And another thing you've got to remember is that foreigners like to hear that we've got troubles. It doesn't do to discuss our affairs out loud."

Michael took these sayings to bed with him. He remembered, when he came out of the war, thinking: 'If there's another war, nothing will induce me to go.' But now, if one were to come, he knew he *would* be going again. So Old Forsyte thought he was just 'fussing'! Was he? Was Foggartism a phlizz? Ought he to come to heel, and take up the state of the traffic? Was everything unreal? Surely not his love for Fleur? Anyway he felt hungry for her lying there. And Wilfrid back, too! To risk his happiness with her for the sake of—what? 'Punch' had taken a snap at him this week, grinning and groping at a surrounding fog. Old England, like Old Forsyte, had no use for theories. Self-conscious national efforts were just pomposity. Pompous! He? The thought was terribly disturbing. He got out of bed and went to the window. Foggy! In fog all were shadows; and he the merest shadow of them all, an unpractical politician, taking things to heart! One! Two! Big Ben! How many hearts had he turned to water! How many dreams spoiled, with his measured resonance! Line up with the top-dressers, and leave the Country to suck its silver spoon!

PART III

CHAPTER I

"CIRCUSES"

IN his early boyhood Soames had been given to the circus. He had outgrown it; 'Circuses' were now to him little short of an abomination. Jubilees and Pageants, that recurrent decimal, the Lord Mayor, Earl's Court, Olympia, Wembley—he disliked them all. He could not stand a lot of people with their mouths open. Dressing up was to him a symptom of weak-mindedness, and the collective excitement of a crowd an extravagance that offended his reticent individualism. Though not deeply versed in history, he had an idea, too, that nations who went in for 'circuses' were decadent. Queen Victoria's funeral, indeed, had impressed him—there had been a feeling in the air that day; but ever since, things had gone from bad to worse. They made everything into a 'circus' now! A man couldn't commit a murder without the whole paper-reading population—himself included—looking over each other's shoulders; and as to these football-matches, and rodeos—they interfered with the traffic and the normal course of conversation; people were so crazy about them!

Of course, 'circuses' had their use. They kept the people quiet. Violence by proxy, for instance, was obviously a political principle of some value. It was difficult to gape and shed blood at the same time; the more people stood in rows by day to see others being hurt, the less trouble would they take to hurt others themselves, and the sounder Soames could sleep by night. Still, sensation-hunting had become a disease, in his opinion, and no one was being inoculated for it, so far as he could see!

As the weeks went on, and the cases before it in the

List went off, the 'circus' they were proposing to make of his daughter appeared to him more and more monstrous. He had an instinctive distrust of Scotchmen—they called themselves Scotsmen nowadays, as if it helped their character!—they never let go, and he could not approve in other people a quality native to himself. Besides, 'Scotchmen' were so—so exuberant—always either dour or else hearty—extravagant chaps! Towards the middle of March, with the case in the List for the following week, he took an extreme step and entered the Lobby of the House of Commons. He had spoken to no one of his determination to make this last effort, for it seemed to him that all —Annette, Michael, Fleur herself—had done their best to spoil the chance of settlement.

Having sent in his card, he waited a long while in that lofty purlieu. 'Lobbying,' he knew the phrase, but had never realised the waste of time involved in it. The statues consoled him somewhat. Sir Stafford Northcote —a steady chap; at old Forsyte dinner-parties in the 'eighties his character had been as much a standby as the saddle of mutton. He found even 'that fellow Gladstone' bearable in stucco, or whatever it was up there. You might dislike, but you couldn't sneeze at him, as at some of these modern chaps. He was sunk in coma before Lord Granville when at last he heard the words:

"Sir Alexander MacGown," and saw a square man with a ruddy face, stiff black hair, and clipped moustache, coming between the railings, with a card in his hand.

"Mr. Forsyte?"

"Yes. Can we go anywhere that's not quite so public?"

The 'Scotchman' nodded, and led him down a corridor to a small room.

"Well?"

Soames smoothed his hat. "This affair," he said, "can't be any more agreeable to you than it is to me."

"Are you the individual who was good enough to apply the word 'traitress' to the lady I'm engaged to?"

"That is so."

"Then I don't see how you have the impudence to come and speak to me."

Soames bit his lips.

"I spoke under the provocation of hearing your *fiancée* call my daughter a snob, in her own house. Do you want this petty affair made public?"

"If you think that you and your daughter can get away with calling the lady I'm going to marry 'a snake,' 'a traitress,' 'an immoral person,' you're more mistaken than you ever were in your life. An unqualified apology that her Counsel can announce in Court is your only way out."

"That you won't get; mutual regret is another thing. As to the question of damages——"

"Damn the damages!" said MacGown violently. And there was that in Soames which applauded.

"Well," he said, "I'm sorry for you and her."

"What the devil do you mean, sir?"

"You will know by the end of next week, unless you revise your views in between. If it comes into Court, we shall justify."

The 'Scotchman' went so red that for a moment Soames was really afraid he would have an apoplectic fit.

"You'd better look out what you say in Court."

"We pay no attention to bullies in Court."

MacGown clenched his fists.

"Yes," said Soames, "it's a pity I'm not your age. Good evening!"

He passed the fellow and went out. He had noted his way in this 'rabbit-warren,' and was soon back among the passionless statues. Well! He had turned the last stone and could do no more, except make that overbearing fellow and his young woman sorry they'd ever been born. He came out into the chilly mist of Westminster. Pride and temper! Sooner than admit themselves in the wrong, people would turn themselves into an expensive 'circus' for the gaping and the sneers, the japing and the jeers of half the town! To vindicate her 'honour,' that 'Scotchman' would have his young woman's past dragged out! And fairly faced by the question whether to drag it out or not, Soames stood still. If he didn't, she might get a verdict; if he did, and didn't convince the jury, the damages would be shockingly increased. They might run into thousands. He felt the need of definite decision. One had been drifting in the belief that the thing wouldn't come into Court! Four o'clock! Not too late, perhaps, to see Sir James Foskisson. He would telephone to very young Nicholas to arrange a conference at once, and if Michael was at South Square, he would take him down to it. . . .

In his study, Michael had been staring with lugubrious relish at Aubrey Greene's cartoon of himself in a Society paper. On one leg, like Guy—or was it Slingsby?—in the Edward Lear 'Nonsense' book, he was depicted crying in a wilderness where a sardonic smile was rising on the horizon. Out of his mouth the word 'Foggartism' wreathed like the smoke of a cigar. Above a hole in the middle distance, a meercat's body supported the upturned face and applauding forepaws of Mr. Blythe. The thing was devastating in treatment and design—not unkind, merely killing. Michael's face had been endowed with a sort of after-dinner rapture, as if he were enjoying the sound of his own voice. Ridicule! Not even a personal friend, an artist, could see that the wilderness was at least as deserving of ridicule as the pelican! The cartoon seemed to write the word futility large across his page. It recalled to him Fleur's words at the outset: "And by the time the Tories go out you'll have your licence." She was a born realist! From the first she had foreseen for him the position of an eccentric, picturesquely beating a little private drum! A dashed good cartoon! And no one could appreciate it so deeply as its victim. But why did every one smile at Foggartism? Why? Because among a people who naturally walked, it leaped like a grasshopper; to a nation that felt its way, despising design, it seemed a will-o'-the-wisp. Yes, he was a fool for his pains! And —just then, Soames arrived.

"I've been to see that Scotchman," he said. "He means to take it into Court."

"Oh! Not really, sir! I always thought you'd keep it out."

"Only an unqualified apology will do that. Fleur can't give it; she's in the right. Can you come down with me now and see Sir James Foskisson?"

They set out in a taxi for the Temple.

The chambers of very young Nicholas Forsyte were in Paper Buildings. Chinny, mild and nearly forty, he succeeded within ten minutes in presenting to them every possible doubt.

"He seems to enjoy the prospect of getting tonked," murmured Michael while they were going over to Sir James.

"A poor thing," Soames responded; "but careful. Foskisson must attend to the case himself."

After those necessary minutes during which the celebrated K. C. was regathering from very young Nicholas what it was all about, they were ushered into the presence of one with a large head garnished by small grey whiskers, and really obvious brains. Since selecting him, Soames had been keeping his eye on the great advocate; had watched him veiling his appeals to a jury with an air of scrupulous equity; very few—he was convinced—and those not on juries, could see Sir James Foskisson coming round a corner. Soames had specially remarked his success in cases concerned with morals or nationality—no one so apt at getting a corespondent, a German, a Russian, or anybody at all bad, non-suited! At close quarters his whiskers seemed to give him an intensive respectability— difficult to imagine him dancing, gambling, or in bed. In spite of his practice, too, he enjoyed the reputation of being thorough; he might he relied on to know more than half the facts of any case by the time he went into Court, and to pick up the rest as he went along—or at least not to show that he hadn't. Very young Nicholas, knowing all the facts, had seemed quite unable to see what line could possibly be taken. Sir James, on the other hand, appeared to know only just enough. Sliding his light eyes from Soames to Michael, he retailed them, and said: "Eminently a case for an amicable settlement."

"Indeed!" said Soames.

Something in his voice seemed to bring Sir James to attention.

"Have you attempted that?"

"I have gone to the limit."

"Excuse me, Mr. Forsyte, but what do you regard as the limit?"

"Fifteen hundred pounds, and a mutual expression of regret. They'd accept the money, but they ask for an unqualified apology."

The great lawyer rested his chin. "Have you tried the unqualified apology without the money?"

"No."

"I would almost be inclined. MacGown is a very rich man. The shadow and the substance, eh? The expressions in the letters are strong. What do you say, Mr. Mont?"

"Not so strong as those she used of my wife."

Sir James Foskisson looked at very young Nicholas.

"Let me see," he said, "those were——?"

"Lion-huntress, and snob," said Michael, curtly.

Sir James wagged his head precisely as if it were a pair of scales.

"Immoral, snake, traitress, without charm—you think those weaker?"

"They don't make you snigger, sir, the others do. In Society it's the snigger that counts."

Sir James smiled.

"The jury won't be in Society, Mr. Mont."

"My wife doesn't feel like making an apology, anyway, unless there's an expression of regret on the other side; and I don't see why she should."

Sir James Foskisson seemed to breathe more freely.

"In that case," he said, "we have to consider whether to use the detective's evidence or not. If we do, we shall need to subpœna the hall porter and the servants at Mr. —er—Curfew's flat."

"Exactly," said Soames; "that's what we're here to decide." It was as if he had said: 'The conference is now opened.'

Sir James perused the detective's evidence for five silent minutes.

"If this is confirmed, even partially," he said, at last, "we win."

Michael had gone to the window. The trees in the garden had tiny buds; some pigeons were strutting on the grass below. He heard Soames say:

"I ought to tell you that they've been shadowing my daughter. There's nothing, of course, except some visits to a young American dangerously ill of pneumonia at his hotel."

"Of which I knew and approved," said Michael, without turning round.

"Could we call him?"

"I believe he's still at Bournemouth. But he was in love with Miss Ferrar."

Sir James turned to Soames.

"If there's no question of a settlement, we'd better go for the gloves. Merely to cross-examine as to books and plays and clubs, is very inconclusive."

"Have you read the dark scene in 'The Plain Dealer'?" asked Soames; "and that novel, 'Canthar'?"

"All very well, Mr. Forsyte, but impossible to say what a jury would make of impersonal evidence like that."

Michael had come back to his seat.

"I've a horror," he said, "of dragging in Miss Ferrar's private life."

"No doubt. But do you want me to win the case?"

"Not that way. Can't we go into Court, say nothing, and pay up?"

Sir James Foskisson smiled and looked at Soames. 'Really,' he seemed to say, 'why did you bring me this young man?'

Soames, however, had been pursuing his own thoughts.

"There's too much risk about that flat; if we failed there, it might be a matter of twenty thousand pounds. Besides, they would certainly call my daughter. I want to prevent that at all costs. I thought you could turn the whole thing into an indictment of modern morality."

Sir James Foskisson moved in his chair, and the pupils of his light-blue eyes became as pin-points. He nodded almost imperceptibly three times, precisely as if he had seen the Holy Ghost.

"When shall we be reached?" he said to very young Nicholas.

"Probably next Thursday—Mr. Justice Brane."

"Very well. I'll see you again on Monday. Good evening." And he sank back into an immobility, which neither Soames nor Michael felt equal to disturbing.

They went away silent—very young Nicholas tarrying in conversation with Sir James' devil.

Turning at the Temple station, Michael murmured:

"It was just as if he'd said: 'Some stunt!' wasn't it? I'm looking in at 'The Outpost,' sir. If you're going back to Fleur, will you tell her?"

Soames nodded. There it was! He had to do everything that was painful.

CHAPTER II

"NOT GOING TO HAVE IT"

IN the office of 'The Outpost' Mr. Blythe had just been in conversation with one of those great business men who make such deep impression on all to whom they voice their views in strict confidence. If Sir Thomas Lockit did not precisely monopolise the control of manufacture in Great Britain, he, like others, caused almost any one to think so—his knowledge was so positive and his emphasis so cold. In his view the Country must resume the position held before the Great War. It all hinged on coal—a question of this seven hours a day; and they were "not going to have it." A shilling, perhaps two shillings, off the cost of coal. They were "not going to have" Europe doing without British produce. Very few people knew Sir Thomas Lockit's mind; but nearly all who did were extraordinarily gratified.

Mr. Blythe, however, was biting his finger, and spitting out the result.

"Who was that fellow with the grey moustache?" asked Michael.

"Lockit. He's 'not going to have it.'"

"Oh!" said Michael, in some surprise.

"One sees more and more, Mont, that the really dangerous people are not the politicians, who want things with public passion—that is, mildly, slowly; but the big business men, who want things with private passion, strenuously, quickly. They know their own minds; and if we don't look out they'll wreck the country."

"What are they up to now?" said Michael.

"Nothing for the moment; but it's brewing. One sees in Lockit the futility of will-power. He's not going to have what it's entirely out of his power to prevent. He'd like to break Labour and make it work like a nigger from sheer necessity. Before that we shall be having civil war. Some of the Labour people, of course, are just as bad— they want to break everybody. It's a bee nuisance. If we're all to be plunged into industrial struggles again, how are we to get on with Foggartism?"

"I've been thinking about the Country," said Michael. "Aren't we beating the air, Blythe? Is it any good telling a man who's lost a lung, that what he wants is a new one?"

Mr. Blythe puffed out one cheek.

"Yes," he said, "the Country had a hundred very settled years—Waterloo to the War—to get into its present state; it's got its line of life so fixed and its habits so settled that nobody—neither editors, politicians, nor business men—can think except in terms of its bloated town industrialism. The Country's got beyond the point of balance in that hundred settled years, and it'll want fifty settled years to get back to that point again. The real trouble is that we're not going to get fifty settled years. Some bee thing or other—war with Turkey or Russia, trouble in India, civil ructions, to say nothing of another general flare-up—may knock the bottom out of any settled plans any time. We've struck a disturbed patch of history, and we know it in our bones, and live from hand to mouth, according."

"Well, then!" said Michael, glumly, thinking of what the Minister had said to him at Lippinghall.

Mr. Blythe puffed out the other cheek.

"No backsliding, young man! In Foggartism we have the best goods we can see before us, and we must bee well deliver them, as best we can. We've outgrown all the old hats."

"Have you seen Aubrey Greene's cartoon?"

"I have."

"Good—isn't it? But what I really came in to tell you, is that this beastly libel case of ours will be on next week."

Mr. Blythe's ears moved.

"I'm sorry for that. Win or lose—nothing's worse for public life than private ructions. You're not going to have it, are you?"

"We can't help it. But our defence is to be confined to an attack on the new morality."

"One can't attack what isn't," said Mr. Blythe.

"D'you mean to say," said Michael, grinning, "that you haven't noticed the new morality?"

"Certainly not. Formulate it if you can."

"'Don't be stupid, don't be dull.'"

Mr. Blythe grunted. "The old morality used to be: 'Behave like a gentleman.'"

"Yes! But in modern thought there ain't no sich an animal."

"There are fragments lying about; they reconstructed Neanderthal man from half a skull."

"A word that's laughed at can't be used, Blythe."

"Ah!" said Mr. Blythe. "The chief failings of your generation, young Mont, are sensitiveness to ridicule, and terror of being behind the times. It's bee weak-minded."

Michael grinned.

"I know it. Come down to the House. Parsham's Electrification Bill is due. We mav get some lights on Unemployment."

Having parted from Mr. Blythe in the Lobby, Michael came on his father walking down a corridor with a short bright old man in a trim grey beard.

"Ah! Michael, we've been seeking you. Marquess, my hopeful son! The marquess wants to interest you in electricity."

Michael removed his hat.

"Will you come to the reading-room, sir?"

This, as he knew, was Marjorie Ferrar's grandfather, and might be useful. In a remote corner of a room lighted so that nobody could see any one else reading, they sat down in triangular formation.

"You know about electricity, Mr. Mont?" said the marquess.

"No, sir, except that more of it would be desirable in this room."

"Everywhere, Mr. Mont. I've read about your Foggartism; if you'll allow me to say so, it's quite possibly the policy of the future; but nothing will be done with it till you've electrified the country. I should like you to start by supporting this Bill of Parsham's."

And, with an engaging distinction of syllable, the old peer proceeded to darken Michael's mind.

"I see, sir," said Michael, at last. "This Bill ought to add considerably to Unemployment."

"Temporarily."

"I wonder if I ought to take on any more temporary trouble. I'm finding it difficult enough to interest people in the future as it is—they seem to think the present so important."

Sir Lawrence whinnied.

"You must give him time and pamphlets, Marquess. But, my dear fellow, while your Foggartism is confined to the stable, you'll want a second horse."

"I've been advised already to take up the state of the traffic or penny postage. And, by the way, sir, that case of ours *is* coming into Court, next week."

Sir Lawrence's loose eyebrow shot up.

"Oh!" he said. "Do you remember, Marquess—your granddaughter and my daughter-in-law? I came to you about it."

"Something to do with lions? A libel, was it?" said the old peer. "My aunt——"

While Michael was trying to decide whether this was an ejaculation or the beginning of a reminiscence, his father broke in:

"Ah! yes, an interesting case that, Marquess—it's all in Betty Montecourt's Memoirs."

"Libels," resumed the marquess, "had flavour in those days. The words complained of were: 'Her crinoline covers her considerable obliquity.'"

"If anything's to be done to save scandal," muttered Michael, "it must be done now. We're at a deadlock."

"Could *you* put in a word, sir?" said Sir Lawrence.

The marquess's beard quivered.

"I see from the papers that my granddaughter is marrying a man called MacGown, a Member of this House. Is he about?"

"Probably," said Michael. "But I had a row with him. I think, sir, there would be more chance with her."

The marquess rose. "I'll ask her to breakfast. I dislike publicity. Well, I hope you'll vote for this Bill, Mr. Mont, and think over the question of electrifying the country. We want young men interested. I'm going to the Peers' Gallery, now. Good-bye!"

When briskly he had gone, Michael said to his father: "If he's not going to have it, I wish he'd ask Fleur to breakfast also. There are two parties to this quarrel."

CHAPTER III

SOAMES DRIVES HOME

SOAMES in the meantime was seated with one of those parties in her 'parlour.' She had listened in silence, but with a stubborn and resentful face. What did he know of the loneliness and frustration she had been feeling? Could he tell that the thrown stone had starred her mirrored image of herself; that the words 'snob,' and 'lion-huntress,' had entered her very soul? He could not understand the spiritual injury she had received, the sudden deprivation of that self-importance, and hope of rising, necessary to all. Concerned by the expression on her face, preoccupied with the practical aspects of the 'circus' before them, and desperately involved in thoughts of how to keep her out of it as much as possible, Soames was reduced to the closeness of a fish.

"You'll be sitting in front, next to me," he said. "I shouldn't wear anything too bright. Would you like your mother there, too?"

Fleur shrugged her shoulders.

"Just so," said Soames. "But if she wants to come, she'd better, perhaps. Brane is not a joking judge, thank goodness. Have you ever been in a Court?"

"No."

"The great thing is to keep still, and pay no attention to anything. They'll all be behind you, except the jury —and there's nothing in them really. If you look at them, don't smile!"

"Why? Aren't they safe, Dad?"

Soames put the levity aside.

"I should wear a small hat. Michael must sit on your

left. Have you got over that—er—not telling each other
things?"

"Yes."

"I shouldn't begin it again. He's very fond of you."
Fleur nodded.

"Is there anything you want to tell *me?* You know I
—I worry about you."

Fleur got up and sat on the arm of his chair; he had at
once a feeling of assuagement.

"I really don't care now. The harm's done. I only
hope *she'll* have a bad time."

Soames, who had the same hope, was somewhat shocked
by its expression.

He took leave of her soon after and got into his car for
the dark drive back to Mapledurham. The Spring evening
was cold and he had the windows up. At first he thought
of very little; and then of still less. He had passed a tiring
afternoon, and was glad of the slight smell of stephanotis
provided by Annette. The road was too familiar to rouse
his thoughts, beyond wonder at the lot of people there
always seemed to be in the world between six and seven.
He dozed his way into the new cut, woke, and dozed again.
What was this—Slough? Before going to Marlborough
he had been at school there with young Nicholas and St.
John Heyman, and after his time, some other young
Forsytes. Nearly sixty years ago! He remembered his
first day—a brand-new little boy in a brand-new little
top-hat, with a playbox stored by his mother with things
to eat, and blessed with the words: "There, Summy dear,
that'll make you popular." He had reckoned on having
command of that corruption for some weeks; but no sooner
had he produced a bit of it, than they had taken the box,
and suggested to him that it would be a good thing to
eat the lot. In twenty-two minutes twenty-two boys had
materially increased their weight, and he himself, in

handing out the contents, had been obliged to eat less than a twenty-third. They had left him one packet of biscuits, and those had caraway seeds, for which he had constitutionally no passion whatever. Afterwards three other new boys had complained that he was a fool for having it all eaten up like that, instead of saving it for them, and he had been obliged to sit on their heads one by one. His popularity had lasted twenty-two minutes, and, so far as he knew, had never come back. He had been against Communism ever since.

Bounding a little on the cushioned seat, he remembered poignantly his own cousin St. John Heyman pushing him into a gorse-bush and holding him there for an appreciable minute. Horrid little brutes, boys! For the moment he felt quite grateful to Michael for trying to get them out of England. And yet—! He had some pleasant memories even of boys. There was his collection of butterflies—he had sold two Red Admirals in poor condition to a boy for one-and-threepence. To be a boy again—h'm—and shoot peas at passengers in a train that couldn't stop, and drink cherry brandy going home, and win a prize by reciting two hundred lines of 'The Lady of the Lake' better than 'Cherry-Tart' Burroughes—Um? What had become of 'Cherry-Tart' Burroughes, who had so much money at school that his father went bankrupt! 'Cherry-Tart' Burroughes!

The loom of Slough faded. One was in rank country now, and he ground the handle of the window to get a little fresh air. A smell of trees and grass came in. Boys out of England! They had funny accents in those great places overseas. Well, they had funny accents, here, too. The accent had been all right at Slough—if it wasn't a boy got lammed. He remembered the first time his father and mother—James and Emily—came down; very genteel (before the word was fly-blown), all whiskers and crin-

Just like that fellow, drawing attention to it—no gump-
tion whatever! But how, without touching, did you find
out whether anything was broken in a pig? He moved a
step and saw the pig's eyes; and a sort of fellow-feeling
stirred in him. What if it had a broken leg! Again the
chauffeur touched it with his foot. The pig uttered a
lamentable noise, and, upheaving its bulk, squealing and
grunting, trotted off. Soames hastily resumed his seat.
"Drive on!" he said. Pigs! They never thought of anything but themselves; and cottagers were just as bad—
very unpleasant about cars. And he wasn't sure they
weren't right—tearing great things! The pig's eye seemed
looking at him again from where his feet were resting.
Should he keep some, now that he had those meadows on
the other side of the river? Eat one's own bacon, cure
one's own hams! After all, there was something in it—
clean pigs, properly fed! That book of old Foggart said
one must grow more food in England, and be independent
if there were another war. He sniffed. Smell of baking—
Reading, already! They still grew biscuits in England!
Foreign countries growing his food—something unpleasant
about living on sufferance like that! After all, English
meat and English wheat—as for a potato, you couldn't
get one fit to eat in Italy, or France. And now they wanted
to trade with Russia again! Those Bolshevists hated
England. Eat their wheat and eggs, use their tallow and
skins? Infra dig, he called it! The car swerved and he
was jerked against the side cushions. The village church!
—that fellow Riggs was always shying at something.
Pretty little old affair, too, with its squat spire and its
lichen—couldn't see that out of England—graves, old
names, yew-trees. And that reminded him: One would
have to be buried, some day. Here, perhaps. Nothing
flowery! Just his name, 'Soames Forsyte,' standing out
on rough stone, like that grave he had sat on at High-

The marquess gave her another glance.

"You know nothing about it," he said. "But you're looking very charming. What's this I hear of a libel?"

She might have known! Grandfather was too frightfully spry! He missed nothing!

"It wouldn't interest you, dear."

"I disagree. My father and *old* Sir Lawrence Mont were great friends. Why do you want to wash linen in Court?"

"I don't."

"Are you the plaintiff?"

"Yes."

"What do you complain of?"

"They've said things about me."

"Who?"

"Fleur Mont and her father."

"Ah! the relation of the tea-man. What have they said?"

"That I haven't a moral about me."

"Well, have you?"

"As much as most people."

"Anything else?"

"That I'm a snake of the first water."

"I don't like that. What made them say so?"

"Only that I was heard calling her a snob; and so she is."

The marquess, who had resigned a finished grapefruit, placed his foot on a chair, his elbow on his knee, his chin on his hand, and said:

"No divinity hedges our Order in these days, Marjorie; but we still stand for something. It's a mistake to forget that."

She sat very still. Everybody respected grandfather; even her father, to whom he did not speak. But to be told that she stood for something was really too dull for anything! All very well for grandfather at his age, and with his lack of temptations! Besides, *she* had no handle to her name, owing to the vaunted nature of British institutions. Even if she felt that—by Lord Charles out of Lady Ursula—she ought not to be dictated to, she had never put on frills—had always liked to be thought a mere Bohemian. And, after all, she did stand—for not being stuffy, and not being dull.

"Well, grandfather, I tried to make it up, but she wouldn't. Coffee?"

"Yes, coffee. But tell me, are you happy about yourself?"

Marjorie Ferrar handed him the cup.

"No. Who is?"

"A hit," said the marquess. "You're going to be very well off, I hear. That means power. It's worth using well, Marjorie. He's a Scotsman, isn't he? Do you like him?" Again the shrewd bright glance.

"At times."

"I see. With your hair, you must be careful. Red hair is extraordinarily valuable on occasion. In the Eton and Harrow Match, or for speaking after dinner; but don't let it run away with you after you're married. Where are you going to live?"

"In Eaton Square. There's a Scotch place, too."

"Have your kitchens electrified. I've had it done here. It saves the cook's temper. I get very equable food. But about this libel. Can't you all say you're sorry—why put money into the lawyers' pockets?"

"She won't, unless I do, and I won't, unless she does."

The marquess drank off his coffee.

"Then what is there in the way? I dislike publicity, Marjorie. Look at that suit the other day. Anything of this nature in Society, nowadays, is a nail in our coffins."

"I'll speak to Alec, if you like."

"Do! Has he red hair?"

"No; black."

"Ah! What would you like for a wedding-present—lace?"

"Oh! no, please, dear. Nobody's wearing lace."

With his head on one side, the marquess looked at her. "I can't get that lace off," he seemed to say.

"Perhaps you'd like a Colliery. Electrified, it would pay in no time."

Marjorie Ferrar laughed. "I know you're hard up, grandfather; but I'd rather not have a Colliery, thanks. They're so expensive. Just give me your blessing."

"I wonder," said the marquess, "if I could sell blessings? Your uncle Dangerfield has gone in for farming; he's ruining me. If only he'd grow wheat by electricity; it's the only way to make it pay at the present price. Well, if you've finished breakfast, good-bye. I must go to work."

Marjorie Ferrar, who had indeed begun breakfast, stood up and pressed his hand. He was a dear old boy, if somewhat rapid! . . .

That same evening in a box at the St. Anthony, she had her opportunity, when MacGown was telling her of Soames' visit.

"Oh, dear! Why on earth didn't you settle it, Alec? The whole thing's a bore. I've had my grandfather at me about it."

"If they'll apologise," said MacGown, "I'll settle it to-morrow. But an apology they must make."

"And what about me? I don't want to stand up to be shot at."

"There are some things one can't sit down under, Marjorie. Their whole conduct has been infamous."

Visited by a reckless impulse, she said:

"What d'you suppose I'm really like, Alec?"

MacGown put his hand on her bare arm.

"I don't suppose; I know."

"Well?"

"Defiant."

Curious summary! Strangely good in a way—only——!

"You mean that I like to irritate people till they think I'm—what I'm not. But suppose"—her eyes confronted his—"I really am."

MacGown's grasp tightened.

"You're not; and I won't have it said."

"You think this case will whitewash my—defiance?"

"I know what gossip is; and I know it buzzes about you. People who say things are going to be taught, once for all, that they can't."

Marjorie Ferrar turned her gaze towards the still life on the dropped curtain, laughed and said:

"My dear man, you're dangerously provincial."

"I know a straight line when I see one."

"Yes; but there aren't any in London. You'd better hedge, Alec, or you'll be taking a toss over me."

MacGown said, simply: "I believe in you more than you believe in yourself."

She was glad that the curtain rose just then, for she felt confused and rather touched.

Instead of confirming her desire to drop the case, that little talk gave her a feeling that by the case her marriage stood or fell. Alec would know where he was when it was over, and so would she! There would be precious little secret about her and she would either not be married to him, or at least not married under false pretences. Let it rip! It was, however, a terrible bore; especially the preparatory legal catechism she had now to undergo. What effect, for instance, had been produced among her friends and acquaintances by those letters? From the point of view of winning, the point was obviously not without importance. But how was she to tell? Two hostesses had cancelled week-end invitations; a rather prim Countess, and a Canadian millionairess married to a decaying baronet. It had not occurred to her before that this was the reason, but it might have been. Apart from them she would have to say she didn't know, people didn't tell you to your face what they heard or thought of you. They were going to try and make her out a piece of injured innocence! Good Lord! What if she declared her real faith in Court, and left them all in the soup! Her real faith—what was it? Not to let a friend down; not to give a man away; not to funk; to do things differently from other people; to be always on the go; not to be 'stuffy'; not to be dull! The whole thing was topsy-turvy! Well, she must keep her head!

CHAPTER V

THE DAY

ON the day of the case Soames rose, in Green Street, with a sort of sick impatience. Why wasn't it the day after?

Renewed interviews with very young Nicholas and Sir James Foskisson had confirmed the idea of defence by attack on modern morality. Foskisson was evidently going to put his heart into that—perhaps he'd suffered from it; and if he was anything like old Bobstay, who had just published his reminiscences at the age of eighty-two, that cat would lose her hair and give herself away. Yesterday afternoon Soames had taken an hour's look at Mr. Justice Brane, and been very favourably impressed; the learned judge, though younger than himself—he had often briefed him in other times—looked old-fashioned enough now for anything.

Having cleaned his teeth, put in his plate, and brushed his hair, Soames went into the adjoining room and told Annette she would be late. She always looked terribly young and well in bed, and this, though a satisfaction to him, he could never quite forgive. When he was gone, fifteen years hence, perhaps, she would still be under sixty, and might live another twenty years.

Having roused her sufficiently to say: "You will have plenty of time to be fussy in that Court, Soames," he went back and looked out of his window. The air smelled of Spring—aggravating! He bathed and shaved with care—didn't want to go into the Box with a cut on his chin!—then went back to see that Annette was not putting on anything bright. He found her in pink underclothes.

"I should wear black," he said.

Annette regarded him above her hand-mirror.

"Whom do you want me to fascinate, Soames?"

"These people will bring their friends, I shouldn't wonder; anything conspicuous——"

"Don't be afraid; I shall not try to be younger than my daughter."

Soames went out again. The French! Well, she had good taste in dress.

After breakfast he went off to Fleur's. Winifred and Imogen would look after Annette—they too were going to the Court, as if there were anything to enjoy about this business!

Spruce in his silk hat, he walked across the Green Park, conning over his evidence. No buds on the trees—a late year; and the Royal Family out of town! Passing the Palace, he thought: 'They're very popular!' He supposed they liked this great Empire group in front of them, all muscle and flesh and large animals! The Albert Memorial, and this—everybody ran them down; but, after all, peace and plenty—nothing modern about them! Emerging into Westminster, he cut his way through a smell of fried fish into the Parliamentary backwater of North Street, and, between its pleasant little houses, gazed steadily at the Wren Church. Never going inside any church except St. Paul's, he derived a sort of strength from their outsides—churches were solid and stood back, and didn't seem to care what people thought of them! He felt a little better, rounding into South Square. The Dandie met him in the hall. Though he was not over-fond of dogs, the breadth and solidity of this one always affected Soames pleasurably—better than that little Chinese abortion they used to have! This dog was a character—masterful and tenacious—you would get very little out of *him* in a witness-box! Looking up from the dog, he saw Michael and Fleur coming down the stairs.

After hurriedly inspecting Michael's brown suit and speckled tie, his eyes came to anchor on his daughter's face. Pale but creamy, nothing modern—thank goodness! —no rouge, salve, powder, or eye-blacking; perfectly made up for her part! In a blue dress, too, very good taste, which must have taken some finding! The desire that she should not feel nervous stilled Soames' private qualms.

"Quite a smell of Spring!" he said: "Shall we start?"

While a cab was being summoned, he tried to put her at ease.

"I had a look at Brane yesterday; he's changed a good deal from when I used to know him. I was one of the first to give him briefs."

"That's bad, isn't it, sir?" said Michael.

"How?"

"He'll be afraid of being thought grateful."

Flippant, as usual!

"Our judges," he said, "are a good lot, take them all round."

"I'm sure they are. Do you know if he ever reads, sir?"

"How d'you mean—reads?"

"Fiction. We don't, in Parliament."

"Nobody reads novels, except women," said Soames. And he felt Fleur's dress. "You'll want a fur; that's flimsy."

While she was getting the fur, he said to Michael: "How did she sleep?"

"Better than I did, sir."

"That's a comfort, anyway. Here's the cab. Keep away from that Scotchman."

"I see him every day in the House, you know."

"Ah!" said Soames; "I forgot. You make nothing of that sort of thing there, I believe." And taking his daughter's arm, he led her forth.

"I wonder if old Blythe will turn up," he heard Michael

say, when they passed the office of 'The Outpost.' It
was the first remark made in the cab, and, calling for no
response, it was the last.

The Law Courts had their customary air, and people,
in black and blue, were hurrying into them. "Beetle-
trap!" muttered Michael. Soames rejected the simile
with his elbow—for him they were just familiar echoing
space, concealed staircases, stuffy corridors, and the
square enclosures of one voice at a time.

Too early, they went slowly up the stairs. Really, it
was weak-minded! Here they had come—they and the
other side—to get—what? He was amazed at himself for
not having insisted on Fleur's apologising. Time and
again in the case of others, all this had appeared quite
natural—in the case of his own daughter, it now seemed
almost incredibly idiotic. He hurried her on, however,
past lingering lawyers' clerks, witnesses, what not. A
few low words to an usher, and they were inside, and sitting down. Very young Nicholas was already in his place,
and Soames so adjusted himself that there would only
be the thickness of Sir James, when he materialised, between them. Turning to confer, he lived for a cosey moment in the past again, as might some retired old cricketer
taking block once more. Beyond young Nicholas he quar-
tered the assemblage with his glance. Yes, people had
got wind of it! He knew they would—with that cat
always in the public eye—quite a lot of furbelows up
there at the back, and more coming. He reversed himself abruptly; the Jury were filing in—special, but a com-
mon-looking lot! Why were juries always common-look-
ing? He had never been on one himself. He glanced at
Fleur. There she sat, and what she was feeling he couldn't
tell. As for young Michael, his ears looked very pointed.
And just then he caught sight of Annette. She'd better
not come and sit down here, after all—the more there

were of them in front, the more conspicuous it would be!
So he shook his head at her, and waved towards the back.
Ah! She was going! She and Winifred and Imogen would
take up room—all rather broad in the beam; but there
were still gaps up there. And suddenly he saw the plaintiff and her lawyer and MacGown; very spry they looked,
and that insolent cat was smiling! Careful not to glance
in their direction, Soames saw them sit down, some six
feet off. Ah! and here came Counsel—Foskisson and
Bullfry together, thick as thieves. They'd soon be calling
each other 'my friend' now, and cutting each other's
throats! He wondered if he wouldn't have done better
after all to have let the other side have Foskisson, and
briefed Bullfry—an ugly-looking customer, broad, com-
petent and leathery. He and Michael with Fleur between
them, and behind—Foskisson and his junior; Settlewhite
and the Scotchman with 'that cat' between them, and
behind—Bullfry and his junior! Only the Judge wanted
now to complete the pattern! And here he came! Soames
gripped Fleur's arm and raised her with himself. Bob!
Down again! One side of Brane's face seemed a little
fuller than the other; Soames wondered if he had tooth-
ache, and how it would affect the proceedings.

And now came the usual 'shivaree' about such and such
a case, and what would be taken next week, and so on.
Well! that was over, and the judge was turning his head
this way and that, as if to see where the field was placed.
Now Bullfry was up:

"If it please Your Lordship——"

He was making the usual opening, with the usual
flowery description of the plaintiff—granddaughter of a
marquess, engaged to a future Prime Minister . . . or so
you'd think! . . . prominent in the most brilliant circles,
high-spirited, perhaps a thought too high-spirited. . . .
Baggage! . . . the usual smooth and subacid descrip-

tion of the defendant! . . . Rich and ambitious young
married lady. . . . Impudent beggar! . . . Jury would
bear in mind that they were dealing in both cases with
members of advanced Society, but they would bear in
mind, too, that primary words had primary meanings and
consequences, whatever the Society in which they were
uttered. H'm! Very sketchy reference to the incident in
Fleur's drawing-room—minimised, of course—ha! an allusion to himself—man of property and standing—thank
you for nothing! Reading the libellous letters now!
Effect of them . . . very made-up, all that! . . . Plaintiff obliged to take action. . . . Bunkum! "I shall now
call Mrs. Ralph Ppynrryn."

"How do you spell that name, Mr. Bullfry?"

"With two p's, two y's, two n's and two r's, my lord."

"I see."

Soames looked at the owner of the name. Good-look-
ing woman of the flibberty-gibbet type! He listened to
her evidence with close attention. Her account of the incident in Fleur's drawing-room seemed substantially correct. She had received the libellous letter two days later;
had thought it her duty, as a friend, to inform Miss Ferrar. Should say, as a woman in Society, that this incident
and these letters had done Miss Ferrar harm. Had talked
it over with a good many people. A public incident.
Much feeling excited. Had shown her letter to Mrs. Maltese, and been shown one that she had received. Whole
matter had become current gossip. H'm!

Bullfry down, and Foskisson up!

Soames adjusted himself. Now to see how the fellow
shaped—the manner of a cross-examiner was so important!
Well, he had seen worse—the eye, like frozen light, fixed
on unoccupied space while the question was being asked,
and coming round on to the witness for the answer; the
mouth a little open, as if to swallow it; the tongue visible

at times on the lower lip, the unoccupied hand clasping something under the gown behind.

"Now, Mrs.—er—Ppynrryn. This incident, as my friend has called it, happened at the house of Mrs. Mont, did it not? And how did you come there? As a friend. Quite so! And you have nothing against Mrs. Mont? No. And you thought it advisable and kind, madam, to show this letter to the plaintiff and to other people—in fact, to foment this little incident to the best of your ability?" Eyes round!

"If a friend of mine received such a letter about me, I should expect her to tell me that the writer was going about abusing me."

"Even if your friend knew of the provocation and was also a friend of the letter-writer?"

"Yes."

"Now, madam, wasn't it simply that the sensation of this little quarrel was too precious to be burked? It would have been so easy, wouldn't it, to have torn the letter up and said nothing about it? You don't mean to suggest that it made *you* think any the worse of Miss Ferrar— you knew her too well, didn't you?"

"Ye-es."

"Exactly. As a friend of both parties you knew that these expressions were just spleen and not to be taken seriously?"

"I can't say that."

"Oh! You regarded them as serious? Am I to take it that you thought they touched the ham-bone? In other words, that they were true?"

"Certainly not."

"Could they do Miss Ferrar any harm if they were palpably untrue?"

"I think they could."

"Not with you—you were a friend?"

"Not with me."

"But with other people, who would never have heard of them but for you. In fact, madam, you enjoyed the whole thing. Did you?"

"Enjoyed? No."

"You regarded it as your duty to spread this letter? Don't you enjoy doing your duty?"

The dry cackle within Soames stopped at his lips. Foskisson down, and Bullfry up!

"It is, in fact, your experience, Mrs. Ppynrryn, as well as that of most of us not so well constituted, perhaps, as my learned friend, that duty is sometimes painful."

"Yes."

"Thank you. Mrs. Edward Maltese."

During the examination of this other young woman, who seemed to be dark and solid, Soames tried to estimate the comparative effect produced by Fleur and 'that cat' on the four jurymen whose eyes seemed to stray towards beauty. He had come to no definite conclusion, when Sir James Foskisson rose to cross-examine.

"Tell me, Mrs. Maltese, which do you consider the most serious allegation among those complained of?"

"The word 'treacherous' in my letter, and the expression 'a snake of the first water' in the letter to Mrs. Ppynrryn."

"More serious than the others?"

"Yes."

"That is where you can help me, madam. The circle you move in is not exactly the plaintiff's, perhaps?"

"Not exactly."

"Intersecting, um?"

"Yes."

"Now, in which section, yours or the plaintiff's, would you say the expression 'she hasn't a moral about her' would be the more, or shall we say the less, damning?"

"I can't say."

"I only want your opinion. Do you think your section of Society as advanced as Miss Ferrar's?"

"Perhaps not."

"It's well known, isn't it, that her circle is very free and easy?"

"I suppose so."

"Still, *your* section is pretty advanced—I mean, you're not 'stuffy'?"

"Not what, Sir James?"

"Stuffy, my lord; it's an expression a good deal used in modern Society."

"What does it mean?"

"Strait-laced, my lord."

"I see. Well, he's asking you if you're stuffy?"

"No, my lord. I hope not."

"You hope not. Go on, Sir James."

"Not being stuffy, you wouldn't be exactly worried if somebody said to you: 'My dear, you haven't a moral about you'?"

"Not if it was said as charmingly as that."

"Now, come, Mrs. Maltese, does such an expression, said charmingly or the reverse, convey any blame to you or to your friends?"

"If the reverse, yes."

"Am I to take it that the conception of morality in your circle is the same as in—my lord's?"

"How is the witness to answer that, Sir James?"

"Well, in your circle are you shocked when your friends are divorced, or when they go off together for a week in Paris, say, or wherever they find convenient?"

"Shocked? Well, I suppose one needn't be shocked by what one wouldn't do oneself."

"In fact, you're not shocked?"

"I don't know that I'm shocked by anything."

"That would be being stuffy, wouldn't it?"

"Perhaps."

"Well, will you tell me then—if that's the state of mind in your circle; and you said, you know, that your circle is less free and easy than the plaintiff's—how it is possible that such words as 'she hasn't a moral about her' can have done the plaintiff any harm?"

"The whole world isn't in our circles."

"No. I suggest that only a very small portion of the world is in your circles. But do you tell me that you or the plaintiff pay any——?"

"How can she tell, Sir James, what the plaintiff pays?"

"That *you*, then, pay any attention to what people outside your circle think?"

Soames moved his head twice. The fellow was doing it well. And his eye caught Fleur's face turned towards the witness; a little smile was curling her lip.

"I don't personally pay much attention even to what anybody *in* my circle thinks."

"Have you more independence of character than the plaintiff, should you say?"

"I dare say I've got as much."

"Is she notoriously independent?"

"Yes."

"Thank you, Mrs. Maltese."

Foskisson down, Bullfry up!

"I call the plaintiff, my lord."

Soames uncrossed his legs.

CHAPTER VI

IN THE BOX

MARJORIE FERRAR stepped into the Box, not exactly nervous, and only just 'made-up.' The papers would record a black costume with chinchilla fur and a black hat. She kissed the air in front of the book, took a deep breath, and turned to Mr. Bullfry.

For the last five days she had resented more and more the way this case had taken charge of her. She had initiated it, and it had completely deprived her of initiative. She had, in fact, made the old discovery, that when the machinery of quarrel is once put in motion, much more than pressure of the starting button is required to stop its revolutions. She was feeling that it would serve Alec and the lawyers right if all went wrong.

The voice of Mr. Bullfry, carefully adjusted, soothed her. His questions were familiar, and with each answer her confidence increased, her voice sounded clear and pleasant in her ears. And she stood at ease, making her figure as boyish as she could. Her performance, she felt, was interesting to the judge, the jury, and all those people up there, whom she could dimly see. If only 'that little snob' had not been seated, expressionless, between her and her Counsel! When at length Mr. Bullfry sat down and Sir James Foskisson got up, she almost succumbed to the longing to powder her nose. Clasping the Box, she resisted it, and while he turned his papers, and hitched his gown, the first tremor of the morning passed down her spine. At least he might look at her when he spoke!

"Have you ever been party to an action before, Miss Ferrar?"

"No."

"You quite understand, don't you, that you are on your oath?"

"Quite."

"You have told my friend that you had no animus against Mrs. Mont. Look at this marked paragraph in 'The Evening Sun' of October 3d. Did you write that?"

Marjorie Ferrar felt exactly as if she had stepped out of a conservatory into an East wind. Did they know everything, then?

"Yes; I wrote it."

"It ends thus: 'The enterprising little lady is losing no chance of building up her *salon* on the curiosity which ever surrounds any buccaneering in politics.' Is the reference to Mrs. Mont?"

"Yes."

"Not very nice, is it—of a friend?"

"I don't see any harm in it."

"The sort of thing, in fact, you'd like written about yourself?"

"The sort of thing I should expect if I were doing the same thing."

"That's not quite an answer, but let me put it like this: The sort of thing your father would like to read about you, is it?"

"My father would never read that column."

"Then it surprises you to hear that Mrs. Mont's father did? Do you write many of these cheery little paragraphs about your friends?"

"Not many."

"Every now and then, eh? And do they remain your friends?"

"It's not easy in Society to tell who's a friend and who isn't."

"I quite agree, Miss Ferrar. You have admitted making one or two critical—that was your word, I think—remarks concerning Mrs. Mont, in her own house. Do you go to many houses and talk disparagingly of your hostess?"

"No; and in any case I don't expect to be eavesdropped."

"I see; so long as you're not found out, it's all right, eh? Now, on this first Wednesday in October last, at Mrs. Mont's, in speaking to this gentleman, Mr. Philip—er—Quinsey, did you use the word 'snob' of your hostess?"

"I don't think so."

"Be careful. You heard the evidence of Mrs. Ppynrryn and Mrs. Maltese. Mrs. Maltese said, you remember, that Mr. Forsyte—that is Mrs. Mont's father—said to you on that occasion: 'You called my daughter a snob in her own house, madam—be so kind as to withdraw; you are a traitress.' Is that a correct version?"

"Probably."

"Do you suggest that he invented the word 'snob'?"

"I suggest he was mistaken."

"Not a nice word, is it—'snob'? Was there any other reason why he should call you a traitress?"

"My remarks weren't meant for his ears. I don't remember exactly what I said."

"Well, we shall have Mr. Forsyte in the Box to refresh your memory as to exactly what you said. But I put it to you that you called her a snob, not once but twice, during that little conversation?"

"I've told you I don't remember; he shouldn't have listened."

"Very well! So you feel quite happy about having written that paragraph and said nasty things of Mrs. Mont behind her back in her own drawing-room?"

Marjorie Ferrar grasped the Box till the blood tingled in her palms. His voice was maddening.

"Yet it seems, Miss Ferrar, that you object to others saying nasty things about you in return. Who advised you to bring this action?"

"My father first; and then my *fiancé*."

"Sir Alexander MacGown. Does he move in the same circles as you?"

"No; he moves in Parliamentary circles."

"Exactly; and he wouldn't know, would he, the canons of conduct that rule in your circle?"

"There are no circles so definite as that."

"Always willing to learn, Miss Ferrar. But tell me, do you know what Sir Alexander's Parliamentary friends think about conduct and morality?"

"I can guess. I don't suppose there's much difference."

"Are you suggesting, Miss Ferrar, that responsible public men take the same light-hearted view of conduct and morals as you?"

"Aren't you rather assuming, Sir James, that her view *is* light-hearted?"

"As to conduct, my lord, I submit that her answers have shown the very light-hearted view she takes of the obligations incurred by the acceptance of hospitality, for instance. I'm coming to morals now."

"I think you'd better, before drawing your conclusions. What have public men to do with it?"

"I'm suggesting, my lord, that this lady is making a great to-do about words which a public man, or any ordinary citizen, would have a perfect right to resent, but which she, with her views, has no right whatever to resent."

"You must prove her views then. Go on!"

Marjorie Ferrar, relaxed for a moment, gathered herself again. Her views!

"Tell me, Miss Ferrar—we all know now the meaning of the word 'stuffy'—are public men 'stuffier' than you?"

"They may say they are."

"You think them hypocrites?"

"I don't think anything at all about them."

"Though you're going to marry one? You are complaining of the words: 'She hasn't a moral about her.' Have you read this novel 'Canthar'?" He was holding up a book.

"I think so."

"Don't you know?"

"I've skimmed it."

"Taken off the cream, eh? Read it sufficiently to form an opinion?"

"Yes."

"Would you agree with the view of it expressed in this letter to a journal? 'The book breaks through the British "stuffiness," which condemns any frank work of art—and a good thing too!' Is it a good thing?"

"Yes. I hate Grundyism."

"'It is undoubtedly Literature.' The word is written with a large L. Should you say it was?"

"Literature—yes. Not great literature, perhaps."

"But it ought to be published?"

"I don't see why not."

"You know that it is not published in England?"

"Yes."

"But it ought to be?"

"It isn't everybody's sort of book, of course."

"Don't evade the question, please. In your opinion ought this novel 'Canthar' to be published in England? . . . Take your time, Miss Ferrar."

The brute lost nothing! Just because she had hesitated a moment trying to see where he was leading her.

"Yes. I think literature should be free."

"You wouldn't sympathise with its suppression, if it were published?"

"No."

"You wouldn't approve of the suppression of any book on the ground of mere morals?"

"I can't tell you unless I see the book. People aren't bound to read books, you know."

"And you think your opinion generally on this subject is that of public men and ordinary citizens?"

"No; I suppose it isn't."

"But your view would be shared by most of your own associates?"

"I should hope so."

"A contrary opinion would be 'stuffy,' wouldn't it?"

"If you like to call it so. It's not my word."

"What is your word, Miss Ferrar?"

"I think I generally say 'ga-ga.'"

"Do you know, I'm afraid the Court will require a little elaboration of that."

"Not for me, Sir James; I'm perfectly familiar with the word; it means 'in your dotage.'"

"The Bench is omniscient, my lord. Then any one, Miss Ferrar, who didn't share the opinion of yourself and your associates in the matter of this book would be 'ga-ga,' that is to say, in his or her dotage?"

"Æsthetically."

"Ah! I thought we should arrive at that word. You, I suppose, don't connect art with life?"

"No."

"Don't think it has any effect on life?"

"It oughtn't to."

"When a man's theme in a book is extreme incontinence, depicted with all due emphasis, that wouldn't have any practical effect on his readers, however young?"

"I can't say about other people, it wouldn't have any effect on me."

"You are emancipated, in fact."

"I don't know what you mean by that."

"Isn't what you are saying about the divorce of art from life the merest claptrap; and don't you know it?"

"I certainly don't."

"Let me put it another way: Is it possible for those who believe in current morality to hold your view that art has no effect on life?"

"Quite possible; if they are cultured."

"Cultured! Do you believe in current morality yourself?"

"I don't know what you call current morality."

"I will tell you, Miss Ferrar. I should say, for instance, it was current morality that women should not have *liaisons* before they're married, and should not have them after."

"What about men?"

"Thank you; I was coming to men. And that men should at least not have them after."

"I shouldn't say that was *current* morality at all."

In yielding to that satiric impulse she knew at once she had made a mistake—the judge had turned his face towards her. He was speaking.

"Do I understand you to imply that in your view it is moral for women to have *liaisons* before marriage, and for men and women to have them after?"

"I think it's current morality, my lord."

"I'm not asking you about current morality; I'm asking whether in *your* view it is moral?"

"I think many people think it's all right who don't say it, yet."

She was conscious of movement throughout the jury; and of a little flump in the well of the Court. Sir Alexander had dropped his hat. The sound of a nose being loudly blown broke the stillness; the face of Bullfry K. C. was lost to her view. She felt the blood mounting in her cheeks.

"Exactly! And was it a coincidence that you thereupon made up your mind to marry Sir Alexander Mac-Gown?"

"A coincidence?"

"I mean the announcement of your engagement, you know?"

Brute!

"It had nothing to do with this case."

"Indeed! Now when you brought this action did you really care one straw whether people thought you moral or not?"

"I brought it chiefly because I was called 'a snake.'"

"Please answer my question."

"It isn't so much what *I* cared, as what my friends cared."

"But their view of morality is much what yours is—thoroughly accommodating?"

"Not my *fiancé's*."

"Ah! no. He doesn't move in your circle, you said. But the rest of your friends. You're not ashamed of your own accommodating philosophy, are you?"

"No."

"Then why be ashamed of it for them?"

"How can I tell what *their* philosophy is?"

"How can she, Sir James?"

"As your lordship pleases. Now, Miss Ferrar! You like to stand up for your views, I hope. Let me put your philosophy to you in a nutshell: You believe, don't you, in the full expression of your personality; it would be your duty, wouldn't it, to break through any convention —I don't say law—but any so-called moral convention that cramped you?"

"I never said I had a philosophy."

"Don't run away from it, please."

"I'm not in the habit of running away."

"I'm so glad of that. You believe in being the sole judge of your own conduct?"

"Yes."

"You're not alone in that view, are you?"

"I shouldn't think so."

"It's the view, in fact, of what may be called the forward wing of modern Society, isn't it—the wing you belong to, and are proud of belonging to? And in that section of Society—so long as you don't break the actual law—you think and do as you like, eh?"

"One doesn't always act up to one's principles."

"Quite so. But among your associates, even if you and they don't always act up to it, it *is* a principle, isn't it, to judge for yourselves and go your own ways without regard to convention?"

"More or less."

"And, living in that circle, with that belief, you have the effrontery to think the words: 'She hasn't a moral about her,' entitles you to damages?"

Her voice rang out angrily: "I have morals. They may not be yours, but they may be just as good, perhaps better. I'm not a hypocrite, anyway."

Again she saw him look at her, there was a gleam in his eyes; and she knew she had made another mistake.

"We'll leave my morals out of the question, Miss Ferrar. But we'll go a little further into what you say are yours. In your own words, it should depend on temperament, circumstances, environment, whether you conform to morality or not?"

She stood silent, biting her lip.

"Answer, please."

She inclined her head. "Yes."

"Very good!" He had paused, turning over his papers; and she drew back in the Box. She had lost her temper—had made him lose his; at all costs she must keep her head now! In this moment of search for her head she took in everything—expressions, gestures, even the atmosphere—the curious dramatic emanation from a hundred and more still faces; she noted the one lady juryman, the judge breaking the nib of a quill, with his eyes turned away from it as if looking at something that had run across the well of the Court. Yes, and down there, the lengthening lip of Mr. Settlewhite, Michael's face turned up at her with a rueful frown, Fleur Mont's mask with red spots in the cheeks, Alec's clenched hands, and his eyes fixed on her. A sort of comic intensity about it all! If only she were the size of Alice in 'Wonderland,' and could take them all in her hands and shake them like a pack of cards—so motionless, there, at her expense! That sarcastic brute had finished fiddling with his papers, and she moved forward again to attention in the Box.

"Now, Miss Ferrar, his lordship put a general question to you which you did not feel able to answer. I am going to put it in a way that will be easier for you. Whether or no it was right for you to have one"—she saw Michael's hand go up to his face—"have you *in fact* had a—*liaison?*" And from some tone in his voice, from the look on his face, she could tell for certain that he knew she had.

With her back to the wall, she had not even a wall to her back. Ten, twenty, thirty seconds—judge, jury, that old fox with his hand under the tail of his gown, and his eyes averted! Why did she not spit out the indignant: No! which she had so often rehearsed? Suppose he proved it—as he had said he would prove her debts?

"Take your time, Miss Ferrar. You know what a *liaison* is, of course."

Brute! On the verge of denial, she saw Michael lean across, and heard his whisper: 'Stop this!' And then 'that little snob' looked up at her—the scrutiny was knowing and contemptuous: 'Now hear her lie!' it seemed to say. And she answered, quickly: "I consider your question insulting."

"Oh! come, Miss Ferrar, after your own words! After what——"

"Well! I shan't answer it."

A rustle, a whispering in the Court.

"You won't answer it?"

"No."

"Thank you, Miss Ferrar." Could a voice be more sarcastic?

The brute was sitting down.

Marjorie Ferrar stood defiant, with no ground under her feet. What next? Her Counsel was beckoning. She descended from the Box, and, passing her adversaries, resumed her seat next her betrothed. How red and still he was! She heard the judge say:

"I shall break for lunch now, Mr. Bullfry;" saw him rise and go out, and the jury getting up. The whispering and rustling in the Court swelled to a buzz. She stood up. Mr. Settlewhite was speaking to her.

CHAPTER VII

"FED UP"

GUIDED by him into a room designed to shelter witnesses, Marjorie Ferrar looked at her lawyer.

"Well?"

"An unfortunate refusal, Miss Ferrar—very. I'm afraid the effect on the jury may be fatal. If we can settle it now, I should certainly say we'd better."

"It's all the same to me."

"In that case you may take it I shall settle. I'll go and see Sir Alexander and Mr. Bullfry at once."

"How do I get out quietly?"

"Down those stairs. You'll find cabs in Lincoln's Inn Fields. Excuse me;" he made her a grave little bow and stalked away.

Marjorie Ferrar did not take a cab; she walked. If her last answer had been fatal, on the whole she was content. She had told no lies to speak of, had stood up to 'that sarcastic beast,' and given him sometimes as good as she had got. Alec! Well, she couldn't help it! He had insisted on her going into Court; she hoped he liked it now she'd been! Buying a newspaper, she went into a restaurant and read a description of herself, accompanied by a photograph. She ate a good lunch, and then continued her walk along Piccadilly. Passing into the Park, she sat down under a tree coming into bud, and drew the smoke of a cigarette quietly into her lungs. The Row was almost deserted. A few persons of little or no consequence occupied a few chairs. A riding mistress was teaching a small boy to trot. Some sparrows and a pigeon alone seemed to take a distant interest in her. The air smelled of Spring. She sat some time with the pleasant feeling that nobody in the world knew where she was. Odd, when you thought of it—millions of people every day, leaving their houses, offices, shops, on their way to the next place, were as lost to the world as stones in a pond! Would it be nice to disappear permanently, and taste life incognita? Bertie Curfew was going to Moscow again. Would he take her as secretary, and *bonne amie?* Bertie Curfew— she had only pretended to be tired of him! The thought brought her face to face with the future. Alec! Explanations! It was hardly the word! He had a list of her debts, and had said he would pay them as a wedding-present. But—if there wasn't to be a wedding? Thank God, she had some ready money. The carefully 'laid-up' four-year-old in her father's stable had won yesterday. She had dribbled 'a pony' on at a nice price. She rose and sauntered along, distending her bust—in defiance of the boylike fashion, which, after all, was on the wane— to take in the full of a sweet wind.

Leaving the Park, she came to South Kensington Station and bought another paper. It had a full account under the headlines: 'Modern Morality Attacked.' 'Miss Marjorie Ferrar in the Box.' It seemed funny to stand there reading those words among people who were reading the same without knowing her from Eve, except, perhaps, by her clothes. Continuing her progress towards Wren Street, she turned her latch-key in the door, and saw a hat. Waiting for her already! She took her time; and, pale from powder, as though she had gone through much, entered the studio.

MacGown was sitting with his head in his hands. She felt real pity for him—too strong, too square, too vital for that attitude! He raised his face.

"Well, Alec!"

"Tell me the truth, Marjorie. I'm in torment."

She almost envied him the depth of his feeling, however unreasonable after her warnings. But she said, ironically:

"Who was it knew me better than I knew myself?"

In the same dull voice he repeated:

"The truth, Marjorie, the truth!"

But why should she go into the confessional? Was he entitled to her past? His rights stopped at her future. It was the old business—men expecting more from women than they could give them. Inequality of the sexes. Something in that, perhaps, in the old days when women bore children, and men didn't; but now that women knew all about sex and only bore children when they wanted to, and not always even then, why should men be freer?

And she said, slowly: "In exchange for your adventures I'll tell you mine."

"For God's sake don't mock me; I've had hell these last hours."

His face showed it, and she said with feeling:

"I said you'd be taking a toss over me, Alec. Why on earth did you insist on my bringing this case? You've had your way, and now you don't like it."

"It's true then?"

"Yes. Why not?"

He uttered a groan, recoiling till his back was against the wall, as if afraid of being loose in the room.

"Who was he?"

"Oh! no! That I can't possibly tell you. And how many affairs have you had?"

He paid no attention. He wouldn't! He knew she didn't love him; and such things only mattered if you loved! Ah! well! His agony was a tribute to her, after all!

"You're well out of me," she said, sullenly; and, sitting down, she lighted a cigarette. A scene! How hateful! Why didn't he go? She'd rather he'd be violent than deaf and dumb and blind like this.

"Not that American fellow?"

She could not help a laugh.

"Oh! no, poor boy!"

"How long did it last?"

"Nearly a year."

"My God!"

He had rushed to the door. If only he would open it and go! That he could feel so violently! That figure by the door was just not mad! His stuffy passions!

And then he did pull the door open and was gone.

She threw herself at full length on the divan; not from lassitude, exactly, nor despair—from a feeling rather as if nothing mattered. How stupid and pre-war! Why couldn't he, like her, be free, be supple, take life as it came! Passions, prejudices, principles, pity—old-fashioned as the stuffy clothes worn when she was a tot. Well! Good riddance! Fancy living in the same house, sharing the same bed, with a man so full of the primitive that he could 'go off his chump' with jealousy about her! Fancy living with a man who took life so seriously, that he couldn't even see himself doing it! Life was a cigarette to be inhaled and thrown away, a dance to be danced out. On with that dance! . . . Yes, but she couldn't let him pay her debts, now, even if he wanted to. Married, she would have repaid him with her body; as it was—no! Oh! why didn't some one die and leave her something? What a bore it all was! And she lay still, listening to the tea-time sounds of a quiet street—taxis rounding the corner from the river; the dog next door barking at the postman; that one-legged man—ex-Service—who came most afternoons and played on a poor fiddle. He expected her shilling—unhappy fellow!—she'd have to get up and give it him. She went to the little side window that looked on to the street, and suddenly recoiled. Francis Wilmot in the doorway with his hand up to the bell! Another scene! No, really! This was too much! There went the bell! No time to say 'Not at home'! Well, let them all come—round her past, like bees round a honey-pot!

"Mr. Francis Wilmot."

He stood there, large as the life he had nearly resigned —a little thinner, that was all.

"Well, Francis," she said, "I thought you were 'through with that fool business'?"

Francis Wilmot came gravely up and took her hand. "I sail to-morrow."

Sail! Well, she could put up with that. He seemed to her just a thin, pale young man with dark hair and eyes and no juices in his system.

"I read the evening papers. I wondered if, perhaps, you'd wish to see me."

Was he mocking her? But he wore no smile; there was no bitterness in his voice; and, though he was looking at her intently, she could not tell from his face whether he still had any feeling.

"You think I owe you something? I know I treated you very badly."

He looked rather as if she'd hit him.

"For heaven's sake, Francis, don't say you've come out of chivalry. That'd be too funny."

"I don't follow you; I just thought, perhaps, you didn't like to answer that question about a love-affair—because of me."

Marjorie Ferrar broke into hysterical laughter.

"Señor Don Punctilio! Because of you? No, no, my dear!"

Francis Wilmot drew back, and made her a little bow. "I shouldn't have come," he said.

She had a sudden return of feeling for that slim unusual presence, with its grace and its dark eyes.

"I'm a free lance again now, Francis, anyway."

A long moment went by, and then he made her another little bow. It was a clear withdrawal.

"Then for God's sake," she said, "go away! I'm fed up!" And she turned her back on him.

When she looked round, he *had* gone, and that surprised her. He was a new variety, or a dead one, dug up! He didn't know the rudiments of life—old-fashioned, *à faire rire!* And, back at full length on the divan, she brooded. Well, her courage was 'not out'! To-morrow was Bella Magussie's 'At Home,' to meet—some idiot. Everybody would be there, and so would she!

CHAPTER VIII

FANTOCHES

WHEN Michael, screwed towards Sir James Foskisson's averted face, heard the words: "Well, I shan't answer," he spun round. It was just as if she had said: "Yes, I have." The judge was looking at her, every one looking at her. Wasn't Bullfry going to help her? No! He was beckoning her out of the Box. Michael half rose, as she passed him. By George! He was sorry for MacGown! There he sat, poor devil!—with every one getting up all round him, still, and red as a turkey-cock.

Fleur! Michael looked at her face, slightly flushed, her gloved hands clasped in her lap, her eyes fixed on the ground. Had his whisper: 'Stop this!' his little abortive bow, offended her? How could one have helped sympathising with the 'Pet of the Panjoys' in so tight a place! She must see that! The Court was emptying— fine birds, many—he could see her mother and her aunt and cousin, and Old Forsyte, talking with Foskisson. Ah! he had finished; was speaking: "We can go now."

They followed him along the corridor, down the stairs, into the air.

"We've time for a snack," Soames was saying. "Come in here!"

In one of several kennels without roofs in a celebrated room with a boarded floor, they sat down.

"Three chump chops, sharp," said Soames, and staring at the cruet-stand, added: "She's cooked her goose. They'll drop it like a hot potato. I've told Foskisson he can settle, with both sides paying their own costs. It's more than they deserve."

"He ought never to have asked that question, sir."

Fleur looked up sharply.

"Really, Michael!"

"Well, darling, we agreed he shouldn't. Why didn't Bullfry help her out, sir?"

"Only too glad to get her out of the Box; the judge would have asked her himself in another minute. It's a complete fiasco, thank God!"

"Then we've won?" said Fleur.

"Unless I'm a Dutchman," answered Soames.

"I'm not so sure," muttered Michael.

"I tell you it's all over; Bullfry'll never go on with it."

"I didn't mean that, sir."

Fleur said acidly: "Then what *do* you mean, Michael?"

"I don't think we shall be forgiven, that's all."

"What for?"

"Well, I dare say I'm all wrong. Sauce, sir?"

"Worcester—yes. This is the only place in London where you can rely on a floury potato. Waiter—three glasses of port, quick!"

After fifteen minutes of concentrated mastication, they returned to the Court.

"Wait here," said Soames, in the hall; "I'll go up and find out."

In that echoing space, where a man's height was so inconsiderable, Fleur and Michael stood, not speaking, for some time.

"She couldn't know that Foskisson had been told not to follow it up, of course," he said, at last. "Still, she must have expected the question. She should have told a good one and have done with it. I couldn't help feeling sorry for her."

"You'd feel sorry for a flea that bit you, Michael. What do you mean by our not being forgiven?"

"Well! The drama was all on her side, and it's drama that counts. Besides, there's her engagement!"

"That'll be broken off."

"Exactly! And if it is, she'll have sympathy; while if it isn't, he'll have it. Anyway, we shan't. Besides, you know, she stood up for what we all really believe now-adays."

"Speak for yourself."

"Well, don't we talk of every one being free?"

"Yes, but is there any connection between what we say and what we do?"

"No," said Michael.

And just then Soames returned.

"Well, sir?"

"As I told you, Bullfry caught at it. They've settled. It's a moral victory."

"Oh! not moral, I hope, sir."

"It's cost a pretty penny, anyway," said Soames, look-ing at Fleur. "Your mother's quite annoyed—she's no sense of proportion. Very clever the way Foskisson made that woman lose her temper."

"He lost his, at the end. That's his excuse, I suppose."

"Well," said Soames, "it's all over! Your mother's got the car; we'll take a taxi."

On the drive back to South Square, taking precisely the same route, there was precisely the same silence.

When a little later Michael went over to the House, he was edified by posters.

"Society Libel Action."

"Marquess's granddaughter and K. C."

"Dramatic Evidence."

"Modern morality!"

All over—was it? With publicity—in Michael's opin-ion—it had just begun! Morality! What was it—who had it, and what did they do with it? How would he have answered those questions himself? Who could answer them, nowadays, by rote or rule? Not he, or Fleur!

They had been identified with the Inquisition, and what was their position, now? False, if not odious! He passed into the House. But, try as he would, he could not fix his attention on the Purity of Food, and passed out again. With a curious longing for his father, he walked rapidly down Whitehall. Drawing blank at 'Snooks'' and 'The Aeroplane,' he tried the 'Parthenæum' as a last resort. Sir Lawrence was in a corner of a forbidden room, reading a life of Lord Palmerston. He looked up at his son.

"Ah! Michael! They don't do justice to old Pam. A man without frills, who worked like a nigger. But we mustn't talk here!" And he pointed to a member who seemed awake. "Shall we take a turn before the old gentleman over there has a fit? The books here are camouflage; it's really a dormitory."

He led the way, with Michael retailing the events of the morning.

"Foskisson?" said Sir Lawrence, entering the Green Park. "He was a nice little chap when I left Winchester. To be professionally in the right is bad for a man's character—counsel, parsons, policemen, they all suffer from it. Judges, High Priests, Arch-Inspectors, aren't so bad —they've suffered from it so long that they've lost consciousness."

"It was a full house," said Michael, glumly, "and the papers have got hold of it."

"They would." And Sir Lawrence pointed to the ornamental water. "These birds," he said, "remind me of China. By the way, I met your friend Desert yesterday at 'The Aeroplane'—he's more interesting now that he's dropped Poetry for the East. Everybody ought to drop something. I'm too old now, but if I'd dropped baronetcy in time, I could have made quite a good contortionist."

"What would you recommend for us in the House?" asked Michael, with a grin.

"Postmanship, my dear—carrying on, you know; a certain importance, large bags, dogs to bark at you, no initiative, and conversation on every door-step. By the way, do you see Desert?"

"I have seen him."

Sir Lawrence screwed up his eyes.

"The providential," he said, "doesn't happen twice."

Michael coloured; he had not suspected his father of such shrewd observation. Sir Lawrence swung his cane.

"Your man Boddick," he said, "has persuaded some of his hens to lay; he's giving us quite good eggs."

Michael admired his reticence. But somehow that unexpected slanting allusion to a past domestic crisis roused the feeling that for so long now had been curled like a sleepy snake in his chest, that another crisis was brewing and must soon be faced.

"Coming along for tea, sir? Kit had tummyache this morning. How's your last book doing? Does old Danby advertise it properly?"

"No," said Sir Lawrence, "no; he's keeping his head wonderfully; the book is almost dead."

"I'm glad I dropped *him*, anyway," said Michael, with emphasis. "I suppose, sir, you haven't a tip to give us, now this case is over?"

Sir Lawrence gazed at a bird with a long red bill.

"When victorious," he said, at last, "lie doggo. The triumphs of morality are apt to recoil on those who achieve them."

"That's what I feel, sir. Heaven knows *I* didn't want to achieve one. My father-in-law says my hitting Mac-Gown on the boko really brought it into Court."

Sir Lawrence whinnied.

"The tax on luxuries. It gets you everywhere. I don't think I will come along, Michael—Old Forsyte's probably there. Your mother has an excellent recipe for child's

CHAPTER IX

ROUT AT MRS. MAGUSSIE'S

THERE are routs social, political, propagandic; and routs like Mrs. Magussie's. In one of Anglo-American birth, inexhaustible wealth, unimpeachable widowhood, and catholic taste, the word hostess had found its highest expression. People might die, marry, and be born with impunity so long as they met, preferably in her house, one of the largest in Mayfair. If she called in a doctor, it was to meet another doctor; if she went to church, it was to get Canon Forant to meet Dean Kimble at lunch afterwards. Her cards of invitation had the words: "To meet" printed on them; and she never put "me." She was selfless. Once in a way she had a real rout, because once in a way a personality was available, whose name everybody, from poets to prelates, must know. In her intimate belief people loved to meet anybody sufficiently distinguished; and this was where she succeeded, because almost without exception they did. Her two husbands had 'passed on,' having met in their time nearly everybody. They had both been distinguished, and had first met in her house; and she would never have a third; Society was losing its landmarks, and she was too occupied. People were inclined to smile at mention of Bella Magussie, and yet, how do without one who performed the function of cement? Without her, bishops could not place their cheeks by the jowls of ballet-girls, or Home Secretaries be fertilised by disorderly dramatists. Except in her house, the diggers-up of old civilisations in Beluchistan never encountered the levellers of modern civilisation in London. Nor was there any chance for lights of the Palace to meet those lights of the Halls—

Madame Nemesia and Top Nobby. Nowhere else could
a Russian dancer go in to supper with Sir Walter Peddel,
M.D.; F.R.S.T.R.; P.M.V.S.; R.I.P. Even he who had
the finest collection of ducks' eggs in first-class cricket
was not without a chance of wringing the hand of the
great Indian economist Sir Banerjee Bath Babore. Mrs.
Magussie's, in fine, was a house of chief consequence; and
her long face, as of the guardian of some first principle,
moving above the waters of celebrity, was wrinkled in a
great cause. To meet or not to meet? She had answered
the question for good and all.

The "met" or "meetee" for her opening rout in 1925
was the great Italian violinist Luigi Sporza, who had just
completed his remarkable tour of the world, having in
half the time played more often than any two previous
musicians. The prodigious feat had been noted in the
Press of all countries with every circumstance—the five
violins he had tired out, the invitation he had received
to preside over a South American Republic, the special
steamer he had chartered to keep an engagement in
North America, and his fainting fit in Moscow after the
Beethoven and Brahms concertos, the Bach chaconne,
and seventeen encores. During the lingering year of his
great effort, his fame had been established. As an artist
he had been known to a few, as an athlete he was now
known to all.

Michael and Fleur, passing up the centre stairway,
saw a man 'not 'arf like a bull' as Michael muttered,
whose hand people were seizing, one after the other, to
move away with a look of pain.

"Only Italy can produce men like that," said Michael
in Fleur's ear. "Give him the go-by. He'll hurt you."

But Fleur moved forward.

"Made of sterner stuff," murmured Michael. It was
not the part of his beloved to miss the hand of celebrity,

great Italian, in not too much of a sea-green gown, with her red-gold head held high. She came to a stand a small room's length from Fleur, and swept her eyes this way and that. Evidently she had taken up that position in deliberate challenge.

"I must go to Fleur."

"So must I," said Mr. Blythe, and Michael gave him a grateful look.

And now it would have been so interesting to one less interested than Michael. The long, the tapering nose of Society could be seen to twitch, move delicately upwards, and like the trunk of some wild elephant scenting man, writhe and snout this way and that, catching the whiff of sensation. Lips were smiling and moving closer to ears; eyes turning from that standing figure to the other; little reflective frowns appeared on foreheads, as if, beneath cropped and scented scalps, brains were trying to make choice. And Marjorie Ferrar stood smiling and composed; and Fleur talked and twisted the flower in her hand; and both went on looking their best. So began a battle without sign of war declared, without even seeming recognition of each other's presence. Mr. Blythe, indeed, stood pat between the two of them. Bulky and tall, he was an effective screen. But Michael, on the other side of her, could see and grimly follow. The Nose was taking time to apprehend the full of the aroma; the Brain to make its choice. Tide seemed at balance, not moving in or out. And then, with the slow implacability of tides, the water moved away from Fleur and lapped round her rival. Michael chattered, Mr. Blythe goggled, using the impersonal pronoun with a sort of passion; Fleur smiled, talked, twisted the flower. And, over there, Marjorie Ferrar seemed to hold a little Court. Did people admire, commiserate, approve of, or sympathise with her? Or did they disapprove of himself and Fleur? Or was it just

that the 'Pet of the Panjoys' was always the more sensational figure? Michael watched Fleur growing paler,
her smile more nervous, the twitching of the flower spasmodic. And he dared not suggest going; for she would
see in it an admission of defeat. But on the faces, turned
their way, the expression became more and more informa-
tive. Sir James Foskisson had done his job too well; he
had slavered his clients with his own self-righteousness.
Better the confessed libertine than those who brought her
to judgment! And Michael thought: 'Dashed natural,
after all! Why didn't the fellow take my tip, and let us
pay and look pleasant.'

And just then close to the great Italian he caught sight
of a tall young man with his hair brushed back, who
was looking at his fingers. By George! It was Bertie
Curfew! And there, behind him, waiting for his turn 'to
meet,' who but MacGown himself! The humour of the
gods had run amok! Head in air, soothing his mangled
fingers, Bertie Curfew passed them, and strayed into the
group around his former flame. Her greeting of him was
elaborately casual. But up went the tapering Nose, for
here came MacGown! How the fellow had changed—
grim, greyish, bitter! He, too, stepped into that throng.
Did he know? Did he realise Curfew?

A queer silence was followed by a burst of speech, and
then by dissolution. In twos and threes they trickled off,
and there were MacGown and his betrothed standing
alone. Michael turned to Fleur.

"Let's go."

Silence reigned in their homing cab. He had chattered himself out on the field of battle, and must wait
for fresh supplies of camouflage. But he slipped his hand
along till it found hers, which did not return his pressure.
The card he used to play at times of stress—the eleventh
baronet—had failed for the last three months; she seemed

of late to resent his introduction as a remedy. He followed her into the dining-room, sore at heart, bewildered in mind. He had never seen her look so pretty as in that oyster-coloured frock, very straight and simply made, with a swing out above the ankles. She sat down at the narrow dining-table, and he seated himself opposite, with the costive feeling of one who cannot find words that will ring true. For social discomfiture he, himself, didn't care a tinker's curse, but she——!

And, suddenly, she said:

"And you don't mind a bit?"

"For myself—not a bit."

"Yes, you've still got your Foggartism and your Bethnal Green."

"If *you* care, Fleur, I care a lot."

"*If* I care!"

"How—exactly?"

"I'd rather not increase your feeling that I'm a snob."

"I never had any such feeling."

"Michael!"

"Hadn't you better say what you mean by the word?"

"You know perfectly well."

"I know that you appreciate having people about you, and like them to think well of you. That isn't being a snob."

"Yes; you're very kind, but you don't admire it."

"I admire *you*."

"You mean, desire me. You admire Norah Curfew."

"Norah Curfew! For all I care, she might snuff out to-morrow."

And from her face he had the feeling that she believed him.

"If it isn't her, it's what she stands for—all that I'm not."

"I admire a lot in you," said Michael, fervently; "your

intelligence, your *flair*; I admire you with Kit and your father; your pluck; and the way you put up with me."

"No, I admire you much more than you admire me. Only, you see, I'm not capable of devotion."

"What about Kit?"

"I'm devoted to myself—that's all."

He reached across the table and touched her hand.

"Morbid, darling."

"No. I see too clearly to be morbid."

She was leaning back, and her throat, very white and round, gleamed in the alabaster-shaded light; little choky movements were occurring there.

"Michael, I want you to take me round the world."

"And leave Kit?"

"He's too young to mind. Besides, my mother would look after him."

If she had got as far as that, this was a deliberate desire!

"But, your father——"

"He's not really old yet, and he'd have Kit."

"When we rise in August, perhaps——"

"No, now."

"It's only five months to wait. We'd have time in the vacation to do a lot of travelling."

Fleur looked straight at him.

"I knew you cared more for Foggartism now than for me."

"Be reasonable, Fleur."

"For five months—with the feeling I've got here!" she put her hand to her breast. "I've had six months of it already. You don't realise, I suppose, that I'm down and out?"

"But, Fleur, it's all so——"

"Yes, it's always petty to mind being a dead failure, isn't it?"

"But, my child——"

"Oh! If you can't feel it——!"

"I can—I felt wild this evening. But all you've got to do is to let them see that you don't care; and they'll come buzzing round again like flies. It would be running away, Fleur."

"No," said Fleur, coldly, "it's not that—I don't try twice for the same prize. Very well, I'll stay and be laughed at."

Michael got up.

"I know you don't think there's anything to my job. But there is, Fleur, and I've put my hand to it. Oh! don't look like that. Dash it! This is dreadful!"

"I suppose I could go by myself. That would be more thrilling."

"Absurd! Of course you couldn't! You're seeing blue to-night, old thing. It'll all seem different to-morrow."

"To-morrow and to-morrow! No, Michael, mortification has set in, my funeral can take place any day you like!"

Michael's hands went up. She meant what she was saying! To realise, he must remember how much store she had set on her powers as hostess; how she had worked for her collection and shone among it! Her house of cards all pulled about her ears! Cruel! But would going round the world help her? Yes! Her instinct was quite right. He had been round the world himself, nothing else would change her values in quite that way; nothing else would so guarantee oblivion in others and herself! Lippinghall, her father's, the sea for the five months till vacation came —they wouldn't meet her case! She needed what would give her back importance. And yet, how could he go until the vacation? Foggartism—that lean and lonely plant —unwatered and without its only gardener, would wither to its roots, if, indeed, it had any. There was some movement in it now, interest here and there—this Member and that was pecking at it. Private efforts in the same direction were gathering way. And time was going on—Big Ben had called no truce; unemployment swelling, trade dawdling, industrial trouble brewing—brewing, hope losing patience! And what would old Blythe say to his desertion now?

"Give me a week," he muttered. "It's not easy. I must think it over."

CHAPTER X

THE NEW LEAF

WHEN MacGown came up to her, Marjorie Ferrar thought: 'Does he know about Bertie?' Fresh from her triumph over 'that little snob,' fluttered by the sudden appearance of her past, and confronted with her present, she was not in complete possession of her head. When they had moved away into an empty side room, she faced him.

"Well, Alec, nothing's changed. I still have a past as lurid as yesterday. I'm extremely sorry I ever kept it from you. But I did practically tell you, several times: only you wouldn't take it."

"Because it was hell to me. Tell me everything, Marjorie!"

"You want to revel in it?"

"Tell me everything, and I'll marry you still."

She shook her head. "Marry! Oh! no! I don't go out of my depth any more. It was absurd anyway. I never loved you, Alec."

"Then you loved that—you still——"

"My dear Alec, enough!"

He put his hands to his head, and swayed. And she was touched by genuine compassion.

"I'm awfully sorry, I really am. You've got to cut me out; that's all."

She had turned to leave him, but the misery in his face stopped her. She had not quite realised. He was burnt up! He was——! And she said quickly:

"Marry you I won't; but I'd like to pay up, if I could——"

He looked at her.

Quivering all over from that look, she shrugged her shoulders, and walked away. Men of an old fashion! Her own fault for stepping outside the charmed circle that took nothing too seriously. She walked over the shining floor, conscious of many eyes, slipped past her hostess, and soon was in a cab.

She lay awake, thinking. Even without announcement the return of presents would set London by the ears and bring on her again an avalanche of bills. Five thousand pounds! She got up and rummaged out the list, duplicate of that which Alec had. He might still want to pay them! After all, it was he who had spilled the ink by making her go into Court! But then his eyes came haunting her. Out of the question! And, shivering a little, she got back into bed. Perhaps she would have a brain-wave in the morning. She had so many in the night, that she could not sleep. Moscow with Bertie Curfew? The stage? America and the 'movies'? All three? She slept at last, and woke languid and pale. With her letters was one from Shropshire House.

"DEAR MARJORIE,
"If you've nothing better to do, I should like to see you this morning.
Affectionately,
SHROPSHIRE."

What now? She looked at herself in the glass, and decided that she *must* make up a little. At eleven o'clock she was at Shropshire House. The marquess was in his workroom at the top, among a small forest of contraptions. With coat off, he was peering through a magnifying-glass at what looked like nothing.

"Sit down, Marjorie," he said; "I'll have done in a minute."

She had a strong desire to answer: "What are you?" but restrained it, and said:

"I thought of going on the stage."

"Well, I suppose that might be suitable. Can you act?"

"I'm not a Duse."

"Duse?" The marquess shook his head. "One must go back to Ristori for really great acting. Duse! Very talented, of course, but always the same. So you don't choose to marry him now?" He looked at her intently: "That, I think, is right. Have you a list of your debts?"

Marjorie Ferrar rummaged in her vanity bag. "Here it is."

She could see his nose wrinkling above it, but whether at its scent, or its contents, she could not tell.

"Your grandmother," he said, "spent about a fifth of what you seem to on about five times the acreage of clothes. You wear nothing nowadays, and yet it costs all this."

"The less there is, Grandfather, the better it has to be cut, you know."

"Have you sent your presents back?"

"I've had them packed."

"They must all go," said the marquess. "Keep nothing he or any one else gave you."

"Of course not."

"To frank you," he said, suddenly, "I should have to sell the Gainsborough."

"Oh, no!"

Gainsborough's picture of his own grandmother as a little girl—that beautiful thing! She stretched out her hand for the list. Still holding it, he put his foot to the ground, and stood peering at her with his bright, intent old eyes.

"The question is, Marjorie, how far it's possible to strike a bargain with you. Have you a 'word' to keep?"

She felt the blood mounting in her cheeks.

"I think so. It depends on what I've got to promise. But, Grandfather, I don't *want* you to sell the Gainsborough."

"Unfortunately," said the marquess, "without doing your uncle Dangerfield in the eye, I've nothing else. It's been my fault, I suppose, for having had expensive children. Other people don't seem to have had them to the same degree."

She stifled a smile.

"Times are hard," went on the marquess. "Land costs money, collieries cost money, Shropshire House costs money; and where's the money? I've got an invention here that ought to make my fortune, but nobody will look at it."

The poor old boy—at his age! She said with a sigh:

"I really didn't mean to bother you with this, Grandfather. I'll manage somehow."

The old peer took several somewhat hampered steps, and she noticed that his red slippers were heelless. He halted, a wonderfully bright spot among the contraptions.

"To come back to what we were saying, Marjorie. If your idea of life is simply to have a good time, how can you promise anything?"

"What do you want me to promise?"

He came and stood before her again, short and a little bent.

"You look as if you had stuff in you, too, with your hair. Do you really think you could earn your living?"

"I believe I can; I know a lot of people."

"If I clear you, will you give me your word to pay ready money in future? Now don't say 'Yes,' and go out and order yourself a lot of fallals. I want the word of a lady, if you understand what that implies."

CHAPTER XI

OVER THE WINDMILL

DURING his period of indecision Michael struck no attitudes, and used practically no words; the thing was too serious. Perhaps Kit would change Fleur's mood, or she would see other disadvantages, such as her father. The complete cessation, however, of any social behaviour on her part—no invitation issued, or received, no function attended, or even discussed, during that rather terrible week, proved that the iron had really seared her spirit. She was not sulky, but she was mum and listless. And she was always watching him, with a wistful expression on her face, and now and then a resentful look, as if she had made up her mind that he was going to refuse. He could consult no one, too, for to any who had not lived through this long episode, Fleur's attitude would seem incomprehensible, even ridiculous. He could not give her away; could not even go to old Blythe, until he had decided. Complicating his mental conflict was the habitual doubt whether he was really essential to Foggartism. If only his head would swell! He had not even the comfort of feeling that a sturdy negative would impress Fleur; she thought his job a stunt, useful to make him conspicuous, but of no real importance to the country. She had the political cynicism of the woman in the street; only what threatened property or Kit would really ruffle her! He knew that his dilemma was comic. The future of England against the present of a young woman socially snubbed! But, after all, only Sir James Foggart and old Blythe so far seriously connected Foggartism with the future of England; and if, now, he went off round the world, even they would lose their faith.

"What with that German actor hanging himself at Lippinghall," Michael went on, "and my Foggartism, and this Ferrar rumpus, our pitch is badly queered. We've had a wretched week of it since the case. Fleur feels so out of her plate, that she wants me to take her round the world."

A bomb bursting on the dove-cote down there could not have been more startling. Round the world! He heard Michael murmuring on:

"She's quite right, too. It might be the very best thing for her; but I simply can't leave my job until the long vacation. I've taken up this thing, and I must stick to it while Parliament's sitting."

Sitting! As if it were a hen, addling its precious eggs! Round the world!

But Michael ran on:

"It's only to-day I've quite decided. I should feel like a deserter, and that wouldn't be good for either of us in the long run. But she doesn't know yet."

For Soames the dove-cote was solidifying again, now that he knew Michael was not going to take her away for goodness knew how long!

"Round the world!" he said. "Why not—er—Pontresina?"

"I think," answered Michael, slowly, like a doctor diagnosing, "that she wants something dramatic. Round the world at twenty-three! She feels somehow that she's lost caste."

"How can she think of leaving that little chap?"

"Yes, that shows it's pretty desperate with her. I wish to goodness I *could* go."

Soames stared. The young fellow wasn't expecting him to do anything about it, was he? Round the world? A crazy notion!

"I must see her," he said. "Can you leave that thing

of yours in the garage and come up with me in the car?
I'll be ready in twenty minutes. You'll find tea going
down-stairs."

Left alone with the Fred Walker still unhung, Soames
gazed at his pictures. He saw them with an added clarity, a more penetrating glance, a sort of ache in his heart,
as if— Well! A good lot they were, better than he had
thought, of late! *She* had gone in for collecting people!
And now she'd lost her collection! Poor little thing! All
nonsense, of course—as if there were any satisfaction in
people! Suppose he took her up that Chardin? It was
a good Chardin. Dumetrius had done him over the price,
but not too much. And, before Chardin was finished with,
he would do Dumetrius. Still—if it would give her any
pleasure! He unhooked the picture, and, carrying it
under his arm, went down-stairs.

Beyond certain allusions to the characteristics of the
eleventh baronet, and the regrettable tendencies of the
police to compel slow travelling over the new cut con-
structed to speed up traffic, little was said in the car.
They arrived in South Square about six o'clock. Fleur
had not been in since lunch; and they sat down uneasily
to wait for her. The Dandie, having descended to look
for strange legs, had almost immediately ascended again,
and the house was very quiet. Michael was continually
looking at his watch.

"Where do you think she's got to?" said Soames, at last.

"Haven't an idea, sir; that's the worst of London, it
swallows people up."

He had begun to fidget; Soames, who also wanted to
fidget, was thinking of saying: "Don't!" when from the
window Michael cried:

"Here she is!" and went quickly to the door.

Soames sat on, with the Chardin resting against his
chair.

They were a long time out there! Minute after minute passed, and still they did not come.

At last Michael reappeared. He looked exceedingly grave.

"She's in her little room up-stairs, sir. I'm afraid it's upset her awfully. Perhaps you wouldn't mind going up."

Soames grasped the Chardin.

"Let's see, that's the first door on the left, isn't it?" He mounted slowly, his mind blank, and without waiting for her to answer his mild knock, went in.

Fleur was sitting at the satinwood bureau, with her face buried on her arms. Her hair, again in its more natural 'bob,' gleamed lustrously under the light. She seemed unconscious of his entry. This sight of private life affected Soames, unaccustomed to give or receive undefended glimpses of self, and he stood, uncertain. Had he the right to surprise her, with her ears muffled like that, and her feelings all upset? He would have gone out and come in again, but he was too concerned. And, moving to her side, he put his finger on her shoulder, and said:

"Tired, my child?"

Her face came round—queer, creased, not like her face; and Soames spoke the phrase of her childhood:

"See what I've brought you!"

He raised the Chardin; she gave it just a glance, and he felt hurt. After all, it was worth some hundreds of pounds! Very pale, she had crossed her arms on her chest, as if shutting herself up. He recognised the symptom. A spiritual crisis! The sort of thing his whole life had been passed in regarding as extravagant; like a case of appendicitis that must be operated at once.

"Michael," he said, "tells me you want him to take you round the world."

"Well, he can't; so that ends it."

If she had said: 'Yes, and why can't he?' Soames would have joined the opposition automatically. But her words roused his natural perversity. Here she was, and here was her heart's desire—and she wasn't getting it! He put the Chardin down, and took a walk over the soft carpet.

"Tell me," he said, coming to a halt, "where do you feel it exactly?"

Fleur laughed: "In my head, and my eyes, and my ears, and my heart."

"What business," muttered Soames, "have they to look down their confounded noses!" And he set off again across the room. All the modern jackanapes whom from time to time he had been unable to avoid in her house, seemed to have come sniggering round him with lifted eyebrows, like a set of ghosts. The longing to put them in their places—a shallow lot—possessed him at that moment to the exclusion of a greater sanity.

"I—I don't see how *I* can take you," he said, and stopped short.

What was that he was saying? Who had asked him to take her? Her eyes, widely open, were fixed on him.

"But of course not, Dad!"

Of course not! He didn't know about that!

"I shall get used to being laughed at, in time."

Soames growled.

"I don't see why you should," he said. "I suppose people do go round the world."

Fleur's pallor had gone, now.

"But not you, dear; why, it would bore you stiff! It's very sweet of you, even to think of it; but of course I couldn't let you—at your age!"

"At my age?" said Soames. "I'm not so very old."

"No, no, Dad; I'll just dree my weird."

Soames took another walk, without a sound. Dree her weird, indeed!

"I won't have it," he ejaculated; "if people can't behave to you, I—I'll show them!"

She had got up, and was breathing deeply, with her
lips parted, and her cheeks very flushed. So she had
stood, before her first party, holding out her frock for him
to see.

"We'll go," he said, gruffly. "Don't make a fuss!
That's settled."

Her arms were round his neck; his nose felt wet. What
nonsense! as if——! . . .

He stood unbuttoning his braces that night in the most
peculiar state of mind. Going round the world—was he?
Preposterous! It had knocked that young fellow over
anyway—he was to join them in August wherever they
were by that time! Good Lord! It might be China!
The thing was fantastic; and Fleur behaving like a kitten!
The words of a comic ditty, sung by a clergyman, in his
boyhood, kept up a tattoo within him:

> "I see Jerusalem and Madagascar,
>   And North and South Amerikee. . . ."

Yes! Indeed! His affairs were in apple-pie order,
luckily! There was nothing to do, in Timothy's or Winifred's Trusts—the only two he had on his hands now;
but how things would get on without him, he couldn't
tell! As to Annette! She wouldn't be sorry, he supposed.
There was no one else to care, except Winifred, a little.
It was, rather, an intangible presence that troubled his
thoughts, about to forsake it for months on end! Still,
the cliffs of Dover would be standing, he supposed, and
the river still running past his lawn, when he came back,
if he ever came back! You picked up all sorts of things
out there—microbes, insects, snakes—never knew what
you'd run into! Pretty business, steering Fleur clear of
all that. And the sightseeing he would have to do! For

she wouldn't miss anything! Trust her! Going round among a lot of people with their mouths open—he couldn't stand that; but he would have to! H'm! A relief when that young fellow could join them. And yet—to have her to himself; he hadn't, for a long time now. But she would pick up with everybody, of course. He would have to make himself agreeable to Tom, Dick, and Harry. A look at Egypt, then to India, and across to China and Japan, and back through that great sprawling America— God's own country, didn't they call it! She had it all mapped out. Thank goodness, no question of Russia!

CHAPTER XII

ENVOI

AWAY from Fleur five months at least!
Soames' astounding conduct had indeed knocked Michael over. And yet, after all, they had come to a crisis in their life together, the more serious because concerned with workaday feelings. Perhaps out there she would become afflicted, like himself, with an enlarged prospect; lose her idea that the world consisted of some five thousand people of advanced tastes, of whom she knew at the outside five hundred. It was she who had pushed him into Parliament, and until he was hoofed therefrom as a failure, their path was surely conjoined along the crest of a large view. In the fortnight before her departure he suffered and kept smiling; wryly thankful that she was behaving 'like a kitten,' as her father called it. Her nerves had been on edge ever since the autumn over that wretched case—what more natural than this reaction? At least she felt for him sufficiently to be prodigal of kisses—great consolation to Michael while it lasted. Once or twice he caught her hanging with wet eyes over the eleventh baronet; once found her with a wet face when he awoke in the morning. These indications were a priceless assurance to him that she meant to come back. For there were moments when possibilities balled into a nightmare. Absurd! She was going with her father, that embodiment of care and prudence! Who would have thought Old Forsyte could uproot himself like this? He, too, was leaving a wife, though Michael saw no signs of it. One didn't know much about Old Forsyte's feelings, except that they centred round his daughter, and that he was continually asking questions about labels and insects. He had bought himself, too, a life-saving waistcoat and one for Fleur. Michael held with him only one important conversation.

"I want you," Soames said, "to keep an eye on my wife,

and see she doesn't go getting into a mess with the cows. She'll have her mother with her, but women are so funny. You'll find her first-rate with the baby. How will you be off for money?"

"Perfectly all right, sir."

"Well, if you want some for any good purpose, go to old Gradman in the City; you remember him, perhaps?"

"Yes, and I'm afraid he'll remember me."

"Never mind; he's a faithful old fellow." And Michael heard him sigh. "I'd like you to look in at Green Street, too, now and then. Your aunt-in-law may feel my being away a little. I'll let you have news of Fleur from time to time—now they've got this wireless she'll want to know about the baby. I'm taking plenty of quinine. She says she's a good sailor. There's nothing like champagne for that, I'm told. And, by the way, you know best, but I shouldn't press your notions too far in Parliament; they're easily bored there, I believe. We'll meet you at Vancouver, at the end of August. She'll be tired of travelling by then. She's looking forward to Egypt and Japan, but I don't know. Seems to me it'll be all travelling."

"Have you plenty of ducks, sir? You'll want them at this time of year in the Red Sea; and I should take a helmet."

"I've got one," said Soames; "they're heavy great things," and, looking suddenly at Michael, he added:

"I shall look after her, and you'll look after yourself, I hope."

Michael understood him.

"Yes, sir. And thank you very much. I think it's most frightfully sporting of you."

"It's to be hoped it'll do her good; and that the little chap won't miss her."

"Not if I can help it."

Soames, who was seated in front of 'The White Monkey,' seemed to go into a trance. At last he stirred in his chair, and said:

"The war's left everything very unsettled. I suppose

follow what light one had! And if the Future was unread-able, and Fate grinned, well—let it grin!

How empty the house felt! To-morrow Kit and the dog were to go down to 'The Shelter' in the car, and it would be still emptier. From room after room he tried to retrieve some sight or scent of Fleur. Too painful! His dressing-room, his study were the only places possible—in them he would abide.

He went to the nursery, and opened the door softly. Whiteness and dimity; the dog on his fat silver side, the Magicoal fire burning; the prints on the white walls so carefully selected for the moment when the eleventh baro-net should begin to take notice—prints slightly comic, to avoid a moral; the high and shining fender-guard that even Magicoal might not be taken too seriously; the light com-ing in between bright chintz. A charming room! The nurse, in blue, was standing with her back to the door, and did not see him. And, in his little high chair, the eleventh baronet was at table; on his face, beneath its dark chest-nut curls, was a slight frown; and in his tiny hand he held a silver spoon, with which over the bowl before him he was making spasmodic passes.

Michael heard the nurse saying:

"Now that mother's gone, you must be a little man, Kit, and learn to use your spoon."

Michael saw his offspring dip at the bowl and throw some of its contents into the air.

"That's not the way at all."

The eleventh baronet repeated the performance, and looked for applause, with a determined smile.

"Naughty!"

"A—a!" said the eleventh baronet, plopping the spoon. The contents spurted wastefully.

"Oh! you spoiled boy!"

"'England, my England!'" thought Michael, 'as the poet said.'

THE END